Dark Fortune

Dark Fortune

Best wishes
Theresa
Tomlinson

THERESA TOMLINSON

© Theresa Tomlinson, 2021

Published by The Old Print Workshop

A CIP catalogue record for this book is available from the British Library.

ISBN 978-0-9955832-2-1

Book layout and cover design by Clare Brayshaw

Prepared and printed by:

York Publishing Services Ltd
64 Hallfield Road
Layerthorpe
York YO31 7ZQ

Tel: 01904 431213

Website: www.yps-publishing.co.uk

Dedicated to all the NHS Staff,
who risked their own lives by working throughout Covid19

PROLOGUE

February 1861

Lightning flickered and thunder rolled above the red-roofed fishing town. A maroon shot high into the sky and exploded with a sudden flash and boom, echoing the sights and sounds of the storm. The yellow flare and thud of another rocket sent fishermen rushing out onto the quayside from the shelter of their harbour-side doorways. They struggled into their oilskins as they ran, for the second yellow flash meant that the lifeboat would have to go out again.

Dark clouds were bringing twilight to the wintry afternoon. The lightning illuminated the powerful surge and swell of the waves that beat against the harbour side and protective arms of the piers. Moored vessels swung wildly in all directions and crashed together on straining hawsers.

In the midst of this chaos, thirteen grim-faced men marched out to take their places in the lifeboat. Many of them were already exhausted, for they'd been out four times that morning on similar missions of mercy, but look-outs had now seen that the schooner *Merchant* had missed the entrance to the harbour and run aground just beyond the west-side pier. The collier ship listed to the side, buffeted fiercely back and forth, her mast broken and her sails collapsed. She was urgently in need of help.

Anxious women and children followed the crew and other fishermen from small cottage doorways. Clutching shawls and blankets about them, they grabbed at each other's arms and clung together for support. The slipway was pounded by fierce waves, but somehow the lifeboat was manhandled down it and into the raging sea. The crew hauled on the oars as the small, sturdy craft swung and dipped wildly, moving closer, bit by bit, towards the stranded boat. The women and men onshore struggled forward along the pier, heads bent against the wind and rain as they strove to keep pace with the boat, grabbing where they could at the solid capstans to keep their balance.

Another lightning flash revealed a terrifying new threat: a rogue wave gained in power and began to hurtle crossways towards the lifeboat. The lightning was followed by a crash of thunder and the watchers' warning cries, as a second mighty wave rose from the opposite direction, and both rolled headlong towards the small, dipping vessel.

The watchers onshore yelled and bellowed in vain, for nothing could stop the relentless force that caught the rising prow. The clash of waves formed a gigantic waterspout that lifted the boat out of the water and tossed it like a child's small toy towards the sky.

Women screamed, men gasped. It seemed to them that a massive giant's fist had thrust its way through the waters to punch their precious lifeboat into the air. Thirteen dark shapes flew skywards then down again, down, half hidden in the flying spume they went, into the sea's hungry maw.

Pandemonium broke loose. Careless of their own safety men and women raced to the slipway, flinging buoys, hurling ropes, and reaching with desperate hands towards the struggling shapes in the water, for these were their fathers, their brothers, their husbands, their sons. Heads were glimpsed, an arm, a boot – then nothing; only the tossing keel, half broken and smashed.

The damaged, upturned hull was thrown back towards the land where it was surrounded at once by an eager gang of men, up to their shoulders in the water. They tried frantically to turn it over, hacking wildly at the hull, hoping against hope that someone underneath might have survived. Hands and legs were smashed in the reckless attempt to save life; and when the bows at last broke apart they found two bodies there.

Then another cry went up as a struggling shape appeared in the waves; one man tossed back towards the slipway. Men and women skittered and slithered down the dangerous slope towards him, only to see him dragged mercilessly back. Again he was carried towards the reaching arms, and they made a human chain to snatch him from the sea. They pulled him half-conscious from the waves, wrapped him in blankets and carried him back to warmth and safety.

The people struggled on, trying to save life, but the tide had turned and as the waves began to draw back from the battery wall, they grew weaker. At last, as though sated by so much death, the fury of the storm eased, making it possible for them to throw a line from the end of the pier to the listing *Merchant* collier. Slowly, one by one, each member of the crew was hauled alive to the safety of the pier. The rescued seamen stepped ashore into a town that lay stunned and silent.

As the dark clouds drifted away and the sun returned, the search for bodies began.

I was fourteen years old when I was sent to Northallerton Jail. The magistrate judged me old enough to take the punishment for what I'd done.

– Paulina Raw

CHAPTER ONE

On the Crag

Dad didn't go out fishing the evening before the storm, for the rain poured down all day and it was clear that worse weather was coming. A gale blew up in the night and continued during the following morning. Halfway through the afternoon we heard the second maroon go off, and we knew then that the lifeboat would have to go out again, even though they'd already been out so many times that day.

Dad left our cottage on the Crag to see what was happening, but came straight back again. "I'd best go to help," he said. "Such a gale it is, I've never seen owt like it!"

Mam got up too. "Then I'm coming with you," she insisted. "Lina honey," she told me, "you must sit tight and mind the little 'uns. Don't move from here."

They went off together, and I struggled to fasten the door securely as the wind was blowing hard against it. I sat there all afternoon with my younger sister Bella and our little Joey, listening to the howling sounds outside. We grew restless and worried while Mam and Dad were gone, for they seemed to be away for ages. The storm buffeted our cottage along with the many other dwellings on the crowded Crag, built all higgledy-piggledy onto the steep hillside. Our roof tiles shifted and creaked and the windows rattled fit to break. We were tempted to go out to see for ourselves what was happening, but I made the young ones stay as I'd been told to do. We were glad that we hadn't moved when our mam returned, for we could see at once that something was very wrong. She came back soaked to the skin and moaning like an injured cat, too upset to say what had happened.

"Are you hurt, Mam?" I asked.

"No. But your dad… oh your poor dad," was all she'd say.

We watched in fear as she flew around our small homeplace. She pulled the rugs off our beds and threw them down in front of the hearth, yelling at us to move. We scattered fast. Joey ran to hide behind the rocking chair.

Soon enough we understood, for two of the strongest fishermen carried Dad into the cottage. When they put him down on the blankets we could see that he was badly hurt; his leg was crushed and blood was oozing from the wound. Neighbours pushed in through our doorway and our small space was suddenly crammed with anxious faces, so that when Grandma Kat arrived she had to fight her way through to us. Kat pulled Joey out from behind the rocking chair and snatched him up into her arms.

"We'll have these bairns out o' here," she cried. "I'll take 'em up to my place."

So we followed her, feeling frightened. Bella and I clung together, though the wind and rain had ceased, as we walked to Kat's tiny tenement home off Flowergate, in Turners Yard.

Grandma Kat was always there whenever we needed her, though she was what people called 'a character'. She lived alone and made a living mostly by selling fish, though she'd once had an Italian seaman named Giuseppe to lodge with her – and it turned out that he was our grandfather too. Giuseppe had sailed away before he ever knew that he'd fathered a child with Kat. She'd raised my mam alone and called her Maria, and then we grandchildren had been given Italian-sounding names in memory of our lost grandfather. I was Paulina, known as Lina; my sister was Isabella whom we called Bella; and our little Joey was really another Giuseppe.

Some of the neighbours raised their eyebrows at our fancy names and our dark eyes and hair and whispered as we passed.

"Decent folk might be 'shamed o' loose morals and exotic blood."

"Aye… but not Kat."

"No… not Kat."

"But she works hard to keep them all."

"Aye she does. Well… we all know Kat."

I didn't care what they said about us. Our dad, Rob Raw, was a respected fisherman and our mam was a kind and patient mother, while Kat was a crafty old woman with an answer for everything. We'd had tragedies like most of the fishing families – Kat's brother had drowned at sea, and Mam had given birth to three little 'uns that hadn't survived – but we'd managed well enough, until that day when the worst storm in living memory blew into Whitby harbour.

Grandma Kat kept us safe in her tiny tenement in Turners Yard that night, and the following morning she took us home. It was only then that we came to truly understand what had happened.

Our dad had been one of the men who'd rushed to help when the upturned hull of the lifeboat had reappeared in the water. Along with the others he'd tried to break it up, fearing that there were drowning men trapped beneath it. My dad had worked tirelessly, using the sharp gutting knife that he kept in a sheath at his belt, but as the bows smashed open, a jagged spike of planking had shot upwards and cut into his thigh. It carved right through his flesh and sliced him to the bone, and he'd lost a lot of blood. After a few more days he fell into a fever, so that we couldn't be certain whether he'd live or die. Mam worked day and night to save him, and Kat begged help from one of the wealthy Quaker wives who lived in the elegant row of new houses that had been built at the top of Flowergate.

The lady kindly sent a doctor down to the Crag for us. He said that, in addition to the wound, Dad's thighbone was cracked. He cleaned the wound once more and then, with Kat's help, he strapped our dad's twisted leg to a wooden splint. We were sent outside the cottage while it was done, but we could hear Dad groaning from the yard. He grew quiet after the doctor had gone, for a bottle of laudanum had been left behind to soothe the pain.

We didn't realise straight away how much our lives had been changed by the storm. Good friends and neighbours tried to comfort us.

"When your dad is better…" they said.

"When you get through this…"

"It will take a while…" they murmured. "You must keep hoping."

The whole town was grieving, and we were vaguely aware that there were meetings called and money collected to provide for the bereaved families. Slowly, slowly Dad's wound began to heal, and slowly too we came to understand that, though his leg might be mending, it was badly twisted and there'd be no more going out fishing in the Dunsley's coble for our dad.

I couldn't help wondering what I should do now, for when I'd turned ten years old, Mam had taken me from school to look after Dad. I made him breakfast when he arrived back with the morning tide, while she and Kat tramped round the villages with baskets of fresh fish on their heads to sell. Bella and Joey went off to school, for we could afford it then, but as the oldest lass I was expected stay at home and keep house while Dad rested. When he woke I'd fetch two pennyworths

4

of baccy for him to smoke in his pipe, and then we'd sit together and fix his lines, all ready for him to go out fishing again with the evening tide. As our dad lay sick and weak after the storm, I came to realise that our old way of life was lost forever.

Our neighbours helped, and the Quakers continued to pay for Dad's medicine. The fund that had been organised for the widows and orphans couldn't support us with regular payments, for we hadn't *lost* our dad, but there was a deal of sympathy. He hadn't taken an official lifeboat ticket that afternoon but everyone knew how hard he'd tried to help, and there was even some talk that Dad might be awarded a medal for what he'd done. Donations of food and clothing came to us, along with small amounts of money, slipped quietly to us from the families' fund.

Sam Dunsley called in most nights and gave us a share of the fish he'd caught. "I could pay for bait gathering and setting up lines," I heard him say to Mam one time, just as I was returning with a bucket of water from the pump.

"I cannot leave our Rob," Mam said.

"Aye… no, I can see that," Sam replied. "I was thinking more of your lass…" and he glanced at me as I set my bucket down.

"I could fetch bait," I offered at once. "And you know that I can clean a line and fix the bait."

Sam nodded. "Good lass," he said approvingly.

Mam sighed and nodded too. "Aye well… needs must," she agreed, reluctantly.

I'd helped Dad with the lines as long as I could remember, though I'd never gone bait gathering on the beach before. We'd always had enough money to buy fresh bait from Fishtail Lizzie, but I knew many lasses who did the work and felt sure that I could do it too.

"You'd best take the young 'uns with you," Mam said.

"What?" I exclaimed, shocked.

"Aye, Bella and Joey must leave the school."

"Can't we afford their lessons?" I asked.

Mam shook her head.

Our little Joey clapped his hands and danced around the yard when he heard that he wasn't to go to school, but Bella said nothing, and I saw that she looked troubled.

"It will be fine," I told her. "We'll go down to the scaur or up towards Sandsend, and you can find firewood and look for scraps of jet or help me gather bait."

I tried to sound cheerful, though my heart sank a little at the thought of the work. We'd have to join the great gang of scavengers who went down onto the beach at the turn of the tide to scrape a meagre living from the shore.

"Are you sad to be leaving school?" I whispered to Bella that night in bed.

"Aye," she whispered back. "My teacher says my writing is the best in class, but don't tell Mam."

I hugged her tight and sighed.

CHAPTER TWO

On the Scaur

The first time we set out to scavenge I felt scared, though I did my best to hide it, knowing we'd have to compete with many others who were hardened to the job. Bella and I got up early and put on boots, jackets, and shawls; we wrapped our Joey warmly too. We knew enough to bandage our fingers and pull on fingerless gloves to protect our hands, for we'd have to slip our baiting knives sharply beneath the limpet shells in order to snatch up the shellfish that we called flithers.

We took Joey by the hand and set off from the Crag to march across the bridge towards the east side of town. Like other folk we were laden with baskets and buckets, and we knew we needed to be there soon after the tide had turned in order to find the biggest mussels and flithers.

"What you lot doing?" Fishtail Lizzie asked sharply, coming up behind us as we crossed the bridge.

"We're going flitherpicking," I told her, feeling guilty.

"You'll not be buying from me anymore then," she commented gloomily.

"No," I told her. "I'm afraid needs must!"

"Aye well, I know about your dad," she said, and the sharpness in her voice seemed to soften a bit. "'Best walk alongside o' me."

"Aye," I replied. I was grateful to do as she said.

We followed Lizzie through narrow New Way Ghaut, past the Fish Pier, and out onto the sands with all the other scavengers. We set off eastwards over the flat, low, slippery rocks that we call the Scaur. Everyone headed in the direction of Saltwick Nab, where the land sticks out into the sea.

"Keep a look-out for driftwood," Lizzie told us, pointing to patches where the sea had dumped wood and branches on the shore. "I daresay your mam will be glad of that, and you'd best scrape up sea coal when you see it, for that'll burn just as well."

I nodded, grateful for her help, but felt a little shamed too that Lizzie had seen so quickly that we were in need.

"And keep an eye out for sea-washed jet," she shouted as she strode a little way in front of us. "Though you'd do best to go up Sandsend way if that's what you want. You'd get a few pence for that o'course."

We marched on beneath the high cliffs where some of the older lads clambered on ropes, swinging dangerously down the cliff face looking for seagull's eggs to eat or sell. It made me shudder to see them up there, for I knew that sometimes a rope could suddenly fray and send them crashing down onto the hard rocks below. Sam Dunsley's son Frank had fallen like that when he was just a lad. He'd cracked a bone in his leg, like our dad had done, and it had never mended straight, so that he still limped from the injury. Nowadays he worked in a jet workshop instead of climbing cliffs.

I dragged my eyes away from the swinging ropes, for I knew that we must get to work, and we had a lot to learn. Lizzie and some of the other fishwives helped us in their own rough way.

"Here lasses," they cried, waving us over. "Come here and pick. Plenty for you up here!"

Bella and I bent our backs and worked as fast as we could, but we were awkward with it. There was a knack to slipping a knife swift and sudden beneath the limpet shells, for the creatures would cling on tight to the rocks if they knew you were after them. We pulled mussels from the seaweed beds whenever we found them, and despite the bandages and gloves, our fingers gathered sharp little cuts. I shouted at Joey from time to time, for he rushed around splashing and getting in everyone's way, while all the time the tide ebbed further. My back and shoulders began to feel as though I'd been beaten with a stick, but at last we'd almost filled a bucket with bait. Lizzie kindly dropped a few large flithers in to top us up. We discovered too that when Joe stopped his plashing around, he opened up his sandy fist to show us a handful of sea-washed jet slivers.

"Why bless him," Lizzie said. "That's not a bad haul. Get 'em round to Dark Entry Yard. They should give you sixpence for that lot. Don't take less!"

We headed back as soon as the tide was on the turn, for we knew we'd got more work ahead to prepare the lines for Sam. Back across the slippery scaurs we went and up through the town where the market was in full swing. We made ourselves walk quickly past the tempting stalls, ignoring the delicious scent of new baked bread and pies that we couldn't afford. Grasping Granny, the old beggar woman who hung around on the corner of New Way Ghaut, came heading towards us, her hands outstretched, her scrawny granddaughter at her side.

"Gi' us a penny, sweethearts!" she begged in her whistling, whining voice.

The ragged child who followed her watched us with suspicion, her bare feet covered with mud and grime. Everyone knew them; the girl went by the unsuitable name of Sophia Goodchild, much more ridiculous than any of our Italian names. The filthy toothless old woman insistently held out her hand to us.

"Gi' us a penny ma pets," she croaked.

"Clear off!" I said. "Clear off, Grasper, and earn your own bread!"

I ran past them, pulling Joey along behind me. We'd trouble feeding ourselves without giving anything to them.

"At least we haven't sunk that low," I said to Bella.

"No, we aren't that low," she willingly agreed. "But my shoulders are killing me!"

We marched back across the bridge to our side of town and headed for Dark Entry Yard, where the jet dealers had their stalls. When we showed Old Man Turner the handful of pieces that Joe had found, he looked thoughtfully at them and weighed them in his hand.

"I'll give you tuppence," he said.

"I'll give you four," another man next to him offered.

Turner was the man we knew, for he kept his workshop in Turners Yard where Grandma Kat lived, but we took the four pence offered and hurried away back to our cottage on the Crag. We settled outside in the yard to soak the shellfish in buckets and clean the line of any rotting bait. Mam brought out a bowl of soup and hanks of bread that we ate hungrily, despite the stink that came from the buckets that we'd scrubbed the shellfish in. She praised us for our work as we fixed the fresh bait onto the many hooks. I felt a touch of pride that we were somehow managing to do it. It was late afternoon by the time we coiled the long line onto a flat round skep, setting the hooks neatly to the side, so they wouldn't catch or snag when the line was paid out. We'd worked without stopping, and we were worn out by the time we carried our skep down to the boat and handed it over to Sam Dunsley. "Good lasses," he said, impressed with our work

Days passed, and in time we got used to the early start. The skin on our hands grew hard as leather, and our fingers became more nimble to the tasks so that we gathered fewer cuts. The seashore wasn't always such a terrible place to be; there were days when the sun broke through the clouds and it was cheerful down on the scaur, what with the plash of the sea and the screeching of the gulls. On those days the scavengers would tease each other, so that friendly insults flew around, but when the freezing north wind lashed across the bridge and we were soaked with rain, we worked in silence.

Gradually the weather grew warmer. The fishermen set their long lines aside, for long lining was winter work and though so many flithers and mussels were no longer needed for bait, Sam Dunsley still gave us useful work to do, what with nets to mend and crabs and lobsters to be boiled and dressed. Our dad slowly recovered, and Mam felt that he was well enough to be left at home so that she was free to go selling fish once again. I thought that things were getting better, but gradually it became clear that a new problem had somehow come to us.

Dad hobbled around the house a bit and tried to do small jobs while I was boiling crabs in the yard, but his leg still hurt him badly when he moved, and most days he sent me to the druggist to fetch a bottle of Godfrey's Cordial. Everyone knew that the cordial was laudanum, and instead of needing less of it as time went by, he seemed to want it more. He'd drink it fast, and then for a little while he'd smile and be my old loving dad again – but then he'd fall asleep and wake angrily, asking for another bottle. It hurt me to see him like that, for I had such sweet memories of the happy times before the storm when we'd worked together. I used to love the afternoons, when our dad would get up from his rest refreshed and the little ones came home from school. I'd get us all bread and cheese, and we'd sit together cleaning and baiting lines while Dad smoked a pipe of baccy and told us stories that gripped us so that we could hardly breathe. He told tales of misty water sprites that sneaked up from the waves in the silvery moonlight to snatch a weary fisherman from his boat and drag him down through the watery depths to his doom. Chills of fear would run up and down our backs as we worked, but whenever he stopped we'd cry "More… Tell us more!"

Now everything was different. Mam would come home from selling fish to discover that a second bottle of Godfrey's Cordial had been bought and drunk. "How many today?" she'd ask.

I hated to tell her but knew that I must.

"Too much," she'd say, shaking her head. "If your father asks for more, you must tell him 'no'."

"Mam… I can't," I said.

"It's not the lass's fault," Dad told her snappily when he overheard us talking about it. "Leave her be. I need it!"

I hated to find myself stuck between the two of them arguing, but then things changed again and there was nothing I could do about it, for once Dad was well enough to shamble about and leave the cottage, he took himself off to buy what he wanted himself, and he started going to the alehouse too. A great deal of our hard-earned money went on Godfrey's Cordial and ale. We didn't begrudge him the comfort of it, for we knew he still suffered pain, but the amount was too much and the sympathy we'd enjoyed from our neighbours ebbed away – there was no more talk of medals being given. The Quakers and Methodists, who were usually generous to us, especially didn't like to see Dad stumbling in the streets and smelling of drink. We tried to hide what was happening, but we couldn't. Neither the ale nor the cordial seemed to help him much, for he became more miserable than ever and not at all like our old dad.

CHAPTER THREE

A Fortune in the Leaves

One afternoon when the younger ones were playing out in the sunshine, Mam spoke seriously to me. "We can't make ends meet like this," she said. "I'm sorry Lina, but we can't go on this way."

Her words made my stomach turn. "What will we do then?" I asked.

She gave a tired shrug. "Find cheaper lodgings in one of the tenement yards. I can take our tub and mangle with us and set up as a washerwoman, and you and Bella will have to help me with the work, honey."

My spirits sank at the sound of it, for the work of a washerwoman was considered low, and I knew it would be hard and unrelenting.

"Sam Dunsley's catches have been meagre of late," she went on. "He's warned me that he can't keep giving us fish to sell, but your Grandma Kat has said there might be a home-place for rent up in Turner's Yard where she lives, and we'd have drying rights there too. We'd be able to hang the washing in the yard to dry."

I sighed. "I suppose taking in washing is better than begging in the streets like some," I said.

"Aye, and better than the workhouse," Mam said firmly.

So we packed up our belongings and rented the house-place next to Grandma Kat, a one-roomed ground floor tenement in Turners Yard, off Flowergate. We'd a walkway with two-storey dwellings above us and a noisy jet workshop at the bottom of the yard, but we had drying rights in there and a bit of space for washing lines.

The yard was a busy, crowded place, though no busier than most of the yards. The Turners lived in a double-fronted cottage facing us on the other side of the yard. Jet dust hung in the air, and we could hear the constant whirr of grinding wheels along with the dull, dreary sound of the men chopping-out the raw jet, from early in the morning till late at night.

It was nine years since the Duke of Wellington had died, and there'd been a brief boom in the jet trade following the great hero's death. Our Queen had ordered the whole country to go into mourning for the famous duke, so that meant wealthy ladies needed jet necklaces and brooches to wear with their mourning gowns. But the time of mourning for the duke had passed, and the jet trade struggled again, so that many of the skilled craftsmen went looking for other kinds of work.

Old Man Turner and his two apprentices worked in a ramshackle shed where they tapped and chopped and scraped away all day. Alfie Biggin was a cheeky lad whom I knew from my short time at school. The other was Sam Dunsley's boy Frank, the quiet lanky lad who'd fallen from the cliffs so long ago. Frank walked with a limp and rarely spoke, but he was known to be good at carving jet, and people sometimes came specially to order the trinkets he made.

The only good thing about Turners Yard was that we'd moved next door to Grandma Kat; she'd found the place for us and helped in every way she could, using her influence with the wealthy wives who lived at the top of Flowergate. She'd persuaded a few of the ship owners' wives to let Mam take their washing in, while Kat went off as usual, tramping round the villages to sell her fish. Sometimes she took our Joey with her, so that he was out of the yard while we were trying to get the washing clean and dry.

We were very cramped in our one room, and Dad stomped clumsily about the place, getting in the way, until he took himself off to the alehouse. Me and Bella didn't have to go down to the beach anymore, but we got up early to fetch water from the pump and help with the washing. Our hands were just as chapped and raw as they'd been when we were fetching flithers, for we dipped them in and out of hot water all day and wrung out the clothes to get rid of the rinsing water, ready for the mangle.

The three of us bairns slept in a narrow cupboard bed. We didn't mind that, for we were close to the fireside and at least we were warm. I had to put up with Bella's feet in my face, for we could only fit into the bed if she lay the other way round. Joey scrunched himself up beside me.

On damp days washing hung everywhere, in front of the fire, above the windows, over the table, and across Mam's bed. When we pulled our bed down out of the cupboard, washing dangled above us and dripped on our heads.

I hated the place... I hated the whole seething yard, and when Mam told me she was having another bairn I was angry and wanted to walk straight out. I thought about going up to one of those grand houses at the top of Flowergate to see if I could get a job as a scullery maid, but of course I knew that I couldn't leave Mam when she needed me so badly.

"Scullery maids get lodgings and food," I complained to Kat. "I'd get a decent uniform to wear, and the houses up there are clean and quiet... and beautiful."

Kat was not impressed. "Scullery maids works all hours God sends," she told me sharply, "and besides that, honey, your Mam needs you here."

I was angry with my dad… angry that he could manage to give Mam another bairn to feed, though he couldn't manage to work, and resentful that he had such a need of laudanum.

One evening when I was hanging yet more washing in the yard, Kat stuck her head out from her doorway and called me into her home-place. I growled a warning to the jet lads, to be careful of our sheets and went to her.

"Come Lina," she said. "I see that angry face of yours. Come in here and rest a while. You shall have a cup of tea with me."

"Will you read my fortune in the leaves?" I asked, refusing to smile.

"If that's what you want," she agreed.

I nodded then for, after all, it wasn't just a cup of tea that Kat was offering. My crafty grandmother had many ways of earning money as she tramped from village to village. She sold fish whenever she could, but hidden under a cloth in the bottom of her basket she kept a few twists of paper that contained dry tea leaves and a small but very beautiful crystal ball. Tea was an expensive drink, beyond the reach of most of Kat's village customers, but grandmother made special arrangements with the maids who worked in the kitchens of the wealthy ship owners, slipping a few pence into their apron pockets to be rewarded with twists of dried tea leaves, used only once and dried again. They'd still make a decent brew and there'd be plenty of dark swirling leaves at the bottom of the cup, so that besides her gazing into the crystal ball, Kat offered to tell her customers' their fortune by reading the tea leaves, a touch of magic with their fish, for just an extra penny. It wasn't unknown for some of the wealthy wives to consult her quietly in times of need, and grandmother was known for her discretion.

Kat waved me into her den. "Come on, lass," she said. Stepping into her home-place, I did at last allow a soft sigh to escape me. Like all of us she had to fetch her water from the pump in the yard, but Kat seemed to manage to keep things a bit more clean and decent than we did. A fire glowed in her hearth, and her dresser was covered with jars of dried sweet-scented hedgerow herbs that she collected on her wanderings.

"Sit down," she ordered.

As I lowered my weary body into her rocking chair, my rage ebbed a bit.

"We'll have no more talk of scullery maids or big houses," she said. "Let's see if the leaves will tell us what lies ahead for you?"

As she opened her small polished tea chest and spooned the precious leaves into a chipped blue teapot, a prickle of excitement grew in my belly. Kat had read Mam's tea leaves many times, but she'd never done such a thing for me before.

She lifted the kettle from the trivet and poured boiling water onto the leaves, stirred, and sat down. "Now we'll wait for it to brew and while we're waiting we'll think of the future… *your* future, lass."

"I can see nowt but crying bairns and dripping washing," I said.

My spirits drifted down again at the thought of it all. Was my whole life to be spent in this dark hole of a place? But Kat ignored my dismal looks and gave the brew another stir; then after another moment she poured dark amber liquid from the spout into a pretty flowered cup and stood it on a saucer that almost matched.

"Where did this china come from?" I asked.

"Ask no questions, hear no lies," she said.

I guessed it had come from the same place as the second-hand tea leaves.

"Now sit back and sip the brew," she said. "It'll do you good."

I sat back and sipped, and it did do me good for it was warming and refreshing and soothing all at once. No wonder the Quaker wives went out to meet each other and drink tea every day.

"Have you supped it all?" Kat asked at last.

"Yes, nearly all," I said.

"Now, close your eyes and swill the cup widdershins three times, then turn it upside down, quick, quick, so the dregs will run into the saucer."

My hands shook slightly as I did it. Dad often complained that this was old women's rubbish and maybe the devil's work too. As I swirled the dregs, my heart started pounding, and I held my breath as I swiftly turned the cup over and set it in the saucer with a clink.

"Have I done it right?" I asked.

"Aye, that's fine. Now tap the upturned cup three times."

"Is everything in threes?" I asked.

"Aye, three is a magical number. Now, give it to me."

As soon as she took the cup from me, her eyes widened. I peered forward anxious to know what she'd discovered there, but all I could see was a clump of dark leaves that had gathered together at the bottom of the cup, no strange shapes or magical patterns. It looked like a lump of coal to me.

Her silence worried me. "What?" I asked, my heart thundering. "What does it show?"

"Well," Kat said. "I've seldom seen it showing quite as strong as that."

She looked me up and down and then suddenly chuckled. "I should have seen it before. Just look at you… If ever a lass were made for it, you are, your lovely dark hair and eyes as brown as my Giuseppe's."

"What… what is it that I'm made for?" I asked.

"Look at this patch of gleaming darkness at the bottom of your cup," she said, tipping it towards me.

"Like a lump of coal!" I said.

She laughed and shook her head. "Not coal," she said, "but jet. I think the leaves are telling us that your fortune lies in jet."

I gaped at her; that was not what I'd wanted to hear.

"Jet! But I hate the stuff," I said. "All muck and dust… I can't bear the noise and mess of it all. Why anyone wants to wear such dismal jewellery, I cannot think! And they say there's little money in it nowadays. You tell me that I'm fated to stay in this hateful place and work with jet. They won't allow women to do the carving or the polishing, and you think that telling me this will cheer me?"

Kat sat back, regarding me thoughtfully. "Jet has a magic and a beauty all its own," she said quietly. "There's ancient magic in that shining darkness. Well, the leaves don't tell me everything, so I can't say whether it will bring you fortune or favour, but this I know: Those who seize their chances do best in this life, and you have Whitby jet here all around you. They need lasses to thread the beads and stitch the cards and fit fasteners to the jewellery, but most important of all they need decent lasses to sell the finished work."

I folded my arms and pouted feeling miserable again. "What are you saying? I'm to go over the yard to Old Man Turner and tell him that my future lies in jet? Am I to ask *him* for a job? Do you think I want to spend my days sweeping up after those brazen apprentices of his?"

Kat sighed and rubbed her eyes and suddenly looked old and tired. "Go back your mam," she said, sounding sharp. "I've done my best to cheer you."

I got up and went back, without giving her a word of thanks, feeling angrier than ever.

CHAPTER FOUR

Jet

Our life continued as it had been before, with one new and bothersome difference, for I found that when I went to hang out the washing or take it in, my eyes would stray unbidden to the jet workshop at the top of the yard. Kat's crazy prediction was there in my head, and I couldn't get rid of it. The jettie lads would sit outside in the yard to eat their dinner, and if they saw me giving even the smallest glance in their direction, Alfie would call out rude names and offer even cruder invitations, while Frank scowled at me in silence. I'd known them both since I was a bairn and I wasn't scared of either of them, but I didn't much like them witnessing our humiliatingly reduced circumstances and our struggles to get the washing dry before it was coated with dust. Sometimes when I was weary of Frank's silent stare, I stuck my tongue out at him, making him blush and turn sharply away. I'd march back to our house-place, trying to scrape together as much dignity as I could muster, but it's hard to move with grace when you've got baskets piled high with washing in your arms and cats and dogs and slippery stone flags beneath your feet.

September came around and the weather turned chill. Mam's face had never looked so pinched and drawn, while Dad kept out of our way most of the time. He hung around the alleyways until the alehouse opened and returned in the evening the worse for drink, though how he paid for it none of us knew.

Mam began to cough, and we knew that the soap and the scrubbing didn't help with that. One morning I got up even earlier than usual and washed myself and brushed my hair and put on my Sunday dress, though even that was worse for wear. I was waiting out in the yard before the apprentices arrived, waiting for Old Man Turner to come out into the yard and open up his workshop. He appeared at last from his doorway, yawning as he took the keys from his waistcoat pocket. He stopped surprised when he saw me waiting there. "What's up?" he asked.

I tried to smile and look alert. "I thought perhaps…" I began. "Perhaps you might need someone to sell your finished jet for you," I said and swallowed hard. "Maybe I could take it round to the shopkeepers and talk to them nicely and show them how pretty your brooches and necklaces look on a lady."

He looked me up and down and for a moment I thought perhaps he was considering what I'd said, but then the two apprentices came noisily into the yard. They fell quiet when they saw me standing there with him.

"What goes on 'ere…?" said Alfie Biggin, a huge grin on his face.

Old Man Turner laughed nastily then. "Ey lass," he said, "the slickest jet dealers are struggling these days to sell their goods. Get back to yer washing lines and yer scrubbing tub and don't come bothering me."

He turned away and put his key in the lock to open up.

"Lina Raw is after our mester," said Alfie. He nudged Frank who looked deeply embarrassed and stared down at his feet.

"Try me, try me instead," Alfie begged. He grabbed my shoulders and pushed his face into mine, his lips pouting forward to offer a horrid kiss.

"Get yerselves in here," Turner called.

Frank hurried into the workshop and I pushed Alfie firmly away from me and scurried back into our house-place, fighting back tears. I hurriedly stowed my best dress away, glad that my family were still drowsy. I took up the bucket with shaking hands and went to fetch the water from the pump.

Mam grew steadily worse and a fever developed, so that she was forced to rest most of the time, and I had only Bella to help me do the washing. Kat tried one medicine after another, but nothing seemed to shift the shivering fits and the cough that shook her body day and night. Bella did her best to help, but she was still a child and kept dropping clean washing in the muddy yard, so that we sometimes had to start it all again. Some of our customers sent their washing elsewhere when we returned their sheets and clothing creased and not quite as spotless as they thought it should be. Kat still had to trudge the streets and lanes, in order to eat, let alone find money to help us with. Sometimes she'd keep back a fish-head or two, so that at least we could make a pot of fish-head stew.

I took the framed pictures that we'd brought with us from the Crag to the pawnshop on the corner of Flowergate, but we only got a few pence for them. I couldn't sell the poss tub or the mangle for then we'd have no means of earning left to us. Our Sunday clothes were next to go, for we had no time to go to the Methodist services anyway. Sam Dunsley knocked on our door with a parcel of fish-heads and tails one morning.

"The catches are poor," he said, "but at least with this you can make a stew."

I took the parcel gratefully, though I was utterly sick of fish-head stew. I caught sight of Frank watching from the workshop and felt shamed, for I guessed then that he'd seen our plight and told his dad that we needed help.

One night Kat came back very tired, after a long day of tramping the roads and just a few pence earned. "I hear the Quaker wives have set up a soup kitchen," she said. "What with some of the jet men struggling and the fishing poor. They might consider helping us and I'd go and ask myself, but I think they'd take more notice of a lass."

"You want me to go begging to them?" I asked, hating the very thought of it.

"They know what happened to your dad," she said.

"Aye… and they see him now," I said angrily. "They see him out in the streets… the state of him. What will they think of that?"

Kat sighed.

"I'll go," I said.

It was a deeply humiliating thing to do, but I swallowed my pride and the following morning, having made sure that we were as clean and tidy as possible, I took Bella and Joey down to the Friends Meeting House with me.

We went in through the open door and stood quietly for a moment, getting our bearings. The building was neat and clean but without decoration. I saw another open door and moved forward until we saw four neatly dressed Quaker women gathered around a scrubbed wooden table; one of them was Mrs Mason, whose washing we sometimes took. Sensing our presence they looked up at us and briefly exchanged a knowing glance.

I cleared my throat. "I've come to beg your help, goodwives," I began, trying to sound as polite as possible, though I hated the sound of my own wheedling voice.

"My dad…" I began.

"Yes… we know your father." Mrs Mason cut in sharply.

"I'm working at the washing, as you know," I said, "but I can't seem to make ends meet and Mam is sick…"

She put up a hand to silence me. "Wait a moment," she said.

We stood there obediently while they went into a huddle and though they spoke in hushed tones, I could sense the disapproval in their voices and caught a little of what was said.

"So they say… expecting again!"

"And him…"

"But… at least they cannot buy drink with our tickets!"

Joey began to slide his weight from foot to foot, and I saw that he'd made muddy marks on their clean floor.

"Be still," I warned him fiercely.

There was silence for a moment, and then Mrs Mason got up and went off into another room at the back of the building. She returned with a little bundle of tickets that she handed to me.

"These will see you through the next few weeks," she said. "Come here at noon on Tuesdays and Fridays and bring one of these tickets and a jug with you. We'll give you broth and a loaf, but you must try to work harder still and manage for yourselves; we cannot be giving out tickets forever. There is always the workhouse…"

"We'll manage," I promised hurriedly, dropping a reluctant curtsey. "When my mam has had the bairn… And I'm so grateful."

"Aye well," she said, not unkindly. "We'll see."

We hurried out, shamefully clutching our tickets.

Bella and I took a jug and a basket down to the Friends Meeting house each Tuesday and Friday and queued outside, along with the very poorest in the town. We shuffled into the clean scrubbed building, shamefaced, to claim our bread and broth and we were glad of it.

Towards the end of the month, Mam's breathing started to make a terrible rasping sound. Kat spent all day trying to ease her, while I struggled to get the washing done.

At last Kat shook her head. "We need a doctor," she said firmly.

I didn't know how we were going to get food for tomorrow, let alone money for a doctor. Kat had been unable to do her rounds selling fish, and the soup kitchen was two days away. It was late at night when dad returned, and I glanced at Joey and Bella who both slept restlessly. He stumbled in through the door, just as Kat was leaving.

"Grandma says mam *must* have a doctor," I told him.

"And where's the payment coming from?" Dad asked.

Kat gave him an angry glance. "I'll go to the top of Flowergate in the morning and beg help again," she said.

"You will not," Dad growled. "We need no help from such as them. I'll find the money… Leave it to me."

For a moment he looked his old, proud self, but I knew that what he really feared was the ladies' criticism, for they'd be likely to ask how he managed to find the money for drink, with his wife so poorly.

Kat made an angry gesture and left without a word.

CHAPTER FIVE

Like a Monkey

I turned to wring out a rag in cool water to place on Mam's brow, and Dad sat down by the fire, but I was aware that he was restless and watched me closely. When I got up to fetch more water, he got up too and took my arm.

"You're to come with me Lina," he said. "Kilt up your skirt and we shall find ourselves some money."

"What!" I said, looking at him in horror. "Kilt up my skirt? I will do no such thing."

I'd heard of men selling their daughters. Did he think I was no better than the beggar child whose mother had gone to lie with any man before she died? I shook him off.

"Nay, nay lass," he said, shaking his head as he swayed a little. "You mistake me! I'd never do such a thing to you. You must know that. It's not the sight of your legs I'm selling, lass. I want you to climb. You can climb like a monkey and run fast too. And you are small enough to get inside the place and none shall see us for it's quiet and dark out there."

"What place?" I asked suspiciously. "What is it that you want of me?"

"Jet," he whispered. "Raw jet, that's worth a good sum. I've seen where they keep it and I know how to get it. They think it's safe up there where they've hidden it, but if *you* climb in through the roof, all you'd have to do is pass it down to me, and I'll be the one to sell it. 'Tis there for the taking lass, at the top of our yard. Why, they'll maybe never notice that it's gone, or not for a while, and by then..."

My stomach lurched at his words and my heart started to thunder.

"Jet," I said. "Do you mean Turners' jet? How could I get their jet? I've seen how carefully he locks the shed up each night."

Dad shook his head and chuckled as though at some joke. "They think it's safe up there on the highest shelf, but locks won't stop my little monkey climbing in through the roof. They've got loose tiles up there."

"You couldn't sell it." I said. "The buyers know the owners of the works and who has mining rights. And you have no right to any jet at all."

"I know where they'll take it!" he said, and he wagged a shaking finger in my face. "I've picked up smaller pieces before and I can tell you, lass, they aren't all as fussy as you think! This is on our doorstep, there in Turner's Loft, but I'll take it to the other side of town. You can do it, little monkey!" He slapped me on the back and then flung an arm around me.

I knew what he meant when he called me "monkey". We'd once seen a sweet-faced monkey shin up a stick at the fair that comes in Regatta Week. A man with a barrel-organ turned the handle to set the music playing, and the monkey hopped up to the top of the stick and danced for the crowd. Dad used to call me 'little monkey' after that, for he said I was as sprightly as the little creature. I longed for those happier times, but I pulled away from him, refusing to be persuaded by those loving childhood words.

He hugged me again and planted a whiskery kiss on my forehead. "Nay, lass," he said. He lurched to the side a little, still unsteady on his feet, and let go of me in order to hold out his hands in measurement, as though he'd caught a good-sized herring. "Nay, lass. I've seen it in there, lovely wide slabs of it, some as big as a loaf. Pieces big enough to make five or six brooches, or maybe more, or some of these fancy bracelets that the old ladies wear."

I shook my head, still appalled at the very idea.

"You can do it," he went on. "Those tiles on the ridge above the shed are loose, I've reached up there to have a feel at them, and a lass like you could shin up the clothes prop and lift those tiles they think so safe. We'd both be back inside before the bairns have even stirred."

I was silent now, frightened at what he suggested, but we were desperate, and despite myself the image of those gleaming black tea leaves slipped into my mind. Was this what Kat's reading had signified?

"They've got so much, they might not even know," Dad chuckled. "Jet like that would pay a doctor's bill."

He'd been thinking about it for a while, I could tell that, and though the thought of doing it terrified me, I saw that he was serious. He stroked my arm gently, like he used to do when I was small. "What do you say, monkey... you and me... hey? Come now, we'll sort out your mam."

"It's wrong," I said. "It's theft. If we were caught they'd send us both to prison... or even to Australia. Where would our mam be then?"

"Where will your mam be with no doctor?" he asked me seriously.

I turned to look at her tossing and turning in her fever and at our sleeping bairns in the pull-down cupboard bed – they'd be waking soon and hungry. Was it possible that stealing jet was the only way to get us out of trouble?

"Your mam need never know," Dad said.

A last flash of sense came back to me. "But Mam'd rather die than have me steal," I said.

I folded my arms ready to refuse, but Dad gripped my shoulder so hard that it hurt and he whispered. "Do you want your mam to die instead?"

"Let go of me!" I hissed.

He let me go, for I think he knew he'd won. With those words he'd played the card that I couldn't reject. I bent down and started to pull my skirt forward, knotting it up between my legs, then tucked it up into my belt as I used to do when I went climbing down the harbour ladders to where the fishing coble was moored. A last thought came to me, and I snatched up my apron with its deep pockets, to tie around my waist.

"Let's get it done then," I said at last and followed my dad out into the yard.

All was still outside, except for the mewing of gulls and the sound of muffled laughter that came from inside one of the tenements on the walkway above. It was cold out there and dark but for the faint flicker of candles from the small windows of the dwellings. Through the smoke that drifted everywhere, a dim glow of lamplight could be seen from Flowergate. I turned towards the silent jet workshop and shivered a little as I waited for my eyes to adjust to the shadows that surrounded it.

"No hurry… no rush," Dad said.

He hobbled a bit to the side and picked up the wooden clothes prop from one of our washing lines. The jet workshop had once been a one-storey cottage built into the end of the yard, and my dad vanished into darkness at the side of it. Cautiously I followed him. When I too slipped into the darkest shadows, I saw that he'd set the clothes prop up against the wall, where it almost reached the roof. There were no windows on that side, only buckets stacked for keeping wood and coal.

"No hurry… no rush," he whispered again.

I swallowed hard and my stomach turned queasy.

"You shin up there when you're ready lass, and you'll find soon enough where the tiles are loose. Lift 'em and hand 'em down to me and I'll stack them here. No noise... no sound... no one to know. What we want is up this end o' the loft, on a shelf above the work-bench."

I took the clothes prop in my hands and my stomach lurched again, for my hands were shaking. "You'll have to hold it steady!" I warned.

But just as I lifted my foot, a door opened in one of the cottages on the far side of the yard, and I froze with one leg wrapped round the wooden prop. Old Man Turner staggered out of his house-place to empty a chamber pot into the gutter. The sound of the splashing seemed loud, and I thought he looked our way. I held my breath, but then he turned and went back inside again.

Dad gave me a small shove and, like it or not, I found myself scrambling up the clothes prop. He held it steady while I clambered right up onto the roof amongst the loose clay pantiles. Squatting up there, my heart began to thud, but Dad was right about the tiles – most of them were loose and many broken, though I feared to move again in case more of them slipped and set the whole workshop roof falling away. Old Man Turner certainly didn't bother to keep his pantiles in good order.

"Can yer feel 'em move?" Dad asked, his voice hoarse and low.

"Aye," I whispered and reached for the first slate that slipped a bit beneath me. I picked it up carefully and handed it down to Dad. He took it and vanished. I lifted the tile next to it and it came up easily and silently, sending a small tingle of fearful excitement rippling through my body. I could do this. I *could* move as lightly as a monkey. I could act the thief and get away with it! Reasoning my fears away, I lifted one tile after another – telling myself that we were desperate and it wasn't fair that Mam was ill and Dad cruelly crippled when he'd only been trying to help save life.

Having handed a fourth loose tile to him, I pushed two others to the side, and by then a deep, dark space had opened up in front of me. My hands searched around until I discovered two fairly sturdy rafters beneath to grip onto. I crouched over the hole, grasping the rough wood and staring down until I thought I could make out the shape of the workbench below and shelves close by. I swung myself down, slipping easily through the space I'd made and landing lightly as a cat. The wood of the shelf seemed to hold my weight, but as I slid one foot forward I knocked against something, a small pot perhaps. I reached down to feel powder on my fingers, which I didn't like, so brushed my hands together and rubbed them on my apron. I waited again for my eyes to adjust and told myself to take my time. Gradually I made out the shape of a box that seemed to be piled with rough dark lumps, and when I reached out to them and found the pieces almost warm to the touch and far from heavy, I knew I'd found what we needed. I started to grab at them, shovelling lumps of raw jet into my apron pockets, my heart beating fast as I sensed the value of what I took – but then something happened! It was the most terrible, shocking thing that I could ever have imagined. A shadow moved fast below me and a hand grabbed at my ankle and at the same time a whistle started blowing: beep, beep, beep, beep!

CHAPTER SIX

Red handed

Between each whistle blast I heard a gasping breath that scared me more than anything, while two hands began to creep up my leg, gripping me hard. Someone had been there in the darkness all the time, watching and waiting. Blast after blast of the whistle pierced my ears, and I crouched there on the workbench, frozen with horror, my pockets full of jet. My dad would come to save me now… he'd come somehow to rescue me… surely he would.

Then the hands crept up to my thighs and I screamed. Louder than ever came the whistle blast, and in panic I began to snatch up the stolen pieces of jet and throw them down onto the floor below. I fought like a cat, with nails and teeth, but those two strong hands gripped my left leg even tighter, and there were shouts, and suddenly a swinging lantern filled the place with light.

The whistle blew again, and a voice that was faintly familiar and close to me called out, "Here. I have the thief!"

"Dad," I howled.

But it was Old Man Turner who'd appeared in the doorway, holding a lantern high, and I saw then that the strong brown hands that gripped my thigh so fiercely belonged to Frank Dunsley. He still held me tightly, but his upturned face looked deeply shocked. His mouth gaped open as he stared at me, and the whistle that he'd held between his teeth fell out. Blood ran down one of his cheeks, where I'd raked him with my nails.

"Bloody hell!" he whispered, and he suddenly let go of me.

I moved at once to climb back up towards the roof, but Old Man Turner had grabbed me. "Damned thief... little bitch," he cried. "I have you now! My God, it's the Raw's lass."

"Dad!" I screamed, frantic now.

"No use shouting for him," Turner said. "We've caught you red handed!"

Then he suddenly started to laugh in a most horrible way as he pointed at my hands, and I looked down to see that my fingers were dusted with red jeweller's rouge, my boots and clothing marked in the same way. The pieces of jet that I'd thrown down were lying there on the stone paved floor below me, with two more lumps left bulging in my apron pockets.

Frank backed away, staring at me white faced. He too was marked with jewellers rouge on his hands and in his hair. Blood ran down his cheek and suddenly he made a choking sound in the back of his throat. I tried again to leap away but Turner had tight hold of me, and by then others had crowded into the workshop and rushed to help him.

"Get her down. Get her down from there!" they cried.

"Stop gawping, Frank!" Turner bellowed. "Get yourself off to Blackburns Yard and fetch the constable. 'Tis damage to property as well as theft, I'll 'ave her jailed for this."

Frank stared at me for another moment, wiped his cheek, and then pushed his way out through the gathering crowd.

Old man Turner hauled me down from the workbench. He pulled at me roughly, and I landed awkwardly and twisted my ankle as I landed. I wanted to die, to sink into the floor, to shut my eyes and never open them again.

"Nay... *she* cannot be a thief, not Maria's lass!" It was Mrs Turner's voice, and I snatched a moment of hope from her.

"I'm sorry… so sorry… I never meant…" I began.

But how could it be explained.

"Fetch her father to her," another said. "He'll give her a good hiding. No need to fetch the constable."

"Yes, fetch my dad," I begged.

"'Tis not your roof she's ruined!" Turner growled. "Or your jet she's tried to take. The constable shall have her." Spittle flew from his lips and he gripped my arm like a vice, pulling the remaining pieces of raw jet from my apron pockets. "See this… and this!" he cried. "I've lost plenty o' jet of late. That's why I set the lad to watch, and now I know who's taking it. Those moping seal's eyes of hers won't wash wi' me!"

"I'll fetch her dad meself," Mrs Turner offered.

I couldn't say any more, shocked as I was. What could I plead in my defence? There came further sounds of argument in the yard, and Grandma Kat came pushing past them all to find me. She threw up her hands in horror when she saw me there.

"My granddaughter! *My* granddaughter… give her to me," she demanded.

"No. The constable shall have her," Turner said.

"I'll see her punished," Kat begged. "Her mother's sick and we're at our wits' end. I'll see her punished thoroughly. No need to fetch the constable… no need to fetch him, please. We'll find you money for compensation."

"Aye, that's what I said," Mrs Turner agreed. "Poor Maria! And you know how the father is… They're struggling!"

"Am I not struggling?" Turner was adamant.

"This will finish my Maria," Kat begged. "Give the lass to me. I'll see her punished hard, and we'll somehow make you payment for the damage she's done."

But Constable Linskill had arrived by then, and everyone started shouting at once, though Old Man Turner bellowed loudest, making his accusations clear. My red powdered hands and legs did nothing to help.

Constable Linskill looked grim and shook his head. "Are you sure?" he asked.

"I want her cuffed and put before the magistrate," Turner insisted. He thrust my arm forward, and the constable snapped his handcuffs round my wrist.

"Come with me," he said. He hauled me down the narrow alleyway that led into our yard, past our open doorway. I heard gasps of horror and dismay from both sides of the yard and even the walkway above, as the staring neighbours parted to let us through.

"Dad," I wailed hopelessly, still praying that he might appear and somehow rescue me. Bella stood in our doorway in her shift, looking puzzled and scared at what was happening. Joey wandered out to join her, his eyes wide and anxious at the noise and fuss.

"Lina! Our Paulina!" Bella cried. She made a frantic grab at me. "You cannot take our sister away! Don't take our sister from us, please!"

I tried to speak to her, but no words would come, and Grandma Kat shoved past us. "Now, now, you two, get back inside," she ordered. With one last despairing glance at me, she took my brother and sister firmly in her arms and thrust them back inside our home-place.

The constable dragged me out through the alleyway and into Flowergate. It was then that I saw the dark shape of a man on the other side of the street – a shadow sliding away into the entrance that led to Waterloo Yard. I couldn't see him clearly, but I knew… I knew it was my Dad, and I was filled with a cold, new, frightening kind of anger. How could he do this to his child? How could he desert me and leave me to bear the blame for the wrong that he'd persuaded me to do? I would hate him forever, I told myself.

Bad news always travels fast, and as I was hustled down the street a small crowd gathered. They followed us down the hill to the harbour side, and I can't remember how I got across the bridge or how I managed to walk down Church Street, but the next thing I recall was that I was stumbling up the steps that led into Blackburns Yard. The constable shouted something and Mrs Linskill opened the door of their cottage and stood on the doorstep, blinking and dishevelled in her nightgown, with a lantern in her hand.

"We have a thief," the constable announced.

"No, not Lina Raw!" his wife muttered. "Paulina cannot be a thief!"

Her daughter Anne came out to stare at me. "Whatever has she done?" she asked.

Anne was the second daughter, just a little older than me, and long ago we'd sat together in school. Her older sister Mary appeared behind her looking shocked.

"Caught red handed stealing jet," the constable said. "No doubt about it, I'm afraid. Hold the lantern up and look at her hands and her legs."

Mrs Linskill swung the lantern forward, and I saw with shame that my skirt was still caught up between my legs and tucked into my belt, revealing those red powdery stains that proved my guilt. I reached down to pull at my skirt with my free hand, but the skirt was stained as well.

"She's never walked through the streets with her skirt up like that," Mrs Linskill murmured.

"Aye well… I thought I'd best get her here. Fetch the keys to the lock-up!" the constable said.

The older daughter pushed forward then. "You can't put Kat's granddaughter in there," she protested.

"Now Mary, you know that I must do my duty, even though they be neighbours," Constable Linskill replied.

I stared about me, in a despairing daze. It didn't matter to me where they put me when my whole life had collapsed about my ears.

Mrs Linskill produced keys, and I was hustled outside to the lock-up that stood in the corner of their yard, facing their front door. The constable released me from the handcuffs and pushed me firmly inside. The place smelt of coal tar, damp, and vomit, for it was mainly built there to house violent drunks, streetwalkers, pickpockets, or vicious thieves… and suddenly it hit me that I was one of them, a vicious thief. I would be treated as such.

I briefly glimpsed the tiny room in the lantern light and saw that it contained a wooden bench bed with a thin mattress and a worn woollen blanket folded on top. A small shelf had been bolted to the wall, with a bucket for slops beneath it and a high window with iron bars above it.

"Shall I leave the lantern for her?" Mrs Linskill asked.

"No. She must be treated as any other," her husband said.

They hurried away and the door was closed on me.

CHAPTER SEVEN

In Blackburns Yard

I stood in darkness, though I could hear the constable still arguing with his daughters outside. A grating noise was followed by a loud clang, which told me that a bolt had been drawn, and then the click of a key turning in a padlock. The sound of their voices trailed away.

I stood there alone and still for what seemed a long time, then gradually became aware that I was shivering. Dimly remembering the rough blanket that I'd seen folded on the bed, I shuffled forward towards the dark shape of it, but before I managed to find it there came another low scuffling sound outside. The bolt was drawn back and the flickering light of a candle lit the small space again.

"Hush now, don't make a sound," a voice warned. "Our Mary won't have you left like this."

Anne came into the cell, the lighted candle in one hand and another blanket draped over her arm. The door opened wider and her sister followed her inside, and with them came a clean, fresh scent. Mary carried a small tray with a plate of bread and cheese, a bunch of some sort of plant, and a mug of water on it, which she set down on the shelf.

"Here honey, take this," she said, picking up the small bunch. "Hold it to your nose. We've no flowers at this time of year, but the stems and leaves will carry the scent. It will make it all smell better, for I'd hate to be in here. This place was scrubbed today, but no amount of scrubbing gets rid of its bad smell."

I saw that the source of the fragrance was a small bunch of fresh-picked lavender leaves, and I took them from her gratefully. Mary Linskill was one of the quieter, older girls in Whitby, who sometimes played the organ in the chapel. I hadn't seen her lately, and I recalled that she'd been working away from home.

"Right. Now set that candle down," she told Anne.

"Th… thank you," I managed.

I sniffed the clean scent of the lavender and suddenly the unexpected kindness set my chin atremble. Struggling to take a breath, it came at last in great gulps and sobs. They took no notice of my tears but bustled about in the small space and set up the bed for me with the fresh blanket.

"Get in," Mary ordered, holding back the blanket. I climbed into the bed, still clutching the posy of lavender and shamefully trying to knuckle tears from my eyes.

"Now then, eat this bread and cheese and try to rest," Mary told me, and she reached out for a moment to gently stroke the hair back from my face.

"I… I have ruined my life," I said.

"No," Mary said firmly. "Not forever. Life can be changed, that's something I've learned of late. We'll leave the candle here for you."

I watched them go, wondering vaguely what she'd meant, and found myself alone again but warmer now, with the flickering light of a candle and the fragrance of lavender. My stomach rebelled, but I dared not waste the slice of bread and cheese they'd set beside me, so I made myself eat it, chewing slowly, drank the water from the mug, then tried to sleep.

For a long time I lay awake, my stomach churning, while in my mind I went over and over what had happened. What an utter fool I'd been, and as for him who'd led me into trouble, I'd never call him father again. Painful though it was, I couldn't stop myself from reliving that terrible heart-stopping moment when Frank's hand had snapped around my ankle. I'd never allowed a lad to grab at me like that before, though plenty had tried. He'd held me tightly as his hand moved up my thigh and I'd felt his warm breath on my skin. A flush of shame swept over me. What had he felt, as his hand moved up past my knee? I knew from the look of utter shock on his face that he'd been stunned to discover that it was me he'd caught. Would he have grabbed me so roughly if he'd known? I hated him and he must certainly hate me.

I worried about what might be happening at home. The bairns would be scared – and what of Mam, so sick? Grandma Kat would never leave them… that at least I could be certain of.

I must have drifted off to sleep at last, for sometime later I realised with a start that the bolt was being withdrawn. The candle had guttered and a faint trace of daylight showed through the window high above me.

Constable Linskill opened the door and stood back to allow Anne to come inside. She carried a bowl of porridge and a mug of water. The constable looked at the guttered candle and the plate, but he said nothing. He watched in silence as Anne cleared it all away, and just as they were turning to go, I managed to find my voice.

"I'm sorry, Sir," I said. "I am so very sorry."

"It's not me you need to say sorry to," he said. "I must go to the Police Station now, for written statements should be taken from the witnesses. Then you will have to go before the magistrate at noon."

I gritted my teeth. Should I ask pardon of Old Man Turner, then? That would be much harder, but I knew it must be done.

I was left alone again to eat the porridge and drink the water. After that I sat still, not knowing whether hours or minutes passed though I tried to take note of how the light from the window moved across the walls. I had to use the shameful slop bucket twice and wondered if I'd been forgotten. But at last the door opened, and Anne was there with a comb in her hand and her mother standing behind her barring the door.

"Father says you may comb your hair," she said. "But you cannot wash that rouge away, it's evidence."

My heart sank and my stomach lurched. I could see bright daylight now the door was open.

"Is it noon?" I asked.

"Yes, almost. Father is waiting to take you to the magistrate."

"Neatly plaited hair will serve you best," Mrs Linskill advised. "Be as quick as you can!"

I took the comb and pulled it through my hair then quickly plaited my thick mane. Anne took a ribbon from her own hair and helped me fasten it neatly.

"I thank you," I whispered, "and I thank your sister for her kindness too."

"Our Mary has gone," Anne said wistfully. "She went on the morning coach to Manchester, for she's got a new position there as governess."

"Hurry now," her mother cut in.

"Speak courteous to the magistrate," Anne whispered.

"Hush Nan," her mother told her.

I smoothed down my rouge-stained dress as best I could and rubbed my hands together, but the red marks stayed in place.

"Is she ready?" I heard the constable's voice outside. He came forward to snap the handcuffs onto my wrist, and I stood there meekly as he did it. Constable Linskill was thought of as a firm but fair-minded man, and I took some comfort from that. He led me out through Blackburns Yard, which was busy as usual with fishwives baiting lines and gutting fish and the whirring sound of jet wheels coming from the workshop up on the hillside above. I looked neither right nor left and kept my head down as I walked past them and out onto Church Street. We walked over the bridge at a fast pace and through the streets of Whitby, with me led shamefaced and handcuffed by the constable. The Magistrates Court was close to the centre of town and the streets were full of folk who knew me.

"Lord bless us! Is that Maria's lass?"

"Well are yer surprised? Wi' Rob Raw for a father, always drunk these days!"

"Aye, and old Kat, no better than she should be…"

"But I've never seen her drunk!"

"Nay… not drunk, but something of a witch they say!"

The magistrate was the Reverend John Faraday, a local clergyman who I knew was regarded as strict. I couldn't keep back a small groan of despair when I saw him there and heard his name announced.

"Answer politely!" Constable Linskill said quietly as we went inside. "It will go best with you, if you admit your guilt. Call the magistrate Sir, but never look him in the eye. Your grandmother is here to speak for you."

I saw that Kat was standing in the waiting room, dressed in her best gown and shawl, her hair combed and pinned into a neat bun, her hands clasping and unclasping each other like fluttering birds wings.

Old Man Turner paced angrily at the other end of the room, red faced and furious. Frank Dunsley stood there wearing his Sunday jacket and looking pale, his hands scrubbed clean and his hair slicked back. He glanced my way and then looked down, and I felt myself flush, remembering where his hand had been. There was no sign of my father there.

CHAPTER EIGHT

The Magistrate

With the constable still at my side, I was led into the courtroom and made to stand before the magistrate and listen, while Old Man Turner ranted on and on about the present hardships that the jet workers were suffering and the wickedness of those who stole from them.

"She's guilty as hell!" he cried, spittle flying again. "My roof is damaged, my best haul o' jet in her pockets and jewellers rouge all over her hands and clothes. This'll cost me a full week's profit! The rouge alone shall cost me that! I demand compensation. Had I not set the apprentice lad to watch, I'd have lost more!"

"Bring the witness," Mr Faraday ordered.

Frank shambled forward, looking pale and sheepish. "Is this true?" the magistrate asked. "Did you apprehend this young woman in the act of stealing jet?"

Frank made a faint sound, something between a cough and a grunt.

"Speak up lad," the magistrate ordered. "It is your duty to bear witness, and I see that you've already made a statement to the police. Did you apprehend this girl in the act of stealing jet, yes or no? Speak clearly, or you yourself may be subjected to the law."

"Yes… Sir," I heard him say.

"You, girl. Do you admit this act of theft?"

"Yes, Sir," I whispered. "And I am truly sorry for it."

"Is there someone to speak for her character?"

Kat hurried forward, her eyes darting nervously from me to the man behind the desk. She cleared her throat and spoke in a manner most uncharacteristic of my usually frank spoken grandmother. "Our Paulina is a very good girl," she said, her voice soft and pleading. "She's been working hard to keep the family and nurse her mother through sickness too... These have been difficult times for us. Her father was injured when the boat went down and can no longer earn as he once did. Paulina only stole to get money for a doctor for her mother."

"Hard times are no excuse for theft!"

"No, Sir," she agreed, bobbing her head dutifully.

"If, as you say, your granddaughter has previously been of good character, then she should receive a punishment that will prevent her from straying from the paths of righteousness again. A reformatory will do that."

I caught my breath, for I knew of others who'd been sent to Doncaster Reformatory School and never been seen in Whitby Town again.

"How old are you, girl?" he asked.

"I'm fourteen, Sir," I said.

"Fourteen!" he raised his eyebrows and his cheeks flushed angrily. "She is small for fourteen, and this is a serious matter of theft and damage! At that age she should know better. Fourteen is old enough to go to jail."

I heard Kat gasp, and even the constable seemed to start a little.

A moment of terrible silence followed, and I felt as though I'd somehow left my body behind and must watch it all happening from some far distant place. Then I was back there in my stained clothes and feeling sick. Bile rose in my throat and I feared I'd vomit.

"She shall be sent for trial to the County Court and see

how she likes Northallerton Jail. Can she be transported there tomorrow?"

"Yes," the constable said hurriedly. "That will be possible."

"Very well; take her away!"

"What about my compensation?" Old Man Turner demanded. "Compensation, that's what I want!"

"Next case," the magistrate called out.

"Come," the constable ordered, taking my arm. I struggled to make my legs work as I was led away past Kat, who reached out briefly to touch my hand.

"I'll see to your mam and the bairns," she whispered.

"Leave her," Constable Linskill warned.

He led me once again in handcuffs from the courtroom and through the streets. I stumbled constantly, as though my eyes were closed, and walked in a frightening nightmare. We turned into Blackburns Yard, and as I lifted my feet to climb the steps I caught a brazen glance, a momentary flash of triumph, from the glassy blue eyes of the beggar girl, Sophia Goodchild. I turned momentarily to see that she crouched in a narrow sheltered nook piled high with coal, between two cottages.

He marched me back to the lock-up, removed the handcuffs and pushed me inside again.

I didn't weep, I couldn't think clearly or understand what had happened, but sat on the hard bed in a stupor. That evening they brought me warm onion broth and bread, but I couldn't touch it. A dark cold anger had settled somewhere down in my stomach. I would never, never forgive my father for what he'd done, but I hated myself too. How had I come to be such a fool?

Darkness fell in the lock-up, but still I sat upright, refusing to try to sleep or make myself more comfortable. I deserved to be punished for my weak-mindedness, my stupidity.

Like all the Whitby yards, Blackburns Yard was crammed with cottages and work sheds and even at night there was a deal of noise; doors opened and shut, buckets banged, chamber pots were tipped, women scolded their children, and seagulls screeched through it all. Those sounds were familiar and almost comforting, though the thought came to me that I would hear nothing like them in Northallerton Jail. Quiet fell at last, as people went to their beds and even the screeching gulls were hushed a little, but then unexpectedly other sounds began, distant at first, but growing louder; the sound of raised voices.

Among the shouts came one particular voice that I recognised, though it was angry and slurring. "It were me!" he cried. "I tell yer it were me as made 'er do it! It's me shlud be in there. Not my lass!"

A warm sense of relief flooded through my body and I gave a great sigh. At last, I thought… at last! Dad had done what he should've done all along. I waited, holding my breath as the argument continued. Surely, surely they would now let me go.

The lock-up bolt was drawn, and in the swinging lantern light I saw my father, swaying and red-faced, supported by the constable and a burly fisherman.

"Come out of there, lass," the constable said.

"Are ye listening?" my father said. "Ishh me as done it!" His knees gave way, and they struggled to heave him upright.

"Get her out," the constable told his wife. Mrs Linskill stepped forward, and with lantern in one hand she pulled me outside with the other.

"Can I go now?" I asked.

"No, lass," she said softly, and she kept tight hold of me.

The constable thrust my father into the lock-up in my place.

"Can I not go?" I asked again.

"No, lass, you can't," Mr Linskill said firmly.

"But he has told you, hasn't he? My Dad has told you! It was him that made me do it."

The constable closed the door on my dad, bolted it, and turned the key in the padlock.

"I'm sorry, lass," he said. "The magistrate ruled that you must be tried at the County Court. You are fourteen years old and have admitted your guilt; there is also evidence of the crime."

I stared at him in shock as the hopelessness of my situation dawned on me. Dad's confession had come too late. I had climbed in through the jet workshop roof with the intention of stealing the precious pieces, and I'd admitted my crime to the magistrate. Dread washed over me. Glancing quickly around the yard, I thought that I might make a run for it, but Mrs Linskill sensed the intention and shook her head at me.

"Don't think of it," she hissed. "Tonight you're the lucky one, for my husband says we may put you in Mary's room. You'd do well to make the most of it."

Tom Linskill's face was grim in the lantern light. "Go quietly with my wife," he said. "It will be the best thing for you." With my father still shouting from inside the lock-up, Mrs Linskill led me through the yard, dark shadows dancing all around. I went obediently into their neat cottage, all resistance spent.

"Are you there?" Mrs Linskill called.

"Up here," I heard Anne answer.

"Go up!" her mother said, and she pushed me ahead of her. I climbed the narrow twisting stairs and stepped into the neatest space I'd ever seen.

CHAPTER NINE

Mary's Room

Anne was waiting for me in Mary's tiny room, and I felt as though my very presence soiled the place. The bed was narrow and spread with a patchwork cover, while a lighted candle stood on the small cupboard top beside it. There was a washstand and a chair, no room for more. The walls were freshly whitewashed, but the astonishing things that made the room so special were the two painted pictures that hung on the wall. One was of flowers and the other of a small girl. Anne saw me looking at them.

"That's me," she said pointing to the painting of the child. "Our Mary did that when I was just a bairn."

The space was bare of the usual clutter, for of course Mary had taken her most personal possessions with her; there were no clothes, shoes, combs, gloves, hats, or even a workbox there.

"Go and fetch water, Nan," Mrs Linskill said as she appeared behind me. "There's a bit of warm in the kettle, and she must wash if she's going to sleep in Mary's bed."

Anne pushed past me.

"You'd best take yer boots off too," her mother said.

"I'm sorry for all the trouble," I mumbled, as I bent to unlace my boots.

"How Kat's grandchild came to this I cannot think," she said. She shook her head sadly at me. "You'll break her heart and your mam's as well."

Anne struggled up the stairs with a jug of tepid water that she set down on the washstand. Her mother left us together, saying only, "Mind you lock the door, our Nan."

Anne handed me a clean but ragged towel. "You'd best get washed and into bed," she said. "The convict wagon will be here to take you to Northallerton in the morning."

"W… will I go alone?" I asked.

"Nay, it's part of father's job to take you there," she said, and she sat down on the bed. "It's a rare thing this. They don't usually let a prisoner sleep in here… especially a thief."

For a moment I was offended, but I swiftly realised that she was simply stating facts. "I thank you for it," I said demurely, as I took off my stained dress and stood by the bowl in my shift to wash myself.

"I shall have this room when you are gone," Anne said.

"Did Mary paint the flowers too?" I asked, as I dried myself.

Anne sighed. "Aye, she's good at painting. She's clever at everything is Mary, reading, writing, stitching, she can do them all, but I pity them bairns she's going to act as governess to, for she'll be strict wi' them."

"She was kind to me," I said. "Please thank your Mam, for letting me wash and stay in here. I'm so shamed of my dad."

Anne picked up the washbowl, frowning a little at my words. "He may be a drunk, but at least he's not a thief," she said.

She went out, and I heard her lock the door behind her while I stood there clenching my fists, trying to contain the anger that rose in me. I wanted to shout after her but realised that she could have no idea how it had come about that I'd gone thieving. What good would any amount of shouting do? This was how everyone would see me now. Dad was just a drunk, but I was a thief.

I stood still in the tiny space for a moment, listening to the sound of Anne's footsteps on the stairs, overwhelmed by a dreadful sense of hopelessness. At last I moved to the window and lifted a corner of the loose net curtain to look down into the yard. I could see the dark hump of the lock-up just a little way away. The yard was quiet again, bathed in moonlight, though glimmers of warmth flickered in many of the cottage windows. The small cell, built of rough bricks, stood in the darkest shadowy corner of the yard, and I became aware of a faint repetitive gasping sound, like an animal in pain.

My dad was weeping out there in the darkness.

"Let him weep, let him howl," I whispered bitterly and let the curtain drop.

Carefully I lay down on the bed and covered myself with the clean patchwork quilt. I wished desperately that I was Mary Linskill, not Lina Raw, and could read and write well enough to become a governess and paint beautiful flowers and have a tiny, homely room like this, all of my own. At last I blew out the candle and shut my eyes.

Anne came to wake me in the morning. "Get up and dress," she said. "The wagon will soon be here." She put a bowl of porridge and a mug of water down on the cupboard top. I sat up bleary eyed, swung my legs out of the bed, and went straight to look out of the window at the lock-up.

"Your father's been set free," she said, seeing where I looked. "He'll have to go before the magistrate next week."

"What is *he* charged with?" I asked.

"Not my business," she answered with a shrug.

She went out, carefully locking the door again.

Once I was dressed, Mrs Linskill took me back down to the lock-up, where I was really supposed to be.

"Not long to wait, now," she said and pushed me back inside.

After a moment of useless and rebellious standing, I went cautiously to sit down on the bed in there. It smelled sour and familiar, and I thought of my mam and the bairns and what it would do to them if dad were sent to jail as well as me. The limp bunch of lavender still lay on the shelf; I picked it up and threw it on the floor.

The constable came all too soon to put handcuffs on me again.

"Wagon's here," he said.

He led me out from the lock-up and down the steps towards the street, where the prison wagon was waiting. It had stopped on Church Street, outside the entrance to Blackburns Yard. The brightness of daylight in the yard made me blink, and I dropped my head in shame as I marched past the fishwives sitting on their doorsteps, cleaning bait and fixing lines.

The pleasant ordinary sounds of their voices were hushed for a moment, but then "Chin up, lass!" I heard a croaky voice say.

The words were spoken rough but kind, and I glanced quickly to see Fishtail Lizzie on her doorstep, cleaning bait as usual. "Chin up, hon," she repeated. "Remember tha's a Whitby lass!"

She never stopped the scrape and flick of her knife as I passed.

Suddenly I wanted to howl. I was leaving the only place I'd ever known. I'd have given anything to stay there in that dirty Whitby yard with its stink of cats, fish guts, and bait-cleaning water. But the constable hustled me on and pushed me into the back of the wagon that was drawn by two strong carthorses.

"Sit!" he said, indicating a wooden bench built into the side of the cart. He cuffed my ankles and fastened my feet to a chain on the floor, alongside another girl who was trussed the same.

The driver was perched up at the front of the wagon and didn't even turn his head as I climbed in, but the girl leered at me cheerfully.

"Aye… aye, now then… I could do wi' a bit o' company," she said.

"Silence!" The horse driver turned round and snapped out the order.

The girl had auburn hair that hung in raggedy ringlets round her face, rouge-smeared lips, and a grubby low-cut gown of the cheapest cotton. I knew at once what she was, but I guessed that she must have done more than streetwalking to be sent for trial to Northallerton.

Constable Linskill closed up the back of the wagon, and we sat in gloom. He went round to the front and climbed up beside the driver. The other man gave a grunt and a lash of the whip as the two horses set off.

"What *you* bin up to then?" the girl asked low voiced.

"Quiet!" the constable shouted back at us. The whip was cracked again and we lurched sideways with a jolt as we turned the corner and the wagon set off towards the bridge.

We could see nothing of the streets, for the sides were closed with just a small open hole in the roof to let in air. There was another opening in the front, so that our escorts could watch us. As we left Whitby Town I listened with longing for the raucous cries of gulls, the market shouts, and the steady thud of hammers that came from Fishburn boatyard. The wagon tilted uncomfortably as we were hauled uphill and out of town, and then for a long while we heard little but the steady clop of the horses' hooves.

CHAPTER TEN

Sall

We travelled in silence for many a mile, and at first I stared at the dirty wagon floor, my thoughts in a deep trough of misery, but gradually repeated coughing made me look up at my companion to see that she was trying to communicate with me. I raised my eyebrows in question as she pulled a face and mouthed at me. "What's tha name?"

"Paulina," I mouthed back.

"What… ina?"

"Paulina," I whispered, with a nervous glance back at the men.

But she had got the message and the constable seemed not to have heard. The girl waggled her shoulders to show she thought it far too fancy a name. "Are tha' from foreign parts, then?" she whispered very low.

I lifted my chin and whispered back. "Italiana!" Kat would never forgive me if I denied my Italian blood. "Ti amo!" I added, the only Italian words that Kat had taught me, for she said those were the words that Giuseppe had whispered constantly to her before he left her.

The girl looked surprised then and somewhat impressed. "I'm Sall," she hissed, "from Scarbro', but I might call messen Paulina, when I get out again!"

I frowned and looked away from her.

The journey went on, jolting and dreary, but at last we stopped at what we glimpsed to be a village inn. The constables bought mugs of ale for themselves and we were given a hard biscuit, a scrap of dried cheese, and a mug of water that we had to share. We leaned close and passed the mug awkwardly between us, for our hands were still cuffed and fastened to the chain.

"Tha' must a bin a-thieving," Sall whispered.

I shrugged.

"Tha's nowt to look so offended 'bout, for I've bin thieving too! Second time it is! And I'm a bloody fool!"

"No speaking!" the driver snapped.

He snatched the mug from our hands and we were off again.

The uncomfortable juddering resumed, until Sall lurched forward, dragging my chain with her, and banged on the front of the wagon. "I need to piss," she shouted. "I'll have to do it here, if yer won't stop fer me."

The wagon lurched to a halt and the driver came round to the back; I stupidly thought we'd be able to get out and stretch our legs, but he passed a chamber pot inside to us.

"What wi' thee staring at us!" Sall complained.

"I doubt you're so fussy with your clients," he told her. "And if you don't like it, then give up thieving!" But he leaned in and released one of her hands from the cuffs.

With a quick grin to me Sall lifted her grubby skirt and squatted over the pot while the constable waited. Once she was fastened up again, he pushed the pot to me and released one of my hands. "No more stops," he said. "You'd best make on."

Watching her crouching there had set my bladder complaining too, so hiding my shame as best I could, I crouched awkwardly over the pot. Bella and I had often stood guard for each other when we used the privy in the yard, to keep the jettie lads away. I wondered how Bella would be managing without me and, more importantly, if Kat had been able to find a doctor for Mam.

The journey continued as the light faded, and I fell into a silent stupor, cut off from light and life. It was dark by the time we reached Northallerton, but we could hear the noise of market traders banging about and shouting to each other, so they must be packing away their stalls. The jolting of the wagon on the cobbles shook us back to life, though we could see nothing through the dark window hole. We knew we'd reached the jail when the wagon stopped, and words were exchanged before the gates clanked open. The cart pitched forwards and the gates clanged heavily shut behind us. Bolts were drawn and shot back with further clattering sounds.

Constable Linskill opened the back of the wagon and released my wrists and ankles from the fetters, and then he turned to Sall.

"Get out!" the driver shouted.

They handed us over to two grim-faced wardresses who came out to meet us, dressed in black.

"Be courteous and obedient," Constable Linskill said quietly to me, as he turned to leave. "That would be best for you."

His stern fairness seemed at least familiar. I supressed a strong urge to grab his arm and beg him take me back to Whitby Town, but I'd enough sense to know that I'd only be making an even greater fool of myself. I gritted my teeth and watched him go, in silence.

The tallest, robustly built turnkey took charge of Sall, and the other smaller woman came for me. We were led into a tiled room, where there were two three-sided cubicles, each with a bath and a thin wooden partition between each tub. A small stool stood beside each bath.

"Go there!"

"Stand here!"

"Strip off!"

Their orders snapped away at us, short and sharp. Sall wearily obeyed and I copied her, undressing in one of the open-sided cubicles. We were made to step naked into a bath of lukewarm water and given strong-smelling carbolic soap to clean ourselves with. I could hear Sall splashing at the other side of the partition and complaining at the coldness of the water.

"Hair too!"

"But it's not dirty," I said.

"Hair too," the wardress repeated and without ado she grabbed my head and pushed it down into the water. I gritted my teeth and washed it with the soap and rinsed it as best I could.

She gave me a rough bit of flannel to rub myself dry with and a coarse but clean linen shift to put on instead of my rouge-stained skirt.

"Sit!" she ordered, pointing to the stool.

She handed me a comb and took up a large pair of scissors. I stared at the comb and then the scissors, as it slowly dawned on me what must happen next.

"No… not my hair," I cried and tried to cover it with my arms. "You can tie it neatly back. Please not my hair!"

My thick dark hair was the only part of me that I really felt proud of and I'd always kept it brushed, shining and clean, however hard that might be.

"Hair will be cut short; that is the rule, in order to prevent head lice and nits. Will *you* comb it out, or do we have to strap you down?"

I set my face into a grim, cold mask and began to comb my still wet hair. I wouldn't give them the satisfaction of seeing me weep, though the loss of my long locks hurt me more than any of the other humiliations. I sat silent on the stool, as damp heavy clumps of hair fell all around me: snip… snip… snip!

Then the woman took a bottle from a pouch that swung from her belt and shook some cold stinging liquid over my scalp. I jumped a little, but bit my lip to stop myself from complaining.

"That'll take care of the lice," she said. "Now, take that dustpan and sweep it up!"

I obeyed, vowing silent revenge, though I wasn't quite clear who it was that should receive such revenge.

"Stand up on the stool. The doctor will come to examine you."

I climbed shakily onto the stool, and after a while a stocky little man carrying a bag appeared in the bathroom. He came to me first and peered at my face through an eyeglass; then without a word he lifted up my shift and examined my naked body. I gasped faintly with shock, for nothing like that had ever happened to me before. I realised then that having my hair cut off might not be the greatest humiliation.

He dropped my shift and reached up to yank my mouth open, still without speaking to me, as if I was a horse. He looked at my teeth and tongue and turned my head to poke something cold and metallic into my ear. Lastly he inspected my hands and feet.

"What age is she?" he asked one of the wardresses.

"Fourteen."

"Hmm… small for her age and undernourished, but otherwise appears normal," was his verdict. He wrote some notes down in a book, I made to step down from the stool.

"Stay where you are," the wardress warned.

I wobbled a little on the stool while the doctor examined Sall.

"Now darling… I usually charge for this," I heard her say. "Oooh… now its tuppence extra for that, sweetheart!"

"Silence!" the wardress cried. She grasped the truncheon that swung from her belt, like the ones the constables carried, and banged it on the side of the screen that separated me from Sall.

I shut my eyes, wondering how the girl could manage to be so bold. It was all I could do to stop myself from screaming with rage.

"This one is at least five months pregnant," the doctor reported.

I was shaken from my own concern, when I heard that. The man came out of the open cubicle, wrote something else in his notebook and left the room.

We were then both handed coarse grey linen gowns to put on with an un-dyed calico apron and bonnet, then led through a long corridor with cells on either side. Rough though she was, I was relieved to find that Sall would share a cell with me. There were two pallet beds set close together in the small space, one high barred window, two blankets, and a chamber pot. Nothing else.

We were locked in.

Sall stumbled to the nearest bed and lay down on it, suddenly quiet and pale.

"Did I hear right?" I asked. "That doctor said 'five months pregnant'?"

"Aye, you heard right," she said. All the fight seemed to have suddenly gone out of her. She lay there shorn of her raggedy ringlets, exhausted and drained, and she looked little older than me.

"Will that not mean they'll let you go?" I asked.

"Not likely," she replied.

CHAPTER ELEVEN

Northallerton Jail

Sall rolled over on her bed and turned her back to me, sighing wearily.

I stumbled to the other bed and lay down for a moment or two. I listened for distant sounds that reached our cell, someone coughing further down the row, interspersed with bursts of angry shouting and then someone sobbing. How I longed for the familiar dust and noise of Turners Yard and even the once-hated smell of wet clothes and soap. Those foolish thoughts made me turn my face to the wall like my companion and close my eyes. I wanted to weep but couldn't; it felt as though a dark, cold stone had lodged itself there in my chest, where my heart used to be.

I don't know how long we lay there, but after a time a bell started to jangle and almost immediately there came the sound of tramping feet from somewhere outside and repeated shouts, followed by the sharp clang of bolts being drawn.

Sall sat up. "Supper," she announced. The door of our cell was thrown open.

"All out!" came the cry.

Sall scrambled off her bed. "At least we'll be fed," she said.

As we stepped out into the corridor, we were almost knocked over. Sall grabbed my arm and together we plunged into a rushing stream of silent young women, all dressed identically in grey gowns and bonnets. We stumbled down a flight of twisting stairs, jostling and shoving as we went, to arrive in a long narrow room, bare but for benches and tables set out with baskets of bread. All the seating faced one way towards a platform.

I clung to Sall's sleeve, and she didn't object but pushed her way through the crowd to find space for two more on the end of a bench.

"Stand here quick!" she whispered.

Elbows pushed and fists thrust viciously, and yet there was still no talking. Each woman found herself a place, and at last we all stood still, heads bowed. There came the sound of coughing and someone sneezed. A man dressed in black stepped onto a platform at the front and recited a prayer, so I guessed that he must be the prison chaplain.

"Sit!" a wardress called, as soon as he'd finished speaking. There were loud scraping sounds as everyone scrambled to climb over the benches.

Some older women appeared carrying trays with bowls, which turned out to contain slightly warm broth. Mugs were passed down the narrow tables, while many hands stretched out to reach for bread from a grubby looking basket.

"We oughta' get small ale twice a week," Sall told me eagerly.

"Silence!" the order rang out.

We were both disappointed to discover that the mugs contained weak coffee, with milk that was on the turn. The broth was watery and thin, with slivers of potato, turnip, and a few gristly bits of meat in it. The bread was hard, but I copied the others and dipped it in the broth. It felt a little better to at least have something in my belly. Bowls were quickly scraped clean and mugs were drained and passed back down to the bottom of the table where the servers, all in prison uniforms, walked up and down collecting them.

"Stand for prayers!" the order came.

We struggled to our feet again, and the chaplain read a few words from the bible:

And if thy hand offends thee, cut it off: for it is better for thee to enter heaven maimed, than having two hands to go into hell, into the fire that shall never be quenched.

I glanced along the line of bowed, bonneted heads, with roughly clipped locks sticking out at the front and saw that most were young and skinny, though Sall was not the only one pregnant. Some kept their heads down, while others stared angrily ahead.

I lifted my chin too and stared ahead, as the words of Fishtail Lizzie came back to me. "Keep tha' chin up hon… Remember tha's a Whitby lass!"

I was determined not to be one of those who looked so beaten and ashamed. As soon as the prayers were over, the turnkeys hurried us out of the hall to go back to our cells.

"Quick now – move sharp! Step on it!"

"They want us out, before the old lags come," Sall whispered.

I glanced back as we were leaving and saw what she meant, for through another door at the far end of the hall came a line of much older women. They had sparse grey heads, some of them almost bald and many stooped and hobbling, a few grim faced, though most had a frighteningly blank expression. Newly filled baskets of bread were being set out again, while a fat, red-faced turnkey shooed us back up the stairs to our cells.

"Get in! Get in!" she shouted, as bolts clanged shut again.

"Those terrible faces," I murmured as I sat down on my hard bed. "All those old women."

"Aye they get like that," Sall said. "They don't know where they are half the time. That's what it does to you, you'll see."

"But, I haven't been tried at the court yet," I protested. "They might have to let me out again when I've been before the court!"

She looked at me with scorn. "You'd best stop thinking like that," she said. "Settle yourssen! You're likely to be here a while."

During the following week we were made to scrub the prison floors, which was hard work and made our knees and hands very sore, but on the Monday Sall and I were taken over to the County Court House, which was attached to the prison, for the quarter sessions.

I was put on trial and judged by a jury of farmers, innkeepers, grocers, and gentlemen. Old Man Turner's statement was read aloud, along with the Whitby magistrate's comments. I was asked if I'd anything to say ,and I opened my mouth to complain that my father had made me do it but then thought better of it and stayed silent.

"Are you sorry for what you did?"

"Yes, I am very sorry for what I did," I said trying to sound as humble as I could manage. And that at least was true.

"Paulina Raw, you are sentenced to serve four months hard labour," the chairman of the board announced, "in the hopes that this sentence will teach you the error of your ways."

I gasped. I'd feared most of all to be sent to a reformatory school, though I knew I'd be considered old to be given that punishment, but somehow I hadn't expected hard labour. I knew well enough what it meant; in Northallerton it meant the treadmill, and I'd heard that some had died whilst being made to turn it.

"Take her away," the man said.

I was marched back to my cell where I sat alone and trembling, waiting for Sall to return. In a while I heard her shouting foul language at the turnkeys halfway down the corridor.

"Make the best o' today," the turnkey said, as they pushed her into the cell. "You'll both be on the mill in the morning."

"Both?" I said, appalled. "Not Sall too?"

Sall flopped onto her bed, and then slumped onto her side.

"Two months," she said. "Two months on the 'mill."

"But… but what about the bairn?"

"What about the bairn?" she asked. "I told you they'd care nowt for that!"

"Have you been on one o' them wheels before?" I asked.

She shook her head. "No, but I've heard about it!" she said. "It's a killer! Twenty minutes on and five minutes to rest… twenty minutes on and… But I'd say the treadmill's better than reformatory for you. At least it's over and done with and then you're out again. Reformatory means years away, and some o' them never go home."

I sat there stunned.

The following morning our punishment began. We were given the usual watery coffee and a slice of bread, the chaplain read out prayers, and then we marched in silence down to the wheelhouse, along with ten other young women. A dull grinding sound already came from the men's treadmill, for they started earlier and their wheel ground the local farmer's corn.

The female treadmill was a separate contraption, and its purpose was to draw water from a deep well that supplied the jail and houses close by. We were hustled up a winding staircase that had been built into a squat wooden tower and stepped out onto a wooden platform at the top of it, to be faced by a row of narrow compartments built across the steps of the treadmill.

"Raw – in number seven!" the punishment mistress called. "Silence on the wheel!"

There was nothing inside the tight cubicle but the steps of the wheel and a wooden bar fixed across at head height. I was sorry to see that Sall was sent to work much further down the row. A tall, gaunt-looking woman with a fierce look was ordered into the cubicle next to me and a younger lass on the other side. We couldn't see each other, and it seemed that being alone was part of the punishment.

A gong sounded. "Wheel starting!" the punishment mistress called. "Take hold and get on!"

I grabbed the bar and stepped onto the wheel and we were off at a steady pace, taking step after step after step, hanging onto the bar above to stop us from falling backwards.

I breathed out after a while, almost with relief: I could do it! I'd always been sound of limb and good at climbing. Climbing was what had brought me to this pass, but what a fool I was again, for step after step… step after step… and on… and on it went. Gradually a sense of fear rose in my stomach, and panic grew as I failed to catch my breath, while my arms and knees began to ache as never before. If I slackened in my steps the wheel began to scrape my shins and then, just as I feared I was going to fall, the gong sounded and the wheel stopped.

"Five minutes!" the mistress called.

I staggered backwards, to slump onto a wooden bench that had been set up outside the cubicles. The tall woman lumbered back to sit beside me, flopping forward as she rested her head in her hands.

CHAPTER TWELVE

The Endless Stair

I gasped and groaned, frantically rolling my shoulders in an effort to ease my aching muscles, then seeing others doing it, I began to rub my legs and ankles hard.

"How long… how long?" I muttered.

My neighbour sat upright then, turned her fearsome gaze on me and made a fist, so that I flinched, afraid she'd hit me. Instead she opened her fingers out one by one, to show me five, her eyes all the time on the back of the mistress's tight bun and starched cap.

"Can't do it," I murmured, shaking my head.

She put her finger to her lips to silence me. "Say nowt," she hissed. "Or you'll find yer'sen in the punishment cell and mebbe beaten too. Yer need to step on it! Don't fight it!"

The younger lass who sat on the other side of me wiped a runny nose on the back of her hand. "Tha' mun' step on it," she repeated quietly in a wavering voice.

She was a skinny waif of a girl, her face covered in sores that she picked at constantly. I looked at her and told myself that if she could do it, so could I.

The five minutes rest flew by and the gong sounded again. 'Wheel starting. Wheel starting!" came the shout.

The tall woman slapped my shoulder, making me flinch again. "Step on it!" she growled. "'Keep an ear to the wheel and step on it!"

I frowned, uncertain as to what she meant, but though she was older than me she seemed to be managing.

"Wheel starting," came the shout again and I grabbed the bar, determined that I wouldn't let them beat me or put me in a punishment cell.

The wheel set off and we walked, step... step... step! My arms soon began to ache again, and I cursed myself for the stupidity that had brought me to this place! Step... step... step!

It wasn't long before I was losing pace again and my shins were catching on the wheel as it turned. I clung to the bar, scared and breathless, knowing they'd beat me if I stepped away from the wheel.

"I... can't," I gasped. "I can't!"

"Aye, you can... you can... you can!"

I was puzzled, and that distracted me, for those calming words seemed somehow to come with the rhythm of the turning wheel. I thought perhaps I was hearing things, words ringing out from inside my head. It was as if the very wheel was speaking, and I must be going crazy. Then the words came again, in a low, growling voice, and the hairs on the back of my neck began to lift.

"You can... you can... you can! Step on it... step on it... step on it!"

At last it dawned on me that those rumbling words were coming from the big lass in the cubicle next door to me. She'd somehow pitched her voice to match the groan and growl of the turning wheel and the steady grinding rhythm too. Striving to keep up my pace, I tried to attune my ears.

"Step on it... step on it!"

A flash of anger bubbled inside me – and burst, bringing with it a spurt of new energy. I tried to follow the strange instructions and stepped on the wheel with a touch of renewed vigour, to find that almost at once I regained my balance and my breath.

"Step on it… step on it!"

Stepping faster, I could breathe again and my feet moved almost of their own accord.

"Step on it…" my neighbour growled.

I clung to the wooden bar and stepped and stepped, the harder and faster, the better it felt. I tried to reply with the rhythm of the wheel and the same rumbling voice. "I'm stepping," I growled. "I'm stepping… now!"

I continued to push myself, and though it was hard I'd somehow got the knack. My feet and legs grew sore and my arms ached horribly, but I could do it. When the next gong sounded, I flopped back down on the bench.

"I thank you," I gasped. "I thought I'd die."

The woman nodded, her eyes as ever on the punishment mistress; only when the woman turned away did she speak. "Yer've got it now," she said. "Some never do. Just look at 'em!"

I saw what she meant, looking down the row of weary women. Some had shins so bruised and battered that the sores might never heal.

"Mary 'ad it 'ard… didn't yer, lass?" she said, nodding at the young girl, who wiped her nose again and rubbed her eyes. "Hush now!" she warned, as the mistress turned and came marching back again.

We sat in silence then, getting our breath. When the gong went, we rose to go back to the wheel and my neighbour touched my shoulder again. "'ilda," she said, tapping her chest. "That's me!"

"Lina," I replied.

And I was strangely comforted to hear that name, for it put me in mind of the saintly abbess, who'd once ruled her monastery on the windy cliff tops of Whitby. At the very thought of my home town, I blinked and pressed my lips together to suppress a tightness that grew in my throat and threatened to emerge as a sob. Here was another Hilda, a great, gruff lass she was but offering kindly advice to me.

The rest of the day passed in a dreadful blur of stepping and stopping, the rests so brief, they did little to help. The noise of the wheel and the whoosh of the pump made my head throb, but each time I feared to fall off the wheel, I remembered to step faster still. We filed back to the food hall at noon to be given a bowl of thin porridge. I fought my way to Sall's side and found her looking flushed and clutching at her belly.

"Say nowt," she hissed, looking sharply at me.

So I sat down beside her in silence and ate fast for I was hungry. As soon as we'd finished we traipsed back to the wheelhouse, past a line of grim-faced, stooping men, who tramped around the high-walled exercise yard. The afternoon wore on and the smell of stale sweat filled the air as we struggled to "step on it". I was luckier than most and knew it, for so many there were weaker and thinner than me. Sometimes I fell into that merciful dreamlike state, where my legs and feet seemed to work of their own accord.

Time went by and somehow we survived, while strange messages came to us through the grating of the wheel and flew in growling tones from prisoner to prisoner.

"Ale for supper! Ale for supper!"

"Pass it on! Pass it on!"

My hands grew skinned and sore, but Hilda gave her rugged advice.

"Piss on yer 'ands," she whispered, when she caught me rubbing them together. "Rub piss onto yer feet and legs as well. It'll make yer skin grow hard."

And she was right, as ever; my skin grew tough and calloused.

"Maisie has croaked! Maisie has croaked," the growling message came round one day. "Pass it on. Pass it on!"

Though I didn't know Maisie, I was shocked and saddened at the news and passed the message on with a heavy heart.

We worked the wheel each day till darkness fell and then marched back to our prison cells. Sall and I were so exhausted that we fell straight down onto our beds and at times we almost missed the supper bell. Sall suffered most.

Day after monotonous day passed, and I began to sense my body changing. As the skin of my feet and shins grew hard and calloused, my muscles grew strong, until they made me think of the twisted ships cords that they made on the Rope Walk, high above Whitby Harbour. I learnt the signs that passed between the prisoners: scratching the right ear meant the turnkey was coming; scratching the left was the governor; scratching the chest indicated the doctor. I ate every morsel of food that I could grab, and one time I was put into the punishment cell for a day and a night for snatching bread.

"Don't fret about me," I told Sall. "At least I'll get a rest in the punishment cell."

"There'll be no rest there," she said.

And she was right, for when I was sent to that place I discovered that lying on a hard board in a dark cell, without food or drink or even knowing whether it was day or night, brought strange and fearful imaginings. When they let me out, it briefly felt like a blessing to be walking the endless stair with my wretched companions.

Sometimes I struggled to keep count of the days, but on one of the coldest mornings, as we skidded across a thin layer of ice in the exercise yard, I saw my dad standing in a long line of men awaiting trial. He glanced across at us as we passed, and I saw that he had a black eye.

"Lina," he called after me, his voice full of pleading.

I ignored him and walked on to the wheelhouse, but I quickly regretted it. The following day I looked but could see no sign of him.

"How can I find out what's happened to my dad?" I asked Hilda.

She shrugged. "The chaplain may tell you, if he's feeling kind that day," she said.

That evening after morning prayers I approached the chaplain. "Is my dad in the men's prison?" I asked. "Can you tell me if he is?"

"Get back in line, Raw!" the turnkey barked.

The chaplain shook his head and walked away.

"I only want to know if he's here and what has happened to my mam," I shouted after him.

"Back in line, or you'll be beaten!"

I ground my teeth and slipped into place again, but that evening after prayers the chaplain came to me. "Your father's on the men's side," he said. "He's serving a month's imprisonment with hard labour!"

"What for?" I asked.

"For repeated drunkenness and conspiring to steal," he said.

"I thank you," I said.

I felt some satisfaction that at least my dad hadn't got away completely free while I'd been left to take the blame, but I worried that it might make things even worse for Mam.

CHAPTER THIRTEEN

Grey Mist

That night I dreamt that I was a bairn again and cleaning rotted bait from our lines in the little yard outside our cottage on the Crag. In my dream Dad sat beside me, his strong hands pulling slimy shellfish from the sharp hooks. We were talking happily together while we worked, and suddenly I snagged my thumb on a sharp hook. Dad snatched up my hand and put my cut thumb straight into his mouth to suck the wound clean, then he turned away for a moment to spit the foul taste he'd picked up from my finger onto the cobbles. He laughed at my disgusted face and fished in his pocket to find us both boiled sweets to take the taste away. I woke to find my cheeks wet with tears as I recalled the truth of that dream, for Dad had done that every time I cut myself.

The following day as we turned the treadmill, step, step, step, a very strange message came rumbling along the wheel to us. "The prince is dead! Pass it on! The prince is dead!"

I passed it on to Mary, thinking nowt of it. What prince? The only prince I knew anything about was Prince Albert, the Queen's husband, and he was quite young and strong, so they said. Maybe one of the Queen's children had died. That would be no surprise for most folk lost a child or two – why shouldn't the Queen? More rumours ran up and down the line. "The prince is shot. The prince is shot!"

"No, poisoned. The prince is poisoned!"

Unusually, during the next brief rest from the wheel, the punishment mistress herself stood up to announce that

Prince Albert had died. "Typhoid. Prince Albert has died of typhoid!" she said. "The country has gone into mourning; the Queen has ordered it. We are all in mourning for the prince."

We stared at each other blinking, some shocked, some biting back angry comments for what did we care about Prince Albert or the Queen? It meant nothing to us, who were trapped in this foul place. The gong sounded and we went back to work again. – Step, step, step!

That night in our cell I lay awake, feeling restless.

"Settle yoursen!" Sall complained. "Tha's tossing and turning like a stormy sea. What's up wi' thee? I need to sleep."

I peered at her through the darkness, almost angry with her. "It's all right for you, you'll be leaving soon."

"An' I'll be glad to get away from you," she snapped back.

We lay there quiet for a moment then. The truth was that I dreaded her leaving and feared that I'd be lost without her. Her belly had grown, though she herself was thinner than ever and struggled with the wheel.

"I don't want you to go, Sall," I said at last. "Though I know it will be best for you."

"Nah," she said doubtfully. "At least I get a bit o' food in here. Who's going to feed me when they send me back to Scarborough? I can't turn tricks with this great lump inside me, and I fear I shall 'ave to go to the workhouse."

I could think of nothing useful to say, for what she said was true, and the thought of the workhouse filled most folk with dread.

"It can't be worse than here," I said.

"Nah… same thing," she said gloomily.

Those words set me wondering. Could I live like her? Could I sell myself to men like she did, in order to eat? The moment came back into my mind when Frank's hand had gone creeping up my leg and gripped my thigh. Though I'd been terrified at being caught, just for a fleeting moment a strange kind of thrill had come with his touch. Might I be reduced to selling myself, as Sall had done, when I was released?

"Have you ever gone with a lad?" Sall asked, as though she sensed where my thoughts had wandered.

"No," I said. "And you shouldn't do it either! Not anymore."

"Needs must," she whispered.

I turned my face to the wall and tried to rest.

Christmas came, and we were allowed a small serving of greasy half-cooked goose and dried-up Christmas pudding. My birthday passed and I turned fifteen, but nobody there either knew or cared. The prison yard grew a permanent skin of ice, so that we skidded and slipped as we crossed it. We stepped on the wheel all day, trying to ignore our running noses, coughs, and chilblains. Step, step, step! The skin on my hands and shins grew hard as leather, while the muscles in my arms and legs became steadily stronger too.

When the time came for Sall to be released, we clung to each other.

"You can both stop that!" the turnkey ordered. "To the bath-house with you now, and we don't want to see you back again!"

After she'd gone I seemed to slip into a state of bleak despair. I obediently went to the treadmill every day and stepped on it, and stepped on it, and didn't seem to notice the exhaustion quite so much, but I ceased to speak to anyone, even Hilda. It seemed as though a dull grey mist had settled around my head and shoulders, a thick cloudy mist that softly separated me from the turnkeys and the dreary surroundings – even from the other inmates. I didn't care about anything anymore; just ate what I was given, not knowing whether I was hungry or not.

Then one freezing January evening something changed – something that shocked me out of the ghastly state I'd drifted into. We were trudging back from the treadmill as usual, over the icy yard and up the corridor to our cells, when one of the younger turnkeys caught my arm.

"The chaplain says to tell you that your father has been released."

I vaguely nodded.

"And you 'ave company too," she added, raising her eyebrows as if at some private joke. "Someone you'll know!"

"Someone I know…?" I murmured, confused.

Could Sall be back in prison again so soon? Surely not – unless she'd lost the child and been caught stealing again.

"Off you go," the turnkey said, still amused. "Go and meet your new cellmate. The matron's got bruises to show for 'er! You best tell 'er it'll do no good to be kicking shins in here. She's already had a taste o' the stick! Mebbe *you* should teach her better."

Back at my cell I waited while the door was unlocked, my mind slowly waking up again and questioning what was happening. Kicking shins didn't sound like Sall, she was far too clever for that. I didn't want to share again with anyone, especially someone who wasn't Sall.

"Go on," the turnkey said and gave me a shove.

I entered the tiny space and the door clanged shut behind me. I thought for a moment there'd been a mistake, for all was still in there. It was only when I moved to climb onto my own bed that I stumbled over a discarded pair of boots and saw that there was a small hump in the blanket on Sall's old bed. Someone was lying there under the cover, her face turned to the wall, and it was a very small person indeed. All I could see was a thin curled back that put me painfully in mind of our Bella.

I went to sit on my bed, watching for movement. She must surely have heard me come in, and at last I reached out to touch the thin shoulder.

"Come on. Let's have a look at you," I said.

Whoever she was, she cringed away from me.

"Turn round so I can see you. You don't have to be feared o' me."

"Shan't!"

The reply came, in a small and angry voice that sounded strangely familiar.

"You'll do as I say…" I began, thinking I'd best start as I meant to go on.

And then at last she moved. She struggled to sit up and turned around, and I don't know who was more shocked, her or me!

"Sophia Goodchild!" I gasped.

It was the beggar girl from New Way Ghaut. Though the light was growing dim by then, there was no mistaking those angry blue eyes. She smelled cleanly of carbolic soap for once, and her long matted hair had been washed and chopped like mine.

She gasped too, clearly as stunned as I was.

"No!" she cried. "Not you!"

Then she turned her back on me again and lay there stiff as a board.

I leant against the cold wall, shaken to my core. The sight of her brought many uncomfortable memories flooding back, as I remembered with shame how I'd refused to give her or her grandmother a single halfpenny or farthing.

I remembered the evil look she'd given, as Bella and I ran away from her laughing – and most of all I remembered her malicious smile when she'd seen me dragged through Blackburns Yard in handcuffs. I glanced again at the knobbles on the skinny curve of her back that showed through the rough prison dress that covered her. She was surely the smallest and scrawniest female in Northallerton Jail.

I sat there staring at the shape of her on Sall's bed, as darkness gathered around us, and gradually I came to realise that the dreadful numbing cloud that had been enveloping me had lifted. The shocking arrival of Sophia had somehow dispersed it. A surge of wild emotion rose in my throat, a mixture of sorrow and anger that made me clap a hand to my mouth, fearing that I might vomit. I wanted suddenly to shout and stamp my feet in fury – but the supper bell rang.

Sophia started at the sound of it and then lay still again. I struggled to my feet and touched her bony shoulder, as the usual hubbub of hurrying feet and clanging of locks began. She winced away from me and I sighed, remembering that they'd already beaten her.

"That bell's for supper," I said firmly. "Come wi' me. You need to eat."

She stirred then and slowly sat up, her wide suspicious eyes watching my every move.

"Come on, gi' me your hand," I said. "I'll show you what to do."

"But… yer hate me!" she said.

"No, I don't hate you," and as I said it, I knew it to be true. "We're Whitby lasses, you and I… and we're stuck in here together. If you behave with me, then I'll look after you. Come with me now and I'll find a place for you."

She watched me with suspicion still. "Will I get bread?" she asked.

"Aye, you'll get bread, but you must come quickly or we'll miss it. Get your boots on!"

She glanced angrily up at me again. "Can't," she said.

I stared puzzled for a moment, but then remembered that I'd never seen her wearing shoes. "Best come without them then," I said.

CHAPTER FOURTEEN

But for Hunger

Sophia allowed me to lead her barefooted down the passageway and through the jostling crowd, her small rough hand in mine. I found us a place beside Hilda, but I had to haul her back immediately, for when she saw the bread there on the table, her hand shot out towards the basket.

"Stop it!" I warned and snatched her hand back.

"You said I'd get bread!" she objected.

"Shut up!" I hissed. "You have to stand here first and keep silent. Do as I say or you'll be beaten. Be silent or you'll get no food!"

Hilda pointed a calloused finger in her face. "You do as Lina tells yer," she said.

One of the turnkeys had seen the rumpus and marched towards us. "What's this to do?" she demanded.

"No trouble," I murmured, "Ma'am!"

I dug a knuckle into Sophia's elbow and she made no sound but stood looking at us wide eyed, her small tongue flickering around her lips. The turnkey moved away and the chaplain said grace. As soon as he finished, the scramble to sit down began. I reached for the basket and grabbed a good hunk of bread for Sophia. "Now you can eat!" I said.

She ate hurriedly and warily as a stray cat. When she was given a bowl of broth she snatched at it and raised it to her lips. Hilda caught my eye over her head and raised her eyebrows.

"Eat with a spoon," I said, and handed her one.

When we got up to return to our cells, one of the turnkeys caught sight of Sophia's bare feet. "We don't give you good boots to walk barefoot," she said. "If she comes down here like that again, there'll be no food for her."

By the time we were locked into our cell again, it was dark, with just a flicker of light that came into our cell through the small square spyhole in the door.

"Take off your dress and get into bed," I said.

"Shan't," she said.

I sighed. "Do as you wish," I said wearily. "But you'll sleep more comfortably in your shift."

I undressed myself, ignoring her. She curled up on the bed and I could hear her licking her fingers like a cat, just in case she might find another scrap of meat or gravy left there.

I got into my bed, and at last she struggled out of her prison gown. I made no comment but lay still, while she huddled down under her blanket once more.

"What did you do?" I asked at last. "What did you do to get sent here?"

There was a pause and I thought for a moment she wouldn't answer.

"I took a loaf o' bread," she said at last.

I sighed. "You *stole* it," I said.

"I *took* it from Metcalfe's bakers. They have plenty there."

"Aye well," I said, with a sigh. "I cannot lecture you on that."

"No, you can't," she replied. "They all say it's *your* fault, that your mam is 'up the ropery'."

"What?"

I hauled myself upright into a sitting position and stared through the gloom at her. It took a moment or two for the full meaning of her words to seep into my mind.

"Up the ropery… up the ropery?" I cried.

Like everyone in Whitby, I knew what "up the ropery" meant – the ropewalk was next door to the workhouse.

"Are you saying my mam's in the workhouse?"

She shrank into the farthest corner away from me, as though she feared I'd hit her. At the same time there came the thunderous sound of a truncheon banging on our cell door.

"Silence!" the turnkey's voice rang out.

We were quiet until we heard her footsteps tapping away down the corridor.

"Tell me!" I hissed.

"They're all in there," she whispered. "Your mam is sick and your dad's in jail."

"Are you telling me that old Kat's in there too?"

"Don't know 'bout Kat," she said and shrugged.

I swore angrily.

"Not my fault!" she protested. "That man wi' the big red nose said I had to go to jail, so I don't know no more than that."

I tried to calm myself. "That man? You mean the magistrate."

"Yeh, him."

I was deeply troubled by what she'd said, but she was right, it wasn't her fault. I lay down again and we both were still.

After a while she spoke again almost wistfully. "I wouldn't have done it," she said. "I wouldn't have taken the bread, but for… hunger. My belly gnawed at me!"

I turned to her and felt pity.

"They let my dad out of jail today," I said, "but it's me that should be let out, not him, then I could be looking after my family."

She made no reply, but just as I was beginning to drift off to sleep, a plaintive voice whispered: "Can I come in your bed?"

"No, there's no room," I said for the beds were as hard and narrow as they could possibly be.

She was quiet again for while and then she spoke soft and fearful. "Granny. I... want my granny."

I wondered how she could possibly want that filthy old woman.

"Granny sings to me," she said, with a soft little sigh.

I relented. "Come on then," I said. "You can try to get in here wi' me, but I'm not doing any singing."

It wasn't difficult, because she was so very thin. A small moan escaped from her when I touched her back where she'd been beaten, and we curled together like spoons and fell asleep at last.

I woke in the morning to the sound of the bell, feeling warmer than usual. I was alone in my bed and wondered if I'd had a strange dream, but when I sat up I discovered Sophia sitting on the chamber pot, grinning up at me, in the dim morning light.

"Will I get bread again?" she asked.

"You'll get a hunk of bread and a bowl of porridge."

"I'll come wi' *you* then," she said and she got up, shaking her legs.

"Aye," I said, "but I shall have to go on the treadmill later. I think you'll be sent to scrub floors."

"Scrub floors?" she said and she shook her head. "No. I'll come to the mill wi' you."

I almost laughed. "You can't choose what you do in here," I said.

I knew the hovel she lived in. It was one room like ours, but hers was always filthy, and whenever I passed it

I'd glimpsed nothing but a broken rocking chair and a mouldering straw-filled mattress on the floor. I doubted that floor had ever been scrubbed.

"You'll have to do exactly as you're told, or there'll be no bread. Get dressed and we'll get some porridge," I said, remembering that the promise of food seemed to have more effect than the threat of a beating.

She stepped into her prison dress but struggled to fasten it, so I had to help her as well as myself. We were ready and waiting when the breakfast gong sounded and the clang, clang, clang came of the turnkeys unlocking the cells. I glanced down to see that her feet were still bare.

"Get your boots on fast," I ordered. "You have to put them on."

She looked as though she'd argue for a moment but then pushed her scarred toes into the boots and began to flick the laces up and down. I watched her, remembering again her bare dirty feet on the Whitby cobbles. Was it possible she'd never had shoes on her feet before and not learnt to tie laces? I bent down to do them for her.

"How old are you?" I asked.

"Granny says I'm eleven."

We reached the dining hall just in time. Sophia ate fast, licking her porridge bowl clean, though she wasn't the only one doing that. The bell rang and we stood for prayers, before we left to go to our tasks.

As the chaplain fell silent, names were called.

"Sophia Goodchild!"

A quiet chorus of titters followed.

"Come here girl! You will join the scrubbing gang!"

She cast a questioning glance at me but went obediently at my nod. I joined the women who were lining up in silence to go the treadmill. I felt worn out before we'd even started that morning, and I struggled at first to "step on it", but at least the misty numbness seemed to have fled.

"Tha's got a job on there," said Hilda, when we got our first rest. "Tha's got a job wi' that little lass!"

"I have," I replied. "Yes, I have."

"But she's done you good, I think, that Goodchild! I didn't like to see you looking so 'gone away wi' the fairies'!"

I nodded, for she was right, the arrival of Sophia Goodchild had cleared the dark clouds away, and I was filled with a strange new energy."

"How long since Sall left?" I asked.

"Five days, I think!"

It seemed a lifetime.

I glimpsed Sophia at dinnertime, lined up with the women and girls who were awaiting trial; then I saw her eating fast and glancing nervously about her. She caught my eye, and I gave an approving nod. When I got back to our cell at the end of the day, I found her waiting for me.

"They say we will get ale tonight," she whispered.

"Have you done all they told you to?" I asked.

"Everything," she nodded.

"Then you *should* get ale tonight, but first you must learn to tie these boot laces."

"Will they let me take the boots home wi' me," she asked.

I frowned uncertainly. "I doubt it," I said.

CHAPTER FIFTEEN

All Jet Pickers Now

And so prison life changed again for me. I shared a cell with a half-wild creature, for Sophia would sometimes take offence where none was meant and leap at me in fury; but each night she curled up in my bed and reached to pull my arm around her. I'd little time to think of myself, for however bad my lot might be, I saw that hers was surely worse. I was ashamed to recall my past cruelty to her, but she didn't seem to hold it against me. The day she was taken before the quarter sessions, the news came to me through the treadmill message line.

"Sophia has got three weeks hard labour! Pass it on!"

"Hard labour," I growled to Hilda, "for such a little lass?"

"Aye, she's the smallest scrap I've ever known put on the mill," Hilda said disapprovingly.

But there were older women, frailer even than Sophia, turning the wheel and many of them shrunken to her height; they managed somehow, and I guessed she would too.

Sophia's three-week sentence meant that we'd be released together. I wasn't sure whether that was good or bad. There'd be enough to worry about when I got back to Whitby, without having to think about her as well. She'd have to go back to Grasping Granny and no longer be my responsibility.

"Don't be scared o' the mill," I told her as we lay curled together under the blanket. "You'll have to learn to 'step on it', like I do, then it won't catch at your shins.

"I'm not scared o' the mill!" she said fiercely.

And she was right. Sophia took to the treadmill quickly. The punishment mistress put her in the cubicle next to me, and there might have been a touch of kindness in the gesture, or maybe she just knew she'd have less trouble if she put her there.

Hilda took an interest in the girl, missing her own young granddaughters, and Sophia began to lose the pinched starved look she'd had. The days passed wearily, but finally there were only seven days left before we'd be released. I began to fret about it then. What would I do? Where would I go? We'd have lost our home-place in Turners Yard, if Sophia had told me the truth about the workhouse. Had Kat still got her little tenement, with her clean scrubbed pots and jars of herbs? Prisoners were not allowed family visitors during the first three months of a sentence, and even though I was in my last month now, which of my family would be able to travel to Northallerton? Would Kat still own me as her granddaughter after what I'd done? I doubted any of the Quaker wives would take me on as a scullery maid, not now that I'd been in prison.

And what of my dad? No… I didn't allow myself to think of Dad.

"You'll soon be back with your granny," I told Sophia one night as we waited for the supper bell to ring."

She looked uncertain but nodded.

"If it wasn't for my mam and my family, I'd not go back to Whitby," I said.

"Not go back to Whitby?" Sophia said surprised, as though there were no other place on earth.

"Everyone there will hate me now," I said.

Sophia didn't disagree with that. "Granny will make me beg again," she said with a small sigh. "Everyone hates beggars... You hated me… before."

I didn't deny it. "We might try picking flithers when we get back," I said, "for if we can manage to step on the treadmill, we can surely march over the scaur and pick flithers through the winter months, though at least on the treadmill we stay dry. Perhaps… you could come down onto the scaur with me, if your granny would allow…"

I spoke reluctantly, wondering why I was burdening myself with her.

She shook her head. "They wouldn't let me go on the scaur," she said. "I tried before to go and pick, like you used to do, but they chased me back up the Ghaut and said bad things to me."

"Who chased you?" I asked.

"Lads," she said. "Jet pickers! They're all jet pickers now, no money left in bait."

I shifted uneasily, knowing that I too might have chased her away in that distant other life that I'd once lived, before I'd listened to my father's lies.

"They all want jet," she said. "Somebody died… some 'portant man, and the Queen said that they have to wear jet. If you can find it you can take it round to Entry Yard and get five pence for a piece like this." She pinched her thumb and first finger together and squinted at me through the small round hole, she'd made. "That'd make a brooch, that would."

"Dark Entry Yard," I murmured and nodded wearily.

I didn't much want to think about jet, for it had been the undoing of me.

"It was Prince Albert," I told her. "The man who died. He was the Queen's husband."

She shrugged her thin shoulders. "Well… they're all mad for it now and they wouldn't let me follow them. One of the lads said he'd slit me throat and he took out a gutting knife."

Her words had stirred a memory. "And when the Duke of Wellington died…" I began.

"No, it weren't no duke," Sophia insisted.

"No, listen," I said. "When the Duke of Wellington died, the price of jet shot up, and now… now you say everyone wants jet again!"

She looked at me drearily. "That's what I been telling you," she said.

It dawned on me then that she'd been talking sense. If the death of the duke had brought a boom in jet, then the death of the Queen's beloved husband must put the price up even more.

"It's what the tea leaves said," I told her, feeling foolish. "The tea leaves said my future lay in jet, but I went about it all wrong."

"So… you will come back to Whitby wi' me, won't you?" Sophia asked anxiously.

"I've got no choice," I said. "They take you back to the parish that you come from and tell you to go the workhouse if you're in need."

"Granny won't let me go in there again," she said. "That's why I've got to beg."

"Again…? I didn't know you'd been in there," I said gently, though it wasn't too much of a surprise to me.

Her tense little mouth twisted as she spoke. "I were born there," she admitted. "And my mam died there when I were born. I were sent to a farm…"

"A baby farm?" I asked, for I knew about those dreadful places where nurses were paid a small allowance to neglect the babies in their care. Few infants sent to them survived.

"Aye… but Granny got me out again."

I sighed and shook my head. She'd never had a chance of being anything but a beggar girl… not like me, who'd been so stupid as to throw a good family away. The supper bell rang and we both got up and stood quietly by the cell door, waiting for it to be unlocked.

"They said they'd slit my throat!" she said again, resentfully. "Those jettie lads."

"Not if I'm with you, they wouldn't," I said and took her hand.

The last few days on the treadmill passed slowly, and my spirits swung up and down. One moment I longed to hear the cry of gulls and the lap of waves again; the next I dreaded my return to Whitby Town and the judgement that I must expect when I got there. I was a convicted thief and must smell of prison. There were no mirrors in jail for us to see ourselves, but I could feel the rough shape of my chopped hair and sometimes caught a glimpse of it reflected in the small dusty windows that we passed. Clipped ragged hair was the mark of a woman who'd been in jail.

A momentary surge of hope came sometimes, when I imagined myself walking freely along the foreshore, with Joey running ahead of me like the jet-hound I knew him to be. A string of jet beads could be made by carefully sorting sea-washed slivers and using a hand file and the sharpened spoke of an old umbrella to pierce tiny holes in them. It was fiddly work and you had to be patient doing it, but it could be done and if I'd guessed right, a string of jet beads might bring decent money now.

At other times I dreaded going back and if, as Sophia said, all my family were in the workhouse, what would there be for me, but to join them there?

The morning of our release came late in February. Instead of trooping off to the treadmill after breakfast, we were summoned.

"Raw and Goodchild! Go to the washroom where matron will be waiting for you."

The process of being released was as humiliating as our arrival. Once more we were made to scrub our bodies and hair with carbolic soap and submit to being examined by the doctor. I could hear Sophia growling in the next cubicle as they forcibly washed her hair.

The prison garments were taken away and our original clothing returned to us. My gown had been washed, but the shameful red patches of stain were still there. Sophia was given her familiar cut-down skirt and torn jacket, more ragged than ever now but somewhat cleaner. She watched angrily as the prison boots were removed along with the gown, apron, and bonnet.

"Can she not keep the boots?" I begged on her behalf. "She cannot go barefoot in this weather. It was autumn when I came in here, and I've no shawl. We'll freeze outside."

"You should have thought o' that before you went out thieving," the matron said. But she went to a tall cupboard and fished around in it for a while and eventually brought out a pair of worn boy's boots, too big for Sophia but with a little wear left in them still. She handed me a worn grey shawl and a smaller woollen shawl for Sophia.

"These things are from the Northallerton Methodists Friendly Society," she said with a sharp sniff. "They collect clothes for us to give newly released prisoners. I hope you will appreciate their goodness and behave yourselves better in future."

We took them gladly enough and I helped to lace Sophia into her boots.

"A bit o' scrunched up newspaper in the toes will make them fit better," I said. She grinned at me, pleased just to have them.

Once we were dressed in this finery, the matron led us into the next room where a man with a turnkey's truncheon stood beside a camera box that was perched on three legs. He made us take turns to sit on a stool while he dipped his head down beneath the dark cape that hung from the back of the camera.

"Sit still while I count to ten!" he ordered.

"Gi' us a penny!" Sophia begged when it was her turn.

"Be quiet!" the matron said.

"The Whitby picture-men gi' us a penny," she said. "If they want us to be still for them!"

I smiled, for I understood what she meant. There were three photographers in Whitby Town who owned smart studios where they made portraits of wealthy visitors, but in the early evening light the tall one with the gentle voice would wander the streets to take photographs of the sea, the boats, and the fisher-folk.

"Our picture man's kinder than you," Sophia said, pushing forward her lower jaw with disapproval.

The turnkey and matron exchanged a disapproving glance. "She'll be back before you can spit," the matron said.

CHAPTER SIXTEEN

The Sound of Gulls

At last the heavy prison doors were opened for us, and we walked out into the yard to find Constable Linskill waiting there with the prison wagon. It was his duty to see us back within our parish bounds. I wanted straight away to ask him about my family, but he looked very stern and unapproachable standing there, so I didn't ask. I was even more shocked to see that the driver up at the front of the wagon was Frank Dunsley. He didn't seem to want to look our way either, and I kept my head down, feeling deeply ashamed; I wasn't going to beg for anything in front of him. Constable Linskill opened up the back of the wagon.

"Get in!" he said.

I was relieved to find that this time we weren't handcuffed or chained, nor were we told to be silent, though I'd little to say. Sophia was unusually quiet too, and her small rough hand crept into mine.

We set off in the bumpy wagon, and it didn't seem long before the raucous sounds of Northallerton Market faded into the distance. Good clean air whooshed inside the wagon from the moorland that we crossed, and I took a few deep breaths and felt a little better.

"No more prison smells," I whispered.

Sophia smiled at me uncertainly, and I realised that the space she shared with Grasping Granny would never smell clean like Kat's small home. We made a stop at the inn again, and thankfully we were allowed to use the privy round the back. Constable Linskill brought us a mug of small ale to share, while Frank Dunsley still turned his gaze away from me and kept his distance too. At last I plucked up courage to ask the constable about my family.

"Your mother had her child in the workhouse," he told me.

"And the child?" I asked.

"I don't know," he said. "You must ask your grandmother, for Kat has charge of your young brother and sister. I believe your mother is poorly still and in the workhouse maternity ward."

"Yes Sir, I understand… thank you," I said hurriedly.

I knew that Mam must have been desperate to go to the workhouse to give birth. "Is Kat still in Turner's Yard?" I asked.

"Yes," he said. "You'll find her there. You might ask Frank. He'll be able to tell you more."

I glanced awkwardly at the lad, but Frank Dunsley was the last person I'd want to ask.

"And your father…" Constable Linskill began.

"No," I said firmly. "I thank you, Sir, but I don't wish to know about him."

The constable looked a little shocked at my sharp reply and spoke more abruptly. "Best get back inside the wagon then," he ordered. "Time to move on."

I swiftly obeyed, my spirits swinging about again; I'd been relieved to hear that Bella and Joey were back in Turner's Yard with Kat, but that meant I must face Old man Turner and the rest of the yard, if I was return to my family.

The wagon set off again, and after many more miles of bumping along we found ourselves lurching to the side, as the cart headed downhill.

"Gulls!" Sophia whispered. Her face lit up as we heard the raucous cries. "Are we there?"

"Aye," I said, feeling more uncertain than ever as to what I should do when we arrived in our town and the constable set us free.

"I must get to Granny," Sophia said. "Where will *you* go, Lina?"

I gave no reply.

"You can come wi' me to the Ghaut," she offered.

I said nothing, for Grasping Granny's hovel was the last place I'd want to go.

"Shall us go to the beach, in the morning?" she asked anxiously. "Like you said."

The hopes that had briefly soared when we spoke of searching for jet seemed to ebb like the tide – and yet, I knew we'd have to do something to earn a crust of bread.

"Aye," I said with a sigh. "We'll go to the beach."

The light was fading as we bumped down the rutted road that led into the town. Strident shouts of market traders reached our ears, as they packed up their stalls for the day. Our nostrils were filled with the familiar smell of fish and whale oil, as the horses came to a stop outside the Police Station.

Constable Linskill came round to the back of the wagon and opened the doors. "Get out and stand over there!" he told us.

We scrambled down and stood together shamefaced, while he turned round to address us formally.

"You, Paulina Raw, and you, Sophia Goodchild, have paid for your misdeeds with imprisonment and hard labour," he said formally. "If you break the law again, the punishment will be more severe. There can be no excuse for theft, and if you find yourselves in need, you must apply to the parish."

We both knew what that meant – the workhouse.

Surprisingly, Constable Linskill then felt in his pocket and brought out two threepenny coins, which he held out to us. We stared at them in amazement.

"This money is provided by the Society of Friends," he said. "It will allow you to eat tonight, but in the morning it is your duty to find work. I hope that I will never be called to arrest you again. Either of you."

Sophia's face lit up as she took the coin from him.

I bobbed a curtsey as I took mine. "We'll be no more trouble, Sir," I said. "I promise you."

"You may go," he told us.

I grabbed Sophia by the hand and we hurried fast away, fearful that we might somehow be called back again. As we turned the corner to go down the bankside, I glanced back briefly to see that the constable still stood by the wagon, watching us. Frank Dunsley seemed to have vanished.

We marched away down the hill, past Bagdale Beck, clutching our shawls about us as a bitterly cold north wind swept up from the harbour. Despite the cold my spirits rose at the comforting sights and sounds of our hometown. The lamplighter strode from lamp to lamp, flooding the worn cobbles of Baxtergate with pools of yellow light. Men bawled and shouted at each other as they stacked and rolled crates and barrels of fish off towards the railway station, ready to be loaded onto the evening train. The rumble of a train could be heard in the distance, and a plume of grey smoke and smuts drifted over the river, followed by the hiss of spurting steam. The sound of it briefly disguised the tapping of hammers that still came from the shipyard. We marched on towards the town bridge, passing Dark Entry Yard. Gulls screeched, as they swooped down through the tall masts of the ships to fiercely snatch at any scaly head or tail that might escape the crates. Those rowdy sounds were music to my ears, and Sophia too grinned at the wild commotion of it all. We strode onwards though the confusion and the noise and headed towards the bridge. For a moment I'd a fleeting sensation that somebody followed us, but when I turned around I could see nobody I recognised.

We reached bridge end to find the wind blowing fiercely up river from the sea. I hesitated there and let go of Sophia, who set straight off across the bridge. When she realised she was alone she stopped and turned round, then darted swiftly back to my side.

"Aren't you coming to the Ghaut wi' me?" she asked.

I glanced up in the direction of Flowergate and Turner's Yard, feeling fearful and ashamed to go that way. As I wavered there, a group of young fisher lasses came marching down Golden Lion Bank towards us, clutching their shawls about them. They knew me, and as soon as they recognised us, their faces changed from smiles to suspicion. Hands flew to their lips to cover their whisperings.

"See who's back!"

"Look at that hair!"

"Well serve 'em both right!"

Then the voices grew bolder

"Go back where you came from!" someone shouted.

"We come from here, like you," I cried. "You know we do!"

"We want no thieves in Whitby Town!"

"No, nor beggars neither!"

We shrank back as they marched across the bridge in front of us, continuing to shout bad words at us all the way.

The momentary joy of being back in Whitby fled, and I knew I couldn't face Turners Yard. We waited until they'd vanished from sight and then stepped onto the bridge again.

"Come wi' me to the Ghaut," Sophia pleaded again, pulling at my arm. It began to rain and at last I gave a brief nod and hurried across the bridge with her.

We ran down through Sandgate as the rain came on heavily. I looked around for a moment, for the creeping sensation was back that there was someone there behind us. Sophia hauled me along with wild determination and before I knew it, we were there in the Ghaut on Grasping Granny's doorstep.

"Granny, Granny!" Sophia shouted. "I am here! I am back!"

I remained outside getting soaked and cold, while she burst into the dimly lit space. "Granny, Granny!" she cried. "I got boots and a scarf, look here."

There came a shuffling sound and the old woman emerged from the flickering shadows. Sophia ran and flung herself into her grandmother's arms.

"Can it really be thee mi honey? Now then, watch it lass, you'll knock me over," Grasper wheezed and staggered backwards, while Sophia hauled her upright to stop her falling.

"See who I brought wi' me," Sophia cried.

Grasper stared in astonishment when she saw me hovering in the doorway. "Well now, well now," she said. "How the mighty are fallen. You'd best come in, before you drown out there."

I had to grit my teeth at Grasper's words, but perhaps I deserved them.

CHAPTER SEVENTEEN

In the Ghaut

Sophia grabbed my arm and hauled me into the small bare room. Grasper picked up the one flickering candle and examined my face more closely, while I stood there silent and ashamed. The stale smell of the place enveloped me, as the old woman's dirty hand flew up to twitch back my damp, rough locks.

"Aye, but tha's still a bonny lass," she said at last, sounding somewhat kinder.

"Lina looked after me," Sophia insisted.

"Did she now?" Grasper said.

"We're hungry," Sophia said, holding out her coins. "And I've got three pence. Have you bread for us?"

Grasper took the money and started to shake her head, but then she reached out and touched my hair again. "Nay, but you stay here, my honey. Granny can get a bit o' tick I think." And she moved to the door surprisingly quickly and vanished into the darkness and the rain.

"You see," Sophia told me, pleased. "Granny will see us right. You can sleep down there wi' me."

She pointed to a hole-riddled straw-stuffed mattress in the corner on the damp earthen floor, a matted woollen blanket thrown over it. My heart filled with despair that I should sink so low, when I knew that Kat would have taken me in, had I been braver and gone to Turners Yard.

"It's just for tonight," I said, sneezing.

"Aye, just for tonight," Sophia accepted that.

Then quickly Grasper was back, with a jug of ale and bread and kippers, wrapped in a greasy fold of paper. We sat ourselves down on the edge of the mattress and ate hungrily, while Grasper watched. Kippers had never tasted so good, and the bread was warm from the evening baking. We passed the jug of ale between us and I saw that despite the filthy surroundings, Sophia was truly happy to be with her grandmother again.

The ale and the feeling of having a full stomach made me sleepy, so ignoring the rancid stench of the place, I settled down beside Sophia to sleep on the rotting mattress, while Grasper seemed content to settle herself in the one dilapidated rocking chair.

I surfaced from sleep to find that somebody was pulling at my skirt.

"Leave be," I murmured, pushing away what I thought must be Sophia's hand.

But gradually I realised that the hand was large and rougher even than Sophia's. It crept up my calf and I froze, but then it moved on past my knee and another strong hand gripped my shoulder, making me realize what an utter fool I'd been.

"No!" I shouted.

"Now, now," Grasper wheezed from her rocking chair. "Did you think you'd pay nowt for board and bread?"

"Sophia!" I screamed. I kicked out and hauled myself upright.

The dim flickering candlelight showed me Sophia just waking from sleep on her grandmother's lap, as the chair rocked calmly back and forth. A man who smelt of the sea and sweat and tar rolled drunkenly at my side. He tried to grab at me again, but I kicked back at him and he swore and cursed.

"Sophia!" I bellowed.

"Granny?" she murmured, bleary eyed.

"Be still honey, tha's fine," Grasper wheezed. "What a fuss about nowt, eh! I'd make a guess tha's done it before… quite a few times, I'd have said!"

I struggled, kicked hard, and shouted "No… no… no."

There suddenly there came a great thundering on the door, followed by a cracking sound as the door burst open, and someone else was there, someone who leapt forward, grasped my hand and hauled me to my feet.

"Who… what?" Grasper cried out, shocked to find a new intruder in her home.

"Get off her!" a voice I dimly recognised shouted. "Leave her be!"

I glanced back to see that the man on the mattress had rolled away groaning, for some of my kicks had landed well. He covered his head with his arms, too drunk to face a proper fight.

"What the hell are you doing, Lina?" the intruder demanded, pulling me towards the door.

I knew him then, not only by his voice but also by his lurching gait, as he dragged me out of Granny's filthy den. It was Frank Dunsley.

"Stop," I said. "There's Sophia! I can't leave without Sophia, not with him there."

Grasper took offence at that. "Not my Sophia," she cried. "I'd never let any fella touch my lass. Go on, get shot o' my place, all o' yer!"

"But Granny…" I heard Sophia call.

The drunken seaman came stumbling out of the doorway after us, beaten on his way with blows from Grasper's walking stick. "Get out o' my place and leave us be," she cried.

"I've paid yer good money for nowt," the man objected.

She slammed the door shut behind us, but it swung open again."Tha's broken my door," she screamed. "I'll have the constable on you." She slammed it again and that time it stayed shut, though I could hear Sophia protesting inside.

The seaman stumbled off in the opposite direction, cursing still as he headed down New Way Ghaut towards the sea. Frank Dunsley released my hand then and backed away from me. I found that I was trembling quite violently as we stood there, outside in the cool darkness of the harbour side. I suppose I was shocked at what had happened – and it was hard to take it all in, for it had happened so fast – but then I recalled the sense I'd had of someone following us as we walked through the town and crossed the bridge.

"It was you," I said, when I got my breath back again. "You followed us over the bridge and all the way down Sandgate."

"And a good thing too," he said sheepishly.

I couldn't deny that, but I felt more shamed than ever that he should have been the one to see this. The moment that had troubled my imaginings so often while I was in prison flashed through my mind again, that terrible night – his hand on my ankle and the strange momentary feeling as his hand crept up my thigh. Completely different from the sensation I'd just experienced in Grasping Granny's den, though surely it should have frightened me more.

I was desperate to get away from him and pushed past and hurried off towards the marketplace. It had stopped raining but was still very wet underfoot.

"Wait!" he cried and, lurching to the side a little, he followed me. "Wait!"

I went on resolutely, heading across the stone flags of the marketplace towards Church Street. He caught up with me eventually and struggled along at my side, trying to keep up.

"I asked…" he began. "I asked the constable to let me drive the wagon, so that I could get the chance to speak to you."

"Well, why didn't you speak to me, then?"

"It didn't seem right, not with the constable there. I wanted to speak with you… alone."

I walked on ignoring him still, a sense of hopelessness welling up inside me. After all my good intentions, I seemed to be making a very poor start to improving my life again.

"I'm sorry… I'm so very sorry!" he cried.

"Sorry, what for?" I asked.

"If I'd known…" he began. "If I'd known it were you there in the dark, that night. Please listen to what I've got to say… I've thought of nothing else," he ended softly.

I stopped at last and folded my arms across my chest. The faint light that gleamed from the oil lamps outside the Black Horse Inn fell across his fair hair. His hands were marked with cuts, but he wore good boots and a warm woollen coat and scarf. Despite his dust-ridden work, he looked clean and somehow decent. What could he know of what I'd endured in Northallerton Jail?

"Tell me then," I demanded. "Tell me what you'd have done, if you'd known it were me that came creeping through the darkness to steal Old Turner's jet?"

He opened his mouth again to speak, but I didn't let him. I went on. "Would you have kept quiet about it? Would you have risked your job, to save me from the constable?"

He looked away, clearly wishing he'd never followed me or approached me with his pathetic apology.

"Look at me…" I cried. "Look at my hair! I'm shamed for life."

"No," he said firmly. "Not shamed for life. They know… most of them round here, they know why you did it!"

He started to fumble in his pocket and pulled out a linen drawstring bag, which he held out towards me. "Take this," he said. "I've bin working an' saving. It's all I could think of to make it up to thee!"

My hand went out and he dropped the bag into my palm, where it landed with a faint, metallic clink. It had some weight to it and it chinked again as I moved my hand.

"Money?" I breathed, staring at it.

"Aye, money," he said. "Money to help you start again… and if I can do out else to help, I will."

My heart began to thunder in my chest. I wanted to tear the bag open and look inside, but pride wouldn't let me. Instead I turned away from him, feeling ever more shocked and stunned and, because I didn't know what else to do, I continued to walk away from him up Church Street.

I sensed him following me still as I walked on and realised belatedly that he must also go this way to get to his home. I slowed my pace at last and allowed him to catch up with me.

"Where are you going now?" he asked.

"I don't know," I admitted and stood still again.

"You should go to Turner's Yard," he said.

CHAPTER EIGHTEEN

Say Nowt, Just Eat!

I stared at Frank Dunsley for a moment and suddenly wanted to howl. I clapped my hand over my mouth to try to prevent the wild misery that welled up in me from escaping. The sound that came from my throat was like one long growl.

Frank simply stood there, watching and waiting, until at last I managed to speak again. "Not Turners Yard," I managed. "I cannot go back there again."

"Yes, you can," he said. "There's things you don't know about."

"I know where my mam is," I said fiercely.

"Aye," he said. "But… you might not know about the fire."

I held my breath, dreading what might come next. "What fire?" I asked faintly.

"No… not your family," he hastened to add. "None o' yours!"

"Then who?" I breathed.

"Old Man Turner," he said. "He sacked me after you were sent to jail. He chose to guard the workshop himself through the night and sat there with a candle and a jug o' ale. They think he must have drunk too much and knocked the lighted candle over, for the workshop was badly damaged and you know how jet dust flares and burns. The whole yard was out there fighting the blaze."

"And him?" I asked.

He shook his head. "Found dead amongst the dust and smoke. I thought you'd best know, the yard is changed for ever, and your dad…"

"Don't speak of him!"

"But he…"

"No. Don't speak of *him*! I thank you for this," I said, holding up the bag of coins. "You giving me this… It's fair of you, but I want to know nothing of *him*!"

"Your brother and sister are with Kat," he said. "You *can* go back to Turners Yard."

I stood there clutching the bag of coins, with no idea of what time of night it was, and it started to rain again.

"I'll walk with you," he offered. "My dad has sold his boat now, and he's bought the old cottage and the business from Turner's widow. We've repaired what was left o' the workshop too, and we know that it were none o' your fault. Your family will want you back there wi' them."

"Does Kat know you drove the prison wagon?" I asked.

He shook his head. "I weren't sure you'd even speak to me… and I wanted to give you this first… and try to explain. I never thought you'd head off to Grasper's!"

I stared at him, coming to understand that while I'd been away in Northallerton jail, there'd been a great deal happening here at home. "I didn't think I'd be welcome in Turners Yard," I said at last.

"With Turner gone, you are more than welcome," he said. "And Kat will be so relieved to see you."

A blessed sense of calmness seemed to reach me at last. "I suppose I will have to face them sometime," I admitted.

We set off side-by-side to cross the bridge, wind blasting from the sea so that I struggled to keep my feet. We strode on past scurrying rats and bobbing boats tied up at the quayside. As we went through the empty streets and up the hill to Flowergate, a clock struck three. We stopped at the entrance to Turner's Yard, and I stared down the alleyway towards the dark patch of shadows that had once been Turner's Jetworks.

"Is there much left of it?" I asked.

"Aye," he said. "You'll see it in the morning. We've done our best to build it up again. Go to Kat now and get some rest."

The cottage doors were all closed against the cold wind, and Mam's old house-place was boarded up. When I stopped by our old doorway, Frank pushed past me and went to knock firmly on Kat's door. We had to wait for a reply, for of course they were sleeping, but he knocked a second time and we heard sounds of movement from inside.

"Who is it?" Kat's voice called faintly.

"It's your lass," Frank called.

At last the door opened and three sleepy faces peered out at me. Bella burst into tears and Joey grabbed me tightly around the waist and pulled me inside. I heard the sound of a door opening behind me out in the yard, and suddenly Frank's father was there.

"Is it Lina?" he asked.

"Hush!" I begged. "Don't bring them all out here."

Kat blinked at me, wiping her eyes, and waved me further in. She didn't need to speak – just the look of relief on her face was quite enough.

"What have they done to your lovely hair?" Bella cried.

Questions came thick and fast, and I could only shake my head, still clutching tightly onto my bag of coins. When I turned to look back, both Frank and his dad had gone inside.

"I never meant…" I began, feeling that somehow I should try to explain to Kat why I'd ever gone out to steal jet.

"Hush now!" she said. "Close the door. Everybody knows about it. Your father has made it clear enough. You need say nothing, we're just glad to have you back."

"But our mam is in… "

Kat sighed. "Aye… but we'll get her out again. There's better chance of it, now that you are back with us," she said. "You've a new little brother. They call him Robbie."

"But… to be born in the workhouse?"

"He's not the first and he won't be the last," she said. "Say no more. We'll speak of it later."

She glanced briefly at Joey and I knew to leave it there.

"Bella honey," Kat said, "can you put the boy to bed? I'll make some tea for Lina, for we've a few tea leaves left."

Bella gave me another brief fierce hug and then let me go. "Aye, of course I can," she said.

While Kat reached for the kettle, Bella took Joey to Kat's cupboard bed.

"Don't want to go to bed," he said. "Now Lina's here."

But my sister smiled across at me with a new maturity. "I'll go wi' him," she said. "That'll settle him."

"Aye. *You* come and sit down wi' me, Lina," Kat said.

Our grandmother's neat home was crowded out with our old bits and pieces, still orderly to some degree but very cramped. I could see that it had been a struggle to fit things into the space. She put a warm oatcake down in front of me along with a steaming cup of tea. Powerful emotions washed through me, both happy and sad. I tried to thank her, but a lump seemed to stick in my throat and prevent me from speaking.

"Say nowt, just eat!" Kat ordered.

She put a piece of driftwood onto the fire and stirred up a blaze; then sat in silence while I ate the oatcake and drank my tea. I could hear Joey and Bella whispering softly together inside the cupboard bed.

I reached down to pick up the bag of coins. "You'll never believe who gave me this," I said.

"Oh, I will," she nodded, unsurprised. "That lad has been kindness itself."

"He feels guilt!" I said, sharply.

"Aye… mebbe so!" she agreed with a sigh. "But what choice did he have about what happened?"

I tipped up the bag and spilled the coins onto my lap, gaping at the sight of them. Quickly I counted ten pennies, three shillings, and one glinting gold sovereign; I'd never had a sovereign in my life. Kat smiled and nodded as I chinked each coin carefully back into the bag and fastened it tightly again, scarcely able to believe that the money could be mine.

"Does his father know 'bout this?" I asked, fearful that Sam Dunsley might claim it back from me.

"I'd think so," Kat said, with a sigh.

"What should I do with it?"

"Don't rush, think carefully," she advised.

We sat again for a while. Joey and Bella fell silent, and soon we heard gentle snores coming from them.

"There's things you need to know," Kat said at last. "Things that have happened since you were taken away from us."

"I'm beginning to realise it," I said.

CHAPTER NINETEEN

The Shame Is Mine

Kat sat back and watched me for a moment or two. "It's so good to have you back again, hon," she said gently. "We've missed you so much, and after you'd gone... and your father was arrested..." she began.

"I don't want to hear about him," I objected at once.

She sighed then and leant back again in her rocking chair. "But I think you *must* hear," she insisted. "Things are different now... and what happened to you... that was the turning point. Your dad was arrested for drunk and disorderly behaviour, but he admitted there and then that he should be the one to answer for the theft of Turner's jet. When he repeated it again and again and told all our neighbours too... well, at last the constable came to believe him. He took him before the magistrate."

I folded my arms across my chest. "All too late," I said. "Mam's the one I care about, not him... tell me about Mam."

"Well... you knew all too well that my Maria was so very sick. I had no money for doctors and my potions did little good, so after you and your father were taken, I moved her and the bairns in here with me. We all grew sick then with the coughing disease, and I had to beg help from the parish... They took us into the ropery."

"The bairns too?" I whispered, shocked.

Kat nodded and looked away from me. "I'm 'shamed that it happened," she whispered, "but... you need to know."

"The shame is mine," I told her, "not yours... my fault."

"Don't speak of fault," she replied firmly. "It happened. They put Joey in the boys ward and Bella with the girls, while I was housed in the ward for the sick and aged."

"You were all split up?" I whispered.

She lowered her voice but went on relentlessly. "Aye… Joey still suffers nightmares and won't go to bed without Bella beside him."

"I should've been here," I murmured, feeling worse than ever.

Kat wagged a bony finger at me. "No good can come of handing out blame. They took us in and they fetched a doctor to us, for we had pneumonia. We were given medicine and food, and I got better and the bairns did too. Little Robbie came early, poor scrap, and your mam is getting better, but she's taking time to recover her strength. That's why she's still there in the maternity ward."

"Can I go to see her?"

"Aye… maybe you can, but here's the thing. The rules of the workhouse will allow your mam to keep her child with her for six weeks, but then the little one must be farmed out, and Maria would have to move to the women's ward to work. That will happen, unless we can find space and money to support them both back here with us."

"Oh no," I cried and clasped my head in my hands in despair. I'd heard dreadful things about baby farms and the workhouse too.

"Stop that!" Kat said. "We'll do all we can to prevent it, but listen well. We'd still be there in the workhouse ward for destitutes but for the kindness of our neighbours… and your father's hard work. He is trying as best he can to make up…"

I rose swiftly to my feet. "Is he sleeping here?"

"No. He's in the Dunsley's workshop," she said, nodding her head towards the yard. "They have kindly set up a pallet bed in there for him."

I was speechless and sat down again, staring into the now fading flames of the fire. "How can they trust him?" I asked.

"Well... they do," she said. "They remember the man he once was, before he slipped into trouble with pain and laudanum, and perhaps they remember too that he came to that trouble trying only to save life. When your dad came out of jail, he seemed to be a different man... more the old Rob Raw we loved and respected well. He found himself work and fetched me out of the workhouse. Sam Dunsley had taken my home-place on when he bought into the business, and he kept it for me in the hopes that I'd return. So you see what I mean by good neighbours!"

"I thought they'd have scorned us," I admitted.

"Old Man Turner was a different matter," she said with a shrug. "He never paid those jettie lads fairly, but now... well, the fire has taken him, and Frank works with his dad."

"I can't forgive my dad," I said resentfully. "When they fetched the constable, he deserted me. I saw him hiding in one of the alleyways. He left me to answer for what he'd done."

Kat raised her eyebrows at that. "I know he bullied you, but you did *do* it," she said. "And I doubt he'll ever forgive himself for what he did. I daresay that if he'd been in his right mind, he never would have done such a thing."

"Yes... I *did* do it," I admitted, unwillingly.

"Well," Kat said. "To my knowledge Rob hasn't touched a drop o' drink since he returned to Whitby, and he works all through the night, cleaning jet workshops, going from one to another with his sweeping brush. You know how important it is to keep those places clean, and he takes any lowly job that comes his way and every penny that he earns he hands to me."

"And the jet men trust him?" I asked, doubtfully.

"Aye, it seems they do," she said. "Sam Dunsley's not the only one given up fishing and turned to jet. These jettie lads are making good money now, and there's a chance for such as us… There's packing and threading work for lasses too."

I gazed into the fire and smiled faintly. "My future lies in jet," I murmured sleepily.

"Aye… maybe now it does," Kat said. "But you must get to bed. Can you squeeze in the cupboard along wi' them?"

I smiled at the thought. "I'd be glad to," I said.

Kat went to her narrow bed in the far corner of the home-place.

It looked cosy and warm in the cupboard bed where my brother and sister slept, but first I went softly to open the door and peer out into the yard. All was in darkness but for the faint flicker of a candle in Turner's old workshop, and I heard the soft regular sound of a sweeping brush.

I stood there looking out into the quiet yard for a while and then went back inside, took off my old stained gown and crept behind the curtain in my shift. I squeezed myself in carefully and settled beside Joey, gritting my teeth at the thought of him frightened and alone in the workhouse. He moved a little in his sleep when I pressed my cheek against his curly hair, loving the homely bread-like smell of him.

It was a relief to wake and find myself back in Turner's Yard, with Bella's feet in my face and my brother's soft hair still pressed against my cheek instead of Sophia's shorn locks. Leaving them sleeping, I crept out of bed to discover that Kat was already up and making porridge.

"Have you slept?" she asked softly.

"Yes," I murmured.

"I cannot sleep as I used to," she admitted. "Look, I brought one of your old aprons with us when they came here. It's hanging on that hook."

I pulled on my gown and fastened the old apron round my waist, dropping the bag of coins into one of its deep pockets. Remembering Sophia, I cut a hunk of bread from the end of a loaf and dropped it into the other pocket. What Grasping Granny had tried to do to me was certainly no fault of hers.

Kat saw me do it but made no comment, and I noticed that my grandmother was short of breath and hobbled as she walked; the pneumonia had taken its toll on them all.

"You cannot go tramping out to the villages anymore," I said.

"No. This leg won't do as I want it to," she admitted, slapping her thigh. "I cannot catch my breath either, but I can still read the leaves and look into a crystal ball. The price of jet has shot sky high, and many folk believe it brings good luck. Not all jet goes to jewellery, you know. There's many a sailor carries a sliver in his pocket as protection from the waves, and many a church-going lady hides a small piece in her purse. Jet's always had a touch of magic about it."

"The leaves told me that my future lies in jet…" I began, but Kat looked up sharply, a horrified expression on her face.

"You never did it 'cos o' what the tea leaves said, Lina?"

"No," I said firmly, though it wasn't quite the truth.

"That were nowt but foolish talk, meant to take your mind from your troubles," she said, still frowning.

"Do you make up your readings then?" I asked accusingly.

"Not quite make up," she said. "I let myself dream a bit and say whatever comes into my mind. Though if something bad comes to mind, I put it to them much more gently… And when I saw that dark patch in your cup, it was certainly

116

jet that came to my mind. I fear the leaves *did* lead you into trouble."

"Such a thing won't happen again," I told her. "I'll search for jet and sell it properly. It was my dad who led me into trouble, not you!"

She looked thoughtful for a moment. "Well… there's work for lasses in the trade, for they need beaders, threaders, sorters, and packers. Though…" and she paused.

"Aye, I know…" I said quickly. "They won't want a jailbird working for them."

She shrugged and pulled two stools from a corner where they were neatly stacked and set them in the space between her bed and the small table.

"As you can see, we're strapped for space in here," she acknowledged. "Can you eat your porridge on your knee?"

"'Course I can."

She handed me a spoon and a bowl of porridge, and I took it gratefully and sat down on the rocking chair to eat. "I see they haven't yet let our old place next door. I could pay a month's rent with the money Frank's given me and get it back for us again."

"Aye, you could," she agreed. "But Maria's not fit to come back to us yet, and I think we'd do best to keep managing as we are for now, for there might be better uses for that money. I send the bairns down to the beach each morning to search for jet and driftwood, and never a day passes but Joey finds a handful o' jet. We're somehow scraping by."

"I'll go with them then," I said.

When I'd finished my porridge, I took a deep breath and went out into the yard to empty the chamber pot and wash my face and hands. I heard the grating sound of a turning jet wheel and saw that they'd made a big effort to shore up the scorched, ramshackle workshop. At the sound of our door closing behind me, the wheel stopped and Frank appeared in the workshop doorway.

"Alright then?" he asked.

"Aye," I said. "I'll go down to the scaur with the bairns to look for jet."

"You'd do best to go further along and look near Saltwick or even Sandsend way," he said, and he stepped towards me and waved his hand vaguely in the direction of the abbey and the cliffs. "You need to look in the rock pools and on the tideline… And don't go close to those cliffs. They risk too much, when they go hacking at the cliff face."

"I know," I said sharply, a little irritated by his unasked-for advice, but then swiftly regretted it, for nobody could know the dangers of the cliffs better than Frank.

"Be a good morning for it anyway," he added and shifted awkwardly back towards the workshop. "After last night… a rough sea brings the sea-washed pieces to the surface."

"Aye," I said, gritting my teeth. "And… I thank you for helping me last night… when you had no need," I managed.

"Oh… I did have need," he insisted.

I felt that I should say more, but he vanished inside the workshop.

CHAPTER TWENTY

Jailbirds

Back in Kat's home I found Bella and Joey emerging tousled from their bed. As soon as they were dressed and fed with porridge, we got ready to go to the beach. I tucked Mam's gutting knife into the top of my apron and wrapped the old grey shawl round my shoulders. Kat gave us a small basket packed with bread, cheese, and a bottle of water, along with more empty baskets for wood or anything else useful we could find.

"Here, lass," Kat said, as she tied an old scarf around my shorn head. "This will keep you warmer. Which way are you going? There's jet to be found up Sandsend way."

I sighed and thought of Sophia. "Aye… that's what Frank just said, but I'm thinking of the scaur. We can pick up kindling and wood as well if we go down there."

"Aye, that's true," she agreed.

So we set off down Flowergate and headed over the bridge. I gritted my teeth and prepared to do battle, for I expected to face insults and maybe worse. That was another reason to walk through the town. Best get it over with, I told myself.

We joined the usual crowd of folk, tramping over the bridge and moving down towards the beach. I received some doubtful looks and stares, but a few friendly nods came my way as well and nobody actually shouted at me or tried to stop me joining them. As we passed through the marketplace, I saw Sophia at the entrance to New Way Ghaut, begging alms again at Grasper's side.

I slowed my steps and caught Bella by the arm. "I know this is going to make you wonder," I said, "but I must take Sophia Goodchild to the beach with us."

Bella looked astounded. "What! That beggar? Grasper's girl?"

Joey looked troubled by the sudden tension between us.

"You cannot mean it!" Bella cried. "You hate her! Everyone hates her and that filthy old granny of hers!"

I bit my lip, seeing that I'd handled this all wrong.

"I'm sorry," I said. "We haven't had much time to talk about it yet, but Sophia was in Northallerton Jail with me."

"I knew she'd been sent to prison too," Bella said, her face full of resentment. "Everyone said it was bound to happen sooner or later."

"Aye… they would," I said. "But Bella, she's had it so hard in there. She was starving when she stole that loaf of bread and she's such a little scrap. Look at her. They've cut her hair like mine and they beat her when she cursed them for doing it. They put her in a cell with me and I tried… somehow… to look after her."

"So now you like her more than me!" Bella cried.

I flung my arms about her. "Never, never! You are always my only sister, Bella. That lass can never be a sister to me… only you can be that."

She pushed me away and I saw that her cheeks were wet, though maybe with resentment rather than sorrow. "I've had it hard too," she protested. "That workhouse… you don't know…"

I saw then that Joey's small face was screwed up tight with anxiety. "We're frightening Joey," I whispered. "I'm sorry, but I can't just ditch Sophia."

Bella folded her arms and looked stubborn for a moment, but then her eyes suddenly widened as she glanced over my shoulder. "Here she comes," she cried. "She's seen you… and I'm a little bit scared o' her."

Sophia had dodged past her granny and headed our way.

"Take Joey and go ahead with him," I said. "I'll see you on the scaur."

Joey still looked scared, but Bella dragged him off towards the beach. Sophia stared at them both as they passed, then came to me.

"I want to come scavenging wi' you," she said. "Though Granny says I can't. Please take me, Lina… please! Granny wants to sell my boots and make me beg wi' bare feet again!"

Anger rose in me. A sour smell rose from her hair and her clothes after just one night in Grasper's den. "You come with me," I said.

The old woman lurched towards us, grabbing at Sophia with her filthy claw-like hands. I was appalled and deeply ashamed to think that I'd gone creeping into her place last night.

"She's mine… Sophia's mine!" she cried. "Give 'er 'ere!"

No," I said. "She's coming down to the beach with me."

"What right… what right have you?"

"I could report you to the constable for what you did last night," I said.

"I doubt the constable would harken t'you," she cried, pointing a bony finger in my face.

I slipped my hand into my pocket, felt for the precious bag of coins, and brought out one penny. I held it up to Grasper. "I'm paying for Sophia to work with me. You will get one penny a day and a share of what we find."

Grasper stared at the coin and fell silent. I could see that her eyes were growing a light film across them and knew her sight must be failing fast.

"Sophia will come back to you tonight," I said, sounding a little softer then. "And if we're lucky on the scaur, she'll have more pennies for you."

Grasper snatched the coin from me and waved us on without another word. We marched on quickly heading down to the beach together.

"Last night…" Sophia began, after a while.

"Don't speak of it," I said sharply. "I should never have gone there with you. Here, I brought you this."

I gave her the hunk of bread from my pocket, and she took it and began to eat hungrily. That silenced her and I was glad of it, for I didn't want anything more to be said about my ignorant foolishness.

A fierce northerly wind blew into our faces as we walked out onto the flat low-lying rocks. All the women set about fastening their shawls more tightly. Frank had been right, the rough sea had brought all sorts of things to the surface. Scavengers gathered all over the scaur, collecting shellfish, driftwood, sea coal, and jet. Once down there on the slippery rocks, I stood still for a moment, realising how bitterly I'd missed it all; the rush and hiss of the waves, the catlike cry of the gulls, and the salty smell of seaweed. There were so many of us down there that I couldn't at first see Bella and Joey.

"Where do we look?" Sophia asked.

"Not here," I said.

I went skidding over the slippery rocks as fast as I could, with her following me, until at last I spied Bella and Joey. But before we could get close to them some lads came up behind us, laughing and jeering, far too close for comfort.

Sophia glanced back. "It's them," she whispered and snatched at my arm. "It's them as said they'd cut my throat."

I slowed my steps, put my baskets down, and turned to face them, hands on hips. For a moment they looked somewhat taken aback, but then a lad I knew to be something of a bully took a step closer.

"We don't want such as *her* down here," he said, pointing at Sophia. "And we don't want you no more, Lina Raw! Jailbirds you are, jailbirds both!"

Others took courage from his boldness and shouted at us too.

"Aye, thieves you are!"

"Get gone!"

"Go back to prison where you belong!"

My heart started to thunder, but I managed to stay calm for I'd expected this. I knew most of them from when they were bairns, and we'd all grown up in the town together.

"Run back to your mam, Danny Hawsker!" I replied.

I took my mother's gutting knife from the leather sheath that I'd pushed through my apron strings and held it in front of me. "Aye, I've learnt a thing or two in Northallerton Jail!"

Danny scowled ferociously, but some of the others shifted uneasily and backed off a little way.

"We'll go where we choose," I said. "And such as you aren't going to stop us!"

I saw from the corner of my eye that a group of older flitherpickers who'd been prizing limpets off the rocks were now striding towards us, carrying their buckets. When I looked properly I saw that one of them was Danny Hawsker's mam. Sophia gave a small trembling moan as they approached and clutched my apron.

"What's up?" Madge Hawsker asked.

"Lina Raw is threatening us wi' her gutting knife," Danny said. "Look, plain for all to see. And she's brought that little beggar rat down here."

"We've a right to gather from the scaur, just as you have," I said. "Aye, we've been in prison, everyone knows it, but

now we need to make good. I'm trying to help my family. That's what I'm doing here!"

There was whispering amongst the women and I caught Kat's name and my dad's name mentioned too. Suddenly heads were nodding.

"Let 'em be, lads!" Madge said.

"Aye, let the lasses be!" The women chorused.

"What? Let those thieves down here?" Danny objected.

Madge rounded on her son. "I said let them be!"

"But," Danny began. "She's a thief!"

"Aye, but she's not the only one and…" she suddenly pointed at Sophia, who moaned and hid behind me. "And I'd rather see that little lass down here scavenging along of us than begging on street corners. You'll give them both a chance and let 'em be!"

Danny looked furious, but he turned awkwardly away and slowly edged his way back towards the other lads. Then all at once they were splashing through the shallows in the direction of the town, as if they'd never meant to cause trouble in the first place.

"You keep that knife for picking flithers," Madge told me sharply.

"I will," I said, putting it back in its sheath. "I thank you. We're searching for jet, not flithers."

She shook her head and sighed. "Oh aye, you and everyone else. Well… you've as much chance as anyone I suppose. I hope your mam'll be back soon, and if those lads trouble you again, you come to Madge!"

"I will," I said.

The women turned back to their work.

CHAPTER TWENTY-ONE

Sea-Washed Jet

Sophia watched warily as Madge and the other women walked away from us. Eventually gaining confidence, she let go of me and gave a small whoop. "That showed 'em!" she cried.

"Hush! Keep quiet! Don't gloat!" I warned.

Glancing around, I spied my brother and sister in the distance, making their way towards us. "Now listen here," I told Sophia. "You'll be polite and sweet-spoken to my sister, or straight back to Grasper you'll go. Our Bella don't see why you should come picking with us."

"And I don't see why *she* should come wi' me," Sophia replied, quick as a cat.

"Off you go then," I said, pointing the way back to the town.

She relented fast. "I'll talk sweet to her," she promised hurriedly.

Joey arrived, already waving a couple of small slivers of jet.

"Clever lad," I praised him.

Sophia smiled sweetly at Bella and chose her words carefully. "Thank 'ee kindly for letting me come wi' you," she said.

Bella eyed her warily. "All right," she murmured grudgingly.

"Frank said Saltwick might be best," I told them, "though it means a longer walk."

"Well, *he* would know," Bella acknowledged. "But it's a long tramp up there, and most of them search nearer town."

"All the better for us then," I insisted.

Bella gave a sigh and turned towards the distant cliffs. We followed, passing by many of the busy scavengers as we went, and as we strode along I noticed that, after all, the dreaded treadmill had done me some good. It felt joyful to be striding along in the cold fresh air, leaving most of the pickers behind us; I felt that I could walk forever. Sophia too marched ahead of me, while Bella struggled a little way behind us. Joey ran everywhere, returning now and again with more handfuls of tiny jet slivers. After a while Sophia became frustrated when she snatched up shining black stones that we had to tell her were sea-washed coal, with little value but to build a fire.

I put them in one of the bags we'd brought, for anything that would burn could be used.

"How do I know when it's jet?" she asked, furiously flinging down the latest lump, when we gathered together to examine our small finds.

I picked up a flat white pebble and scratched one of Joey's little pieces across it, so that it left a dark gingery trail behind.

"Coal marks black; jet marks brown!" I said.

She grabbed another piece of jet from Joey and made her own brown mark on the flat white surface. "Ah!" she cried. "I see."

Bella frowned. "Now give that back to him," she insisted.

Sophia looked offended but did as she was told.

"We will share all we find, when we get back," I assured her.

"And what if she's found nothing?" Bella asked.

Sophia flashed a brittle smile at her. "I will find the stuff," she said.

We set about searching again, and once we were closer to Saltwick Sophia was at last rewarded with three dark slivers that left a ginger trail.

"Now you give them to me," I ordered. "Share and share alike!"

She handed them over obediently.

I kept our precious finds in one of my deep pockets, and when the watery sun moved overhead we sat down to eat our bread and cheese. Sophia hovered beside us looking hopeful, and Bella reluctantly offered her a hunk of bread. It was accepted with a quiet "thank you", and then she was offered a bit of cheese as well.

We searched again, but already the tide was turning.

"We'd best head back," I said, "and gather driftwood on the way."

"If *they've* left us any," Bella said.

So we set off back along the shore, picking up some good-sized logs that I slung across my back. We gathered a basket of kindling too, and just as we were leaving Saltwick Sophia tripped and fell into a pool. As she rose, dripping with seawater, we saw that she'd snatched up a shining black lump that covered the whole of her palm.

"Bound to be coal," Bella said doubtfully.

"That be jet," Joey said.

And sure enough, when we scraped it across our white pebble, it left a smudgy ginger trail behind.

Bella whistled, impressed at the size of it, while Sophia grinned hugely.

"And is she going to share that with us?" Bella asked.

"Oh yes, she is," I said sternly, looking at Sophia.

She sighed but handed it to me. "Fair shares," she agreed.

We started to walk back fast then, Sophia marching ahead full of pride and energy. I saw that Joey and Bella were trailing behind and struggling, so I tied the bundle of wood onto my back and lifted our Joey onto my shoulders, while Bella still puffed along behind with the kindling basket.

Sophia stopped and, seeing that she was alone, turned to watch us as we made our slower way towards her. As we approached, she came awkwardly back to us and shyly took hold of one handle of Bella's basket. Nothing was said between them, but they walked along together then, sharing the load and I felt satisfied to see them doing that.

We left the beach with the tide lapping about our ankles and headed once again up New Way Ghaut. Grasper was there in her usual begging spot, but Sophia, still helping to carry the log basket, barely glanced in her grandmother's direction. We crossed the bridge and went straight to Dark Entry Yard.

There were more stalls there than ever and more dealers too, all shouting at each other as they weighed lumps of jet and compared notes on what was offered for sale. The main commerce came from the miners who risked their lives burrowing into the cliffs up near Sandsend, but a queue of pickers waited patiently with their smaller finds of sea-washed jet and sometimes a few rusty-skinned lumps that they'd managed to hack from the lower cliffs. This had always been a regular trade in our area, but I'd never seen the yard so wild and crowded out before. Dust-covered jet carvers wandered up and down, looking for good-sized pieces that might suit some special purpose or commission, and there was a deal of argument over prices too. Shards of jet were weighed on scales and in the palms of hands and scrutinized through magnifying glasses.

We joined the pickers queue and I glanced about surreptitiously, comparing our finds with those of others. Slowly we moved towards the front of the queue, watching all the time to see who went away pleased or disappointed, counting their coins. When at last it was our turn, we got a touch of both.

"These scraps will do for nowt but beads," we were told, and a few meagre pence were handed over for them, but when we produced Sophia's find, it was a different matter and caused something of a flurry of excitement. Three dealers were called to examine the piece.

"Almost too big for a funeral brooch!"

"Nay, a funeral brooch can never be big enough!"

"It might make two!"

They looked for flaws through a magnifying glass, and then a small bidding war began.

"I'll give you five shilling!"

"Nay, eight!" came the final call.

"I want it in small coins," I insisted, for I didn't know how we'd split it otherwise.

The dealer who bought it laughed and agreed to that.

I added the coins carefully to the bag that Frank had given me and we hurried away with our money back to bridge end, scare able to believe our luck.

"How do we share it?" Bella asked, concerned.

"We split it four ways," I said firmly.

Sophia's face fell, for she saw at once that most of the money would go to our family, not hers.

"Don't look so sour," I told her. "It'd take you three weeks or more to make that from begging."

I thought she might dig in her heels, and I doubted myself if this was fair. She looked uncertainly from me to Bella. "Can I come wi' you tomorrow?" she asked.

"Yes, you can," Bella said.

"And every day after?" she asked again.

"Yes, you can, if you behave decent," Bella agreed.

"Then we'll split it four ways," Sophia agreed.

She pounced on her share when I counted it out and ran off, over the bridge towards New Way Ghaut, before we could change our minds.

"Can we get a pennorth o' liquorice?" Joey ventured, and I saw a drop of saliva gleaming in the corner of his mouth.

I gave them a penny each and Joey ran eagerly to the sweet shop to spend his reward, while Bella followed more slowly behind him. Relieved that we'd managed to get through the day so well, I sat down for a moment on one of the capstans on the side of the fish staithe.

"Maybe my future lies in jet," I murmured. "After all… after all!"

As I sat there the wind dropped a little, and I glanced across the river to where the low sun was glinting on the far side of the harbour. There seemed to be building work going on up there, quite high on the steep hillside. A mass of ladders, planks, and ropes surrounded the growing development of a terrace of houses with fine slate roofs and chimney pots. The new houses looked as though they were almost finished, gleaming there in the evening sun.

What a site for a house, I thought. You'd be able to see the whole of Whitby Town spread out below you. How wonderful it would be to live in a decent new house up on the hillside, looking down upon the Upper Harbour!

Then my gaze shifted higher still to the sight of the ruined abbey, perched on the cliffs. I remembered my friend Hilda in Northallerton Jail and hoped she'd soon be released, as the ancient abbess with the same name came to mind.

It was my dad who'd told me about the abbess, a princess in her own right as well as a nun. He'd wondered why a princess would choose to live on such a cold windy cliff.

At the thought of my dad my spirits fell again, for I knew I'd have to meet him soon: it couldn't be avoided. I got up and heaved the basket of kindling onto my shoulder, as my brother and sister emerged from the sweet shop by the bridge, their mouths already stained and sticky.

"Back home now," I said with satisfaction.

It was so good to see them looking happy once again.

CHAPTER TWENTY-TWO

Dunsley's Jet Ornaments

The light was fading when we returned to Turners Yard, tired and hungry but pleased with ourselves. Frank's dad looked out from the workshop in the yard.

"It's good to see yer back again lass," he said.

"Aye, thank you Sam," I said gratefully.

I turned to go inside, but another door opened and Hetty Ruswarp stepped into the yard with a water bucket to fill at the pump.

"Alright then, Lina?" she said, as if she'd seen me only yesterday.

"Aye, thanks Hetty," I replied and was comforted by the small exchange, for I knew it was her way of saying that all was forgiven.

Kat had a pan of mutton stew bubbling on the hob, and we made quick work of it and cleaned our bowls with hunks of bread. I sat back, feeling full and contented.

"I meant to warn you about Sophia," I said to Bella, feeling that she deserved much more of an explanation. "There was so much to think about this morning, I never got it said. She has had a terrible life with only Grasper to look after her."

Bella nodded. "Well... she *did* share her find with us," she said fairly. "And I didn't think she'd do that. Maybe after all, she's not so bad."

"What's this?" asked Kat.

"We took the beggar girl with us," Joey said. "And she found a lump of jet, this big." He put his two small hands together, making a wide circle of his fingers and thumbs.

I counted out the shillings that had been our share of the earnings and pushed them towards Kat.

"That's our share," Bella said. "We split four ways – fair's fair! We came away with all of that."

Kat stared at it amazed. She took two shillings and pushed the rest back to me. "Two shilling will keep us for a few more days," she said. "You put the rest with your savings."

I dropped the coins back into my pouch. Joey was almost falling asleep on his stool, so Bella helped him get ready for bed, while I carried our bowls out into the yard to rinse them at the pump. It was shadowy out there, though a few faint lights from the cottage windows lifted the darkness a little. One dim gas lamp shone with a yellow glow from Flowergate. I couldn't help but recall the night that had started all my trouble and glanced across to the workshop that now said DUNSLEY'S JET ORNAMENTS over the door.

The flickering gleam of a candle showed through the window and the door stood slightly open, so I could still hear the regular clack and whirr of a treadle wheel. I put my pots down, quickly rinsed my hands and face and smoothed my ugly hacked hair down on either side of my head. Moving cautiously I went over to the doorway, still wary at the thought of discovering my father in there. The window was coated with brown jet dust and fuzzy with fingerprints where just a few patches had been rubbed clear. I squinted inside and was reassured to see Frank bent over the wheel. At last I pushed the door further open, and when it creaked the treadle wheel stopped.

He looked round at me, with an expression of surprise on his face.

"I haven't come robbing," I hastened to say.

I glanced quickly around to be certain my dad wasn't there.

"I never thought you had," he said.

"I've come to say thank you…" I began. "For all you've done… and for good advice. You've been a help to Kat… and to my dad too." I glanced around at the neat bedroll that was stashed in the corner beside a table and a jug. "Is that his?" I asked.

He nodded. "That's where he sleeps, when he sleeps."

"And he's working now?"

"Aye. He's goes sweeping at Webster's, and he goes onto Routh's and Watmough's. Then he'll clean up here before he settles for the night. I'll wake him as soon as it's light and he'll be off again to fettle a few more workshops very early. He seems to manage with little sleep."

"Well, when he was fishing he was awake most nights," I acknowledged.

"Aye, my dad's the same," he agreed.

"What are you doing?" I asked, moving over to look at his work.

"Grinding and smoothing first," he said. "This piece of sea-washed will make a good brooch."

But I stared when I saw the piece of jet he worked, for the smooth round piece of gleaming sea-washed jet looked familiar. "Where did you get that?" I asked.

"Round at Entry Yard, of course," he said.

"Just now?" I asked.

He nodded.

"I'd swear that's the piece we found at Saltwick and sold today," I said. "That's what I meant by good advice. We walked all the way to Saltwick, as you said, and it was there that we found it. What did they charge you for it?"

"Ten shillings," he said. "It will make a lovely brooch, and if I do a good job on it I might get a sovereign for a funeral brooch in one of these new shops that are springing up."

"They gave us eight," I said. "And we were thrilled to get it, but if I'd brought it straight to you…"

He put the jet carefully down and sighed. "Aye," he said thoughtfully. "If you'd brought it straight to me, I guess we'd maybe both be better off."

"Why should we be putting coins into the dealer's pockets?" I said.

"Aye, why indeed?" he agreed.

"How much would they sell it for, in a shop?" I asked.

"A pound and ten shillings at least, maybe more these days!"

"They take a good share then!"

"Aye, well they have their fancy premises to keep," he said. "With window displays and polished wood counters and assistants dressed in good gowns, all wearing jet themselves. They've lady assistants that talk soft and sweet to the customers these days, just like London folk, selling to the rich summer visitors."

"Could I do that?" I wondered.

He stopped and looked me up and down. "Aye, maybe you could," he said doubtfully. "But…"

I sighed and hung my head, hating both the sight and the feel of my ragged stained gown and my horrid chopped hair that marked me out as a thief. I knew only too well what a ridiculous figure I must cut. "I'm stopping you working," I said at last, "I'll get out o' the way."

"Aye," he said and started to work on the piece again, his fingers flicking light and fast, turning the jet, this way and that. I watched him for a moment, but then he stopped the wheel and looked at me again.

"You've made me think a bit," he said. "If you brought your sea-washed finds to me, I'd pay you as much as I could for them. And maybe we'd be able to cut out the dealers."

"Would it not cause trouble doing that?" I asked.

"Who'd know?" he said. "We'd have to trust each other."

I backed away towards the door. "Yes," I said. "I'll bring our finds to you. You can trust me now. I promise you that."

He stumbled past me to hold the door open, and as I turned to go he raised his hand as though he meant to touch my hair, but then he dropped it quickly, thinking better of it.

"It's still bonny," he said softly, "your hair."

I gave an awkward shrug, glad that it was getting dark by the doorway and hurried back across the yard to Kat's home-place.

"Lina?" he called softly after me, and when I turned again he pointed to the water pump. "You've forgotten your pots."

Feeling foolish, I went to collect them and carried them back inside.

The younger ones were asleep, and my gran was getting ready for bed.

"You've been a while wi' those pots," she said. "What have you been getting up to?"

"Frank says we could take our jet finds straight to him," I said. "We won't go bothering with dealers anymore."

"That sounds good," she agreed. "He'd be more than fair, I'd say."

I sat down by the fire and began rubbing hopelessly at the red marks on my dress, until the thin linen of my gown began to split. "Do you know how big a cut these jet shops take?" I asked.

"I know they take a lot," Kat said. "But they have their costs – good premises, carpets and fittings, window displays and lady assistants."

"I'd love to work in a shop like that," I said with a sigh. "But they'd not have *me*. If I'd got a better gown to wear, I might try tramping from door to door, like you used to do, but instead o' selling fish, I'd be selling Frank's jet."

Kat looked up at me, her expression thoughtful.

"Take no notice o' me," I said with a shrug. "I know I look worse than Sophia, and I've no business worrying about what I look like, not with mam still in the workhouse and you putting up with us all crammed out in here."

CHAPTER TWENTY-THREE

Black Bombazine

Kat struggled to her feet and began rooting around in her old wooden clothes chest that stood in the corner. I watched, wondering what she was up to and worrying about her a bit when she pulled out a black gown and held it up in front of herself.

"This belonged to one of my customers," she said. "Quite a wealthy widow, and it was her best mourning gown. I used to read the leaves for her or gaze into my crystal ball, and she was one I didn't dare tell what I really saw there. Then when she died, her daughter gave me this dress. It's far too wide for me, and I was thinking that the best thing to do with it was to sell it, though I doubt I'd get a lot for it."

I reached out to stroke the heavy material. "But it is worth something," I suggested.

"Bombazine," Kat said. "Not cheap either."

The texture of the bombazine was strong, but with a silky, lightly grained finish to it; the sleeves had satin tucks at the cuffs and the silken trimmings around the bottom of the skirt gleamed in the firelight.

I looked up at Kat, suddenly seeing what was in her mind.

"For me?" I murmured.

"Well… I can't go tramping round the villages no more," Kat said. "But I can sit and stitch all right. This gown could be remade to fit you, lass, and though it's mourning garb, it would be quite correct for a young woman to wear for selling jet."

My stomach lurched with pleasure at the thought of walking out into the yard wearing such a beautiful satin-trimmed gown.

"No, remake it to fit yourself," I said firmly. "It wouldn't be right, for I'm no widow and this is a widow's gown."

Kat cackled. "I'm no widow either," she said. "And I'm not doing this for your pleasure, lass. I wouldn't expect you to go skittering over the scaur in it... But you've made me think. There's money in death these days... and maybe you *could* go selling jet from door to door, just as I used to go selling fish and reading leaves."

"And I'd look respectable," I agreed thoughtfully.

"Aye. The West Cliff would be the place, what with all these fine new buildings and villas going up. There are wealthy folk coming to Whitby now for the fresh sea air, and they know nowt of who you are or what has gone before."

I nodded. "Aye, I've seen them strolling along the Royal Crescent and the Esplanade and the New Gardens," I said with a sigh.

"You could offer brooches, bracelets, and bead necklaces that Frank has made... though o' course you'd have to persuade him first. He's clever with his carving is Frank, that's why his father's given up fishing, to make the most of the skills his lad has got. Now is the moment for selling jet, and his father is learning the trade as well."

"But... the landladies would know me," I said, the hopeful image fading fast. "I doubt Whitby folk would even answer the door to me. Bella should go instead."

"Don't give up so easily," Kat said. "Bella's too young to be sent around like that, and I've other hopes for her. This is where the gown comes in. You'd just need to look right and maybe this way you'll get a chance to prove yourself. All moneyed folk want Whitby jet these days. Maybe the leaves spoke truth to us, after all."

"After that treadmill, I can walk for ever," I admitted.

"Take off those old things and let's get started."

"But you were tired and going to bed."

"Bed can wait".

She pulled out her workbox and found a tape measure. I did as she told me, stripping off my rags to step into the black bombazine. It swamped me, but it felt like nothing I'd ever worn before, rather stiff and heavy but with a soft swishing sound as I moved in it.

Kat made me lift up my arms and turn around, while she carefully measured and tacked and pinned. I began to feel excited but tried to quash the sensation, for so many things could go wrong with this plan, and even in a decent new gown I'd struggle to make my cropped hair look right. When the measuring was done, I carefully stepped out of the gown.

"If I went up to the ropery, would they let me see Mam?" I asked.

"You're supposed to make an appointment, so you may have to go there twice," she said. "They give you a time that fits with the workhouse routine, and I must warn you, honey, that Maria has told me to stay away. She doesn't want Joey going anywhere near that place again."

I nodded. "But I must go to see her, I think."

"You have every right," Kat said.

I took a deep breath. "And I must speak to my dad," I said.

She pressed my arm and nodded. "Aye, you must. Now get to bed."

The next morning we headed off down New Way Ghaut again and I found Sophia and her granny waiting at the top of the alleyway for us. Grasper pushed Sophia towards me, all smiles.

"We can't get two shillings every day," I warned.

"Get what you can… what you can," she squawked. "And you do as yer told," she threatened Sophia.

Unworried by threats, Sophia set off with us again towards the scaur.

"We had bread and ale and cheese and a fancy cake last night!" she said.

"We're saving our money," Bella told her righteously. "But we had mutton stew."

"I like mutton stew," Sophia admitted.

We passed the gangs of pickers and headed for Saltwick again.

"Have we got to go that far?" Bella grumbled. "Most o' the others don't go that far."

"The *others* didn't find a grand piece, like we did yesterday," I said.

So we marched on, and she didn't complain again. We searched until the middle of the afternoon and found nothing as good as the last time, though Joey as ever found plenty of small bits, but then on the way back we found two pieces in a rock pool that had cracked apart, each about a third of the size of Sophia's find. We arrived back in the town late again, just beating the tide. We avoided the dealers and headed straight back to Turners Yard. Sophia went with us, determined to make sure that she got her share. Four anxious faces watched as Frank and his father examined our finds.

They carefully flicked the smallest pieces to the side.

"Only good for beads," Sam Dunsley said.

"Five a penny?" Frank offered.

"That's more than the dealers gave us for scraps," I said.

"I'm giving you what I would've paid the dealers," Frank said.

His dad grunted but didn't interfere.

"There's thirteen pieces here," Frank said, "so let's call it a baker's dozen, and I'll get one free. Now these two pieces would make a pair of earrings, so I could give you two shillings for those."

We agreed and a satisfactory deal was done.

Joey and Bella went into Kat's for their tea, and Sophia hung around our doorstep clutching her earrings.

"Are you having mutton stew?" she asked.

"Not today," I said.

I went inside and helped myself to a bit of warm bread and cheese and slipped her a slice. "Off back to your granny's now. I'll walk down the road with you, for I need to cross the bridge."

"Where are yer going?" she asked.

"Up to the ropery, to see my mam."

Her expression changed to one of fear. "I wouldn't go up there," she said, "but… if you want me to, I'd come wi' you."

I was touched by the reluctant offer, but shook my head. "No, this is something I need to do alone."

I worked my way up the hillside through the hodgepodge of old fishing yards and some tenement houses, just like ours, with walkways linking the dwellings together. There were older sturdy pan-tiled cottages, built tightly into the hillside, so that kitchen windows often spied into neighbours sleeping quarters, and work sheds that seemed little more than a lean-to, all linked together by narrow alleyways. Around every corner came another sharp turn and steep flight of steps. When I eventually emerged at the top of Elbow Yard I found myself on a higher level, alongside the row of the spanking new houses that I'd seen being built from down below. The windowpanes sparkled in the evening sun, though the houses were still unfinished. Doors and windowsills were being painted and neat stone doorsteps ground and sanded. Everything about that row was clean and decent, yet practical. Just below the new terrace a gang of workmen toiled with spades, and one of them looked up and saw me watching them.

"Are you putting in an offer, then?" he shouted up at me.

"I wish I could!" I replied.

The view from up there took my breath away, as my gaze swept across from the distant heather moors, down to the river, through the harbour and on over the jumble of chimneys and rooftops, to the sea. I wondered if the ancient princess-nun had seen something like that view when she lived up there on the cliff tops, amongst soaring gulls, so long ago. I turned away regretfully and followed the long straight path that led beside the old rope-making factory.

CHAPTER TWENTY-FOUR

The Workhouse

The workhouse stood at the furthest end of the old ropewalk. From the outside it was a tall, elegant brick building with extensions newly built. The smart frontage gave a stylish impression – for a place that most folk dreaded. I knew it by reputation only, for I'd never stepped inside its doors before.

My steps slowed as I approached the main entrance, which towered above me and somehow made me think of Northallerton Jail. My stomach churned at the thought of going in, but my mam was in there and so was a tiny mite that was my new brother, so I gritted my teeth and marched up the steps.

I found myself in a small entrance hall, with a polished wooden counter and bell. A notice was pinned up above it that I couldn't read. I tapped the bell gently, but it didn't make much sound , so I hit it again with more energy and it clanged loudly then, making me jump. The echoing tap of fast footsteps came at last from what seemed a distance and a plump, red-faced woman appeared, looking flustered.

"Yes," she said, quickly looking me up and down, taking in my shorn hair and stained skirt. "Are you applying to the parish?"

I swallowed hard and tried to think fast, while she picked up a notebook and began to flick through the pages.

"No… no, I'm not for applying to the parish, but I'd like to see my mam. She's in here."

"You can't just come visiting here!" she said. "This is a workhouse, not a ladies parlour."

"But…" I began. "I thought families could visit."

"Parents may see their children for one hour only on a Sunday afternoon."

"Thank you," I said and hurriedly bobbed a curtsey. "I'll come back again then."

"Aye well," she said, just a touch softer. "We can't have visitors just walking in and expecting to see the inmates. They're supposed to be working you know, unless they are in the maternity wing."

"Oh… but my mam *is* in there," I said. "She's sick and she's had a bairn. She's in the mothers' ward."

"Well why didn't you say so? Wasting my time like that! Maternity Ward is different!"

"So may I see her, please?" I asked.

She sighed heavily and passed a yellow paper ticket over the counter to me. "Here, take this. Go out of the door, round the back and cross the yard. Knock at the blue door and hand this ticket to the matron. Half an hour, no more!"

Taking a deep breath, I tried to quell both my fear and my impatience. "Thank you," I said and bobbed again.

I walked round the big building, crossed the yard and tried to follow the woman's instructions, pushing open the only blue door that I could find, to discover a long corridor that smelled of carbolic soap. A wave of nausea rose at the back of my throat and I needed to stop and swallow hard again, for the smell reminded me once more of Northallerton Jail.

Setting off down the corridor, I eventually found a door that opened into a long room filled with beds. Women dressed in the plain grey and white of the workhouse uniform moved amongst the sick. The reek of urine lay beneath the sharper scent of carbolic soap and a stench of vomit wafted in the air, as a woman carried a slop pot past me. From somewhere in the distance came the wail of babies and the sound of a strident voice.

"Yes, girl."

A woman with a badge on her hat addressed me, and I guessed that she must be the matron. She was middle-aged, with thin dark hair scraped back into a bun and a grim, straight mouth that seemed to snap open and shut; both the look of her and the keys that hung on a chain at her waist made my stomach churn.

I held out my ticket. "Please, I've come to see Maria Raw"

"Half an hour only," she said. "No sitting on the beds."

She pointed to the far end of the long room and I walked in that direction, glancing uncertainly from bed to bed. Then at last I saw her, my mam – a thin pale woman with great dark eyes and her hair shorn just like mine. She was dressed in the rough-woven calico bed-gown that all the invalids wore, and she stared at me from the very corner bed.

"Mam," I whispered.

She struggled to pull herself up. "You shouldn't 'a come," she said and started coughing.

I hurried to her side, shocked to see how thin she'd become. I slipped my arm around her shoulders to ease her into a sitting position and felt the bones of her shoulders. She seemed to be fighting for breath.

"Oh, Mam," I said. "You do look poorly."

The coughing made it impossible for her to reply, so I snatched up a mug of water from a table that stood beside her bed and helped her take a few sips. Eventually the coughing subsided and she stretched her hand up to stroke my chopped hair.

"Oh my honey," she said faintly. "Look at us both! What's become of us?" She gave me a smile that made me want to weep.

"Did they hurt you in that terrible place?" she asked.

"No," I said firmly. "I'm stronger now and wiser too. I'm so sorry for what I did, Mam. I'll never do anything so foolish again, I promise you."

"You did it for me," she said, trying to suppress another cough. "I know you did it for me."

"But it was wrong and it did no good."

She sighed, smiled sadly and stroked my hand.

"Are they giving you enough food here?" I asked.

"Yes," she said. "It's tasteless but I eat it, and there's porridge every day."

"We've got to get you out of here."

She coughed again and I crouched beside her bed to offer her water, for there were no chairs for visitors to sit on. After she'd taken a sip and settled down, she gripped my arm and pointed with a shaking finger to the farthest side of her bed.

"Go see!"

Almost hidden, in the tiniest space between the bed and the wall, I found a plain wooden crib with a beautiful dark-haired elfin child asleep in it.

I caught my breath, for he looked too delicate to be real. Mam's eyes filled with tears and she started coughing again. The sounds made the baby open his eyes, and I saw that they were already turning dark like mine. He gave a mew like a hungry kitten.

"Little Robbie," I murmured.

"Pick him up and bring him here, and I'll try to feed him," Mam said.

I bent over the crib and slipped my hands under his small frame. He was swaddled in rough linen and felt like a moppet doll. I held him and for a powerful insane moment felt the urge to turn and run away with him, to carry him far from that grim place, though I knew that the thought was utter foolishness. I dropped a kiss on his forehead and handed him to mam, who put him to her breast.

"Poor lamb," I said, "born here!"

Mam sighed and looked at me. "Not the only one," she said. "I never told you this, for there was no need… but this is where I was born."

"Oh Mam," I murmured. My thoughts flew around as I tried to take in what that meant. "But Kat…" I started.

"Aye," mam said. "However did you think Kat managed, when my handsome sailor-father sailed away, leaving her with child?"

I saw then that I should have realised there'd be no way for Kat to survive other than to go into the workhouse, just like Sall.

Mam nodded. "But Kat got out of here, as quickly as she could. She set about making a living by selling fish. She carried me with her, fastened in a shawl."

"Aye, she would," I murmured.

"I will too," Mam assured me, and I saw determination in her eyes, even though her face was so thin and drawn. "Now tell me how the bairns are?"

So we chatted while little Robbie fed and I reassured her that Bella and Joey thrived.

All too soon the matron walked past and pointed to a large clock that ticked away the minutes on the wall above us. "You've had your half hour," she said.

I turned away obediently, but feeling desperate for the time had flown so fast.

"Don't come again, honey," mam said.

"I needed to come," I said. "Seeing you and the little 'un's reminded me what we are struggling for.

"I can't think of more than trying to feed the child," she said, "and get myself strong again. Then like Kat… I will come back to you all."

I bent to kiss her. "I understand," I said.

I could see that she must feel as cut off in the Workhouse infirmary as I'd been in Northallerton Jail and not able to think of much more than how to get right again.

"Don't fret, about us," I said. "We are looking after each other. Get yourself better. Think only of that."

"And your father…?"

"We'll see…"

That was all I could say of him.

"Get better, Mam!"

CHAPTER TWENTY-FIVE

Aelfleda Terrace

I left the grim building and walked back past the ropery, my energy somewhat renewed by the thought of the sweet fragile face of my new brother. When I reached the top of Elbow Yard, I saw that a sign had been erected beside the new houses.

It said FOR SALE – *Aelfleda Terrace*

7 New Dwelling Houses, with a delightful prospect.

The houses are newly built, combining comfort with elegance and practicality.

Each house contains a Parlour, Back Sitting Room, and Pantry, with two bedrooms and two excellent attics above.

Each house will be provided with a Jet Ornament Manufactory, situated on the land below, complete with Working Apparatus, consisting of:

Stringing Frames, Lathes, Wheels, Grindstones, Polishing Boards,

Breeching Straps and Stoves, etc.

Now I understood why the men were levelling the land beneath the houses, to provide a solid base for seven jet workshops that would be set up a little lower than the houses.

I stared at that notice and back again at the new terrace and the land below, and as I stared I seemed to drift into a dream, where I saw myself walking into one of those neat new houses, with my baby brother in my arms. Inside that house the furniture would be clean, simple and practical. There would be Kat, sitting by the fire in her rocking chair, knitting away and nodding peacefully, while my brother and sister worked at a table, chalking on slates. Down below the house there'd be a tidy wooden workshop, and along with the whirring sound of the wheel there'd be Frank, his hands all dusty… and my dad…

Shaking my head, I forced myself back to reality. It was senseless to even imagine such things. I made myself turn away from the new terrace and dip my head under rows of washing lines, as I made my way down through the steep broken steps of Elbow Yard, past the shabby tenements below and back into town. That brief vision of a different life was utter foolishness and I knew it, but I smiled to myself a little at the realisation that I'd seen Frank there with us in that place. Surely he, more than any, would be relieved to see the back of me and my family.

Bella and Joey were already in their bed and sleepy when I got back to Turners Yard. Kat looked up at me from her stitching, a question in her eyes.

"I think my mam's slowly getting better," I told her quietly, "but we must keep working hard to make a decent home for her to come out to."

"The bairn…?" she asked.

"Like an elf," I whispered softly.

She patted my arm. "We'll get them out!" she said.

"As I came through the yard I heard Frank's wheel," I said.

"Aye… most days he works into the night," she said.

I grabbed a few mouthfuls of bread and went out into the yard again. Darkness was falling, but there was still the sound of a wheel turning and the flickering light of candle lanterns showing softly through the half open door of the jet workshop. I pushed the door open and it scraped on the floor. The whirring sounds stopped as Frank looked up at me and I saw that he was still working on the brooch.

"Could I make beads for you?" I asked.

He stared for a moment, but then shook his head. "No, no, jet beads cut your hands up something terrible, not really women's work," he said.

"But I'm good wi' my hands," I said. "I used to shell mussels and fix my dad's lines for him, and if they were mucky I'd clean them too. I'm used to sliding flithers off rocks wi' a knife, and that work cuts your hands up too!"

He looked at me thoughtfully for a moment. "Are you any good at stitching?" he asked.

"Aye," I said offended. "O' course, I know how to use a needle and thread."

"Perhaps you could thread beads for me, that's women's work, but fiddly. I've a box o' beads need sorting and threading and then stitching into place. I could pay you a bit for doing that. Alfie was Turner's bead-man, but he's gone to work with his uncle now and left me with all these beads that I can't seem to find the time for..."

"When can I start?" I asked.

"When you like, I suppose!"

"Can I start now?"

He turned around and grinned at me. "You're a keen 'un, I'll say that for you!" So he set the brooch aside and fished about amongst piles of boxes, until he found the beads. "You thread 'em on strong silk cord," he said. "And it's costly stuff, so it mustn't be wasted."

"Do I need a needle?" I asked. "Kat will have one."

He shook his head and smiled. "Kat won't have what you need for this," and he pulled a bit of thin rolled wire out of the box. "Piano wire," he said. "Scraps from the piano tuner."

He bent the end of the wire to make a loop and then threaded the silk cord through the hole he'd made, twisting it tightly and neatly around itself.

"Ah, I see," I said. "Better than a needle that, more bendy like."

"You thread and stitch, thread and stitch. Each bead must be fixed carefully into place. That way they'll stay safe and secure. Now, sorting board!"

He reached a grooved wooden board down from one of the shelves above us and put it on the worktop in front of me. "The beads must be sorted into sizes first. You put them in the grooves and get them all graded, and only then do you start to thread and stitch and make a knot between each one. Do you think you can do it?"

"I'll learn," I said. "Is it to be a plain string of beads, with no fastenings?"

"Aye there's more than enough o' them for that," he said. "You can sit there on that stool, if you like."

He carefully placed one of the lighted lanterns at my side.

"Don't you dare knock it over," he said. "Or this place will go up in flames again."

He leant over the board and dropped a few beads into place and for a moment his hand touched mine. I thought uncomfortably of that other time, and he moved awkwardly back, as though he'd remembered it too.

"Are you alright then?" he asked.

"Yes," I said.

I set about the task of sorting the beads, so that they increased gradually in size. As he'd said, it wasn't difficult but very fiddly. The sorting took longer than I'd guessed, for I forgot that they must increase in size and then decrease again, so that both sides of the necklace would be balanced. Frank set the polishing wheel turning again, while I frowned and sorted, determined to get it right.

He stopped after a while. "Can you manage?" he asked.

"Aye… I'm learning," I said. "Have you finished that brooch?"

"Almost," he said. "It needs polishing, that's what I'm going onto now."

We worked away ignoring each other, but next time he stopped the wheel I said, "You'd best make sure I've sorted 'em right."

He came and looked. "Not bad," he said. He swiftly swopped two or three and then stood back. "That's grand," he said.

"Are they ready for threading now?"

"They are," he agreed.

I took up the wire needle with its silken strand and began to thread and stitch, knotting each bead into place and then adding a stitch to make it absolutely secure. Frank worked away at the treadle as splatters of jeweller's rouge shot up onto his face and hands. After a while he stopped the wheel again and looked over at me, frowning.

"What's wrong?" I asked.

"If you wanted," he said, "you could take those beads and that board and do the work by your grandmother's fire. I should have thought of that… you'd maybe be more comfortable there."

"You'd trust me to take them then?"

He thought for a moment and then nodded. "Aye," he said.

I grinned at him. "I'm fine sitting here," I told him. "When you've finished that brooch, what will you do with it?"

"Well," he began. "I'll take it to one of the shops, along with those beads if you've finished them too, and see what they'll offer for them."

He set the treadle going and I carried on with my threading and stitching. I threaded and stitched until my vision blurred, and by the time he'd stopped the polishing wheel I'd produced a neatly graded string of gleaming black beads, all threaded and stitched into place.

Frank took them from me to examine them, pulling gently to test the strength of my work. "They're good and strong," he admitted. "And as for payment …"

I held up my hand to stop him. "Don't speak o' that yet," I said. "Let me look at that brooch?"

He put the beads down on his workbench and dropped the finished brooch piece into my hand. I caught my breath with wonder, remembering the lump of dark, mottled, sea-washed jet that we'd found on the beach only yesterday. He'd carved it into the shape of a rose and surrounded the flower with a neat pattern of triangles, edged round the rim and a delicate rope twist to finish it off. He'd turned the rough piece into a beautiful, dark, glimmering, jewel that anyone would treasure.

"Not ready to sell on yet though," he said, as he took it back. "I'll have to melt some glue and fix a pin and clasp to the back. I'd like to use silver, but brass will have to do."

"Silver's beautiful," I said. "But brass is strong, and if it were mine I'd fear to lose it. It's beautiful… really beautiful… any woman would want it," I added wistfully.

He looked away from me. "I'd let you have it," he said. "But I cannot. My dad's put the money he got from selling his boat into this workshop, and I have to make it pay."

"Oh no!" I said and got up from the stool, horrified that he should think I was asking for the brooch. "You've given me enough and what would I do with such a lovely thing? No, no, I don't want you to give it to me, but… what I'd like to do is try to sell it for you."

He looked at me in surprise, astonished at the very idea, and I saw his glance skim over my rough clipped hair, my stained, ragged gown, and feet encased in my dad's old boots. I knew what he must be thinking, even though he'd called my hair "still bonny".

"No… selling's best left to those who know it," he said politely. "You stick to threading beads for me, for you do that well. There's enough beads left to make another string tomorrow, but I'm tired now and packing it in for the night."

I suddenly felt exhausted too. "Yes," I said and moved towards the door. "I'll work for you again. Shall I come in the morning?"

"Aye," he agreed. "That'll be fine."

"When will my father get back?" I asked.

"Very late," he said. "And then he'll be off again at first light."

"And you trust him in here with all this jet around?"

He quietly picked up the brooch and slipped it into his pocket. "It's mostly kept inside the house," he said.

CHAPTER TWENTY-SIX

A Crafty Old Woman

I left Frank there in the workshop, knowing that we still had some way to go before my family was back where we needed to be. At Kat's I found her stitching away in the firelight, her mouth full of pins.

"Can you see to do that?" I asked.

She looked up and carefully took the pins from her mouth. "I'm practised at it," she said, "and it's almost finished." She made a few more stitches and snipped the thread with a flourish.

"There now," she said, shaking out the black bombazine folds of the skirt. "Get out of those old things and try this on."

My weariness fled at the thought of it. I pulled off my rags and stepped into the finest gown I'd ever had the chance to wear. Kat had stitched the side and shoulder seams to match my measurements. The fitted bodice closed around me like a glove, with so many hooks to fasten up the back that I needed her help. She'd left the sleeves quite wide, as was the latest fashion, but narrowed the tops of the sleeves so they fitted as closely as the waist. I looked down and lifted the skirt as I'd seen so many elegant women do, but it revealed scarred ankles and battered men's boots.

"Drop the skirt," Kat ordered. "It's still a bit long, but I'll shorten it tomorrow. Now look at the fit of that bodice, I'm pleased wi' that."

She picked up her old hand mirror and moved it around me, while I dipped my head to try to see myself.

"I look like a lady... almost," I whispered. "It fits me perfectly." But then I caught sight of my hair in the mirror and grimaced.

"What you need is a bonnet," Kat said. "A bonnet and some ladies' boots, though they must be strong as well, for you'll have to walk far. I've an idea how to get a pair. I can make a bonnet from the bombazine that I've cut out of the dress."

I stood there feeling elegant and new-made and threw my arms around Kat. "Thank you," I whispered. "How'd we ever manage without you?"

She smiled lovingly and smoothed my hair back from my face. Suddenly, with a painful gulp, I remembered what my mam had told me and saw Kat differently: a young girl in the workhouse, forced to go there to give birth, alone and disgraced. She'd never spoken of it to us, and I sensed that I shouldn't mention it either. Over the years our grandmother had earned a deal of respect from neighbours, and it seemed that it *was* possible to recover from shame and hold one's head high again.

"We're going to get Mam home," I whispered fiercely in her ear. "And we're none of us ever going back into that workhouse again."

"Aye," Kat agreed quietly. "Now take that off and get to bed."

I peeled the gown off and hung it on a bent wire hanger hooked onto a nail on the wall, then gently pushed Bella's warm feet to the side, as I crept into bed beside them. As I lay down, I wondered how I'd sleep with so much whirling round in my head, but I must have been tired enough, for the next thing I knew was a shaft of early morning light creeping in through our window and Joey clambering over me to get to his porridge bowl.

Bella swung her feet carefully past my face and slithered out of our cupboard bed. "I think you went to see Mam yesterday," she said quietly.

"Yes," I said. "And little Robbie too. Like an elf he is, and Mam says she's getting better."

"And do you think she is?" she asked.

"Aye… slowly."

"I want to see her," Bella said, "but I'm afraid to go near that place again."

"And Mam doesn't want you going there either," I told her. "She made that very clear to me. You help her best by taking care of Joey, as you do. Do you think you could go down to the scaur by yourselves today?"

"Why?" She turned a suspicious look on me, and I saw once again that my sister was no longer a child.

"Last night, I was sorting and threading beads for Frank, in the workshop, and he says I can do it again this morning. He'll pay me for doing it ,and this way we can both bring more money in."

"Did you see dad there?" she asked.

"No," I said sharply.

Bella sighed and looked away. "Of course I can take Joey on the scaur," she said sadly. "I did it most of the time when you were away."

"And will you take Sophia with you too?" I pleaded knowing that I was asking a lot.

She chuckled then, and I was relieved. "O' course I will," she said. "I'm getting used to her, and if you're not going at least it means I'll have another lass wi' me."

As soon as Bella and Joey had set off, Kat too began to get ready to go out, knotting her hair back neatly into a bun and wrapping her best shawl around her shoulders.

"Where are *you* going?" I asked.

She picked up her basket, giving me a knowing look, and I glimpsed her crystal ball inside it.

"Up to one of the big new houses."

"But can you manage?" I asked as she hobbled past me.

"Of course I can manage, honey, I just take my time."

I sat down for a moment when she'd gone, still curious as to what she was up to, but there was no time to sit and think, so I dragged a brush through my shameful hair, tied my apron round my waist, and opened the door again. The yard was busy with noise and work and people coming and going; loud hammering sounds issued from Jack Robinson's cottage. He and his son were now working as carpenters, and there was a pile of wooden planks stacked up outside their door. I caught sight of my father's back as he limped down the alleyway, a brush slung over his shoulder. I was glad that I'd once more avoided coming face to face with him.

I found Frank and his father already at work, though they both stopped and looked up when I appeared in the doorway. "I've come to thread more beads," I said.

"You can take that board and work at Kat's place, if you want," Frank said. "As you can see, we're a bit crowded in the yard today."

He reached down the box of beads.

"I'll bring them back all finished," I promised, more to reassure his dad than him.

"See you do, lass," Sam Dunsley said.

So I sat all morning, close to Kat's window, sorting, threading, and stitching, and by noon I'd finished another necklace. Kat returned looking pleased with herself and set her basket on the table.

"Wait till you see what I've got," she said. She pulled out a small bundle wrapped in tissue paper. "More tea leaves for a start," she said. "But now then, look at these!"

And out of her basket she lifted a pair of black, laced leather boots, rather worn but elegantly shaped with little heels.

"Eh, they're grand," I said, "but will they fit?"

"You'd better try. All they need is a bit o' blacking and a good brush up."

Setting the beads carefully aside, I kicked off my clumsy fishermen's boots and slipped one foot, then the other into them. "Bit big," I said.

"Better big than small," Kat said. "I'll find a few bits o' rag, to push into the toes, and then what do you think?"

"I think you're a marvel Kat! How did you do it?"

She pulled her crystal ball from her basket and smiled knowingly. "Telling folk what they want to hear," she said. "I can shorten that skirt for you this afternoon."

"You're a crafty old woman," I said. "But you must have a sup o' broth first, before you start again."

"Aye," she said and chuckled. "And if you can help me, we'll get it finished by tonight."

I ladled broth for us into bowls, and when we'd supped I took the threaded beads back over to the workshop, for I wanted to prove to Sam that I was capable and trustworthy. They examined them carefully and nodded.

"Looks good," Sam said approvingly. "We'll have to find ourselves a new bead-man at this rate."

"Could I…" I began, but a sharp upwards glance from Frank silenced me, and I knew he was warning me to keep quiet.

"Have you more beads for me to thread tonight?" I asked instead.

"Aye," said Frank, glancing meaningfully at me again. "There's enough to make a few more strings, but then we'll need more jet and maybe a bead-man, one who knows his job."

"I'll be back again tonight then," I said, and left them discussing the names of possible workers.

CHAPTER TWENTY-SEVEN

Kat's Memories

Kat and I sat by the window and hemmed all afternoon, each starting at the furthest point and working our way round the edge of the skirt. We chatted comfortably for some of the time, but there were long stretches of silence too when my head swam with hopes and fears for the future. I also thought about the past.

"It must have been hard for you," I risked saying, "when Giuseppe went away."

"Aye," she agreed at once. "It was hard."

"What do you think happened to him?" I asked, relieved that she didn't seem angry that I'd mentioned him.

She sighed and stopped her stitching for a moment. "There's many as would say he'd maybe had enough of me," she said, and she gave a dark chuckle. "I didn't know what to think back then. He said he'd taken an able seaman's berth on a trading vessel, that was setting out to fetch cotton from India. He promised to return as soon as he could with his pay… but he never did come back. I persuaded myself that something had held him up – and for years I hoped that he'd return."

"Do you think he maybe died or was drowned at sea?"

"Aye," she added wistfully. "That was common enough back then, and many a seaman never came back."

We were silent for a moment, but then she looked up at me and smiled.

"I have my memories though," she said. "Those months, when he lodged with me, were the sweetest of times. Sometimes on warm days in the summer he'd persuade one of the lads to let him take a skiff out on the water and he'd row me upriver to Glen Esk. We'd lie there in the sunshine with buttercups and daisies all around us, and we'd eat bread and cheese and drink ale and watch the herons fishing on the riverbank. Sometimes we'd catch the gleam of blue as a kingfisher flashed by… and we always thought it lucky if we saw a kingfisher. Others might think different, but I believed he loved me and that he would have come back to me… if he could have done."

"I'm sure he would," I agreed. "But whatever way round, it was sad for you."

"Not so very sad," she insisted. "You have his dark hair and eyes to remind me of him, and that's why I know you will look perfect in this gown."

I glanced up at the neat pair of polished boots that stood on a stool by the door, and my confidence waned somewhat. Dare I really go knocking on rich folks doors to try to talk them into buying jet jewellery? And would this fine dress convince Frank that I could do it? And his father too?

When the hem was almost finished, Kat snapped her thread and let it drop.

"You do the last little bit, honey," she said. "I'll see what I can do with this bit of spare."

I stitched on, as she gathered up the strip of cut bombazine and set about it with her needle and thread. I glanced up at what she was doing and smiled for she'd gathered the strip and stitched it onto a frilled coil.

"A bonnet," I said. "A black frilled bonnet. I'll look as though I'm in mourning, right enough."

"That's right," she said, as she attached two narrow strips of bombazine to make some ties. "We're all supposed to be

166

in mourning for the poor dead prince! People will respect you for that."

I sighed. "A frilled bonnet is a bit old fashioned, these days," I said. "I heard that the Danish princess Alexandra, the one they say might marry the Prince of Wales, has her hair parted neatly at the front and fastened in a plait at the back. All the elegant ladies who come as visitors are starting to copy her style."

Kat frowned up at me with disapproval, and I felt a touch guilty that I'd complained in any way about the bonnet. "You'll look decent and honest and a little old fashioned," she said. "And they won't be able to turn you away. Trust me, I know about such things."

I chuckled. "Didn't I say you were a crafty old woman… though I am far from honest, I fear."

"You're the most honest girl I know, honey," she said. "And in time everyone will know it."

Joey and Bella came back from the beach to find me gazing at myself in the small hand-mirror, dressed in an elegant black gown. The neat boots were laced onto my feet, the toes stuffed with rags. I'd brushed my hair back and caught it up as tightly as I could with a strip of old ribbon, then covered it with the frilled bonnet that fitted perfectly around my head.

They stared open-mouthed at me and Sophia appeared behind them, watching from the doorway.

"What do you see?" I asked.

"An elegant lady," Bella said, but there was no warmth in her voice. "I thought you said you were threading beads."

I saw how it must seem to her: she'd never gone out thieving or committing crimes, and yet she'd been put into the workhouse. The dress she wore was almost as ragged and stained as my old one.

"I am threading beads, and I'm going to sell jet," I explained hurriedly. "I'm going to *try* to sell it," I corrected myself. "if Frank and his dad will allow me. I'll go tramping from door to door with jet, just like Kat did selling fish. And to do that I need to look respectable. I'm hoping to make more money this way."

"You look beautiful, Lina, "Joey said breathlessly.

Kat put her arm around Bella. "We'll find a new gown for you too, honey," she promised. "As soon as we possibly can."

I saw that Sophia remained on the doorstep, and when I moved towards her she backed away. "No… I don't like you to look like that," she cried. "I think you're going to shout at me."

"I'm not going to shout at you," I assured her, stopping very still and trying to make my voice sound softer. "These clothes are just for selling jet in, and I'll be back in my own old clothes soon enough. How have you done today?"

Bella put a good handful of sea-washed jet down onto the table. "How's that?" she said.

"You've done us proud," I said. "Let's take this over to Frank and see what he'll give us for it."

But Bella shook her head. "You take it," she said. "He likes you, and when he sees you dressed like that…"

I looked at Kat, feeling uncertain.

"Yes, you go," she said. "Show them your new clothes and see if they think you look like a jet seller ought to look?"

I gritted my teeth and went to the workshop, fearing that if I hesitated for just a moment I'd lose my courage. I knocked on the door with a touch of formality before I pushed it open; both Frank and his father stopped their work and stared.

Sam chuckled. "Well now," he said. "Well now… oh my!"

I stood awkwardly, slipping the scraps of jet from hand to hand, feeling the colour rise to my cheeks. "I… I wanted to show you," I began. "I wanted to show you how I *could* look if I were to go out selling jet. I'd make myself tidy and neat like this and wear this dress that Kat has remade for me. Would it do?"

Frank continued to stare, open-mouthed and silent.

"I'd say it would," said Sam and he gave a low soft whistle.

A ripple of excitement ran down my back as Frank continued to gape at me, but as his silence continued I began to fear that he disapproved.

"You don't like it!" I said.

He seemed to recover his voice then. "No… no, I like it," he assured me. "It's just surprised me. You look like a proper lady," he acknowledged.

"Kat thought these clothes would help, if I were to go out selling mourning brooches or necklaces."

Sam glanced thoughtfully at Frank. "Aye… and she might be right," he said. "You look grand, lass and we shall certainly think about it."

There was an awkward silence then, and I remembered that my hands were full of jet finds. I moved forward to lay them out on the workbench so that they could see what had been gathered that day. Frank started counting and sorting but then stopped and glanced up at me again, as though to check that he hadn't been dreaming.

"Ten scraps for beads," he said at last. "Three bigger strips for earrings and that piece there will make a fair-sized simple facetted brooch." He felt in his pocket. "Would three shilling be acceptable?"

"It would," I said happily and took the coins he offered. "But now I must change in order to keep these clothes tidy. I'll be back to start threading beads in a little while, if that's alright."

"Aye, that's alright," he agreed.

Back at Kat's I found Sophia seated at our table sharing bread and cheese, and I gave her a shilling.

"Aren't you taking a cut?" she asked puzzled.

"Not today," I said.

She ran off to find Grasper, pleased with what she'd got.

I handed the rest of the money to Bella and she too stared puzzled at the coins. "Today it's your earnings, not mine," I said.

She shook her head. "Put them into the bag for Mam," she said. "It's all to get Mam back again."

CHAPTER TWENTY-EIGHT

The Most Precious Thing

I changed back into my rags and, having eaten quickly, returned to the workshop, ready for an evening shift. I began to sort the beads, while Frank set about turning the biggest piece of jet that the younger ones had found, making it into a smaller facetted brooch.

"Quicker this, than hand carving," he told me.

I watched him for a moment as he worked, his tall frame hunched over the wheel, and a feeling of warmth crept over me. His fingers flicked the rough jet, over and over again at speed, as he flattened the piece to form the back of a brooch. He'd been so very kind, but it was more than that – somehow I wanted to reach out and stroke his dusty hair, but I knew that might be wrong, so I went to sit down and began sorting beads.

We both worked away, but from time to time I glanced up at him. He set the leading wheel to work across the curved front-piece of the brooch, again and again, creating tiny facets all the time. It was stop, start, stop and start.

A happier memory came to me then, as I saw my father's fingers moving fast and strong, baiting sharp fishing hooks and then neatly coiling a long line, flicking each hook to the side. My dad had been used to working with his hands with speed and precision.

A lump gathered in my throat, as the warmth of the recollection fled and was replaced by the knowledge of where we were now. My hands stilled and the wire needle fell from my grasp, as sadness at the thought of our miserable situation crept over me.

Frank stopped the wheel and looked anxiously across at me. "Are you alright?" he asked.

"Yes… yes," I replied, gathering myself together again. "Yes… of course, I must get on with this." I picked up the needle and forced my thoughts back to the job in hand.

I continued to thread and stitch the beads into place again, but as I worked a tiny seed of an idea began to plant itself in my mind, and once it had settled itself there, I found I couldn't get rid of it.

Glancing up again, I watched to see how Frank managed to work the treadle, controlling it mostly with one foot in order to spare his injured leg. He didn't need the full use of both his legs to turn a leading wheel. Time flew by, and I became so deeply engrossed in my threading and my thoughts that I didn't notice how the darkness had gathered about our lanterns.

"Hey lass," Frank said at last. "I think that's enough for tonight."

"Nearly done," I said, for I'd almost completed another string of beads.

"No… leave it be, you've done enough!"

I put down the string of beads and got up, rubbing my aching back. "Let me see your piece," I begged as I walked over to his wheel.

He placed the finished faceted piece in the middle of his rough red-stained palm. A myriad of gleaming miniature surfaces had emerged from the dark stone.

"Like black diamonds," I whispered.

"That's the red stuff that does that," he said. "French polish."

"Could I try selling something smaller for you?" I asked

awkwardly, knowing he'd refused me once. "Maybe just these beads, or this beautiful facetted brooch?"

"You did look bonny," he acknowledged, "when I saw you dressed like that, but…" and his voice faded as he seemed unable to find the words.

"But maybe I'd sell your jet and disappear wi' the money!" I finished the thought for him.

"*No, no,*" he protested. "I wasn't thinking that!"

I couldn't blame him for being reluctant and got up to go home. As I moved, a faint chink came from the money-pouch in my apron pocket and it made me think again.

"I have the money you gave me still," I said. "I'm saving it up, to help us find better living space, when my mam is well enough to come home to us."

"That'd be a good use for it," he agreed.

I put my hand inside the pouch and felt for the precious sovereign that he'd given me. Picking up the coin, I stepped towards him, holding it out to him. "You told me the rose-carved brooch ought to fetch a sovereign," I said. "Take this back and sell me that brooch, so that I can try to trade it on without any risk to you."

He looked amazed for a moment and then suddenly laughed. "You are full of ideas," he said.

"That way you'd have nowt to lose, and I'd get the chance to show you that I could sell."

"You're such a funny one," he said softly and he lifted his hand as though he'd touch my hair again.

I froze, afraid and yet thrilled to think that he might want to stroke my poor hacked hair.

"You… you surprise me again," he said. He let his hand drop and reached forward instead towards a small wooden box on one of the shelves and lifted the rose carved brooch out from it.

"Put your sovereign away and take the brooch," he said. "If you can sell it, then we'll have our reckoning. If you cannot, just bring it back to me."

"You do trust me then!"

"Aye... I do."

He put the brooch back into the box and handed it to me. I placed it carefully in my pocket along with the sovereign, feeling pleased and excited at the prospect of trying to sell it. I wanted to reach up and kiss his cheek but feared he'd think me forward and mistake my motive, so I did nothing and went back to Kat.

The following morning I woke early, and while Kat was still snoring in her bed, I wrapped my shawl over my shift and crept outside. Having opened the door, I looked out across the yard and saw that all was still and quiet. Glancing nervously to right and left, I made my way towards the jet workshop, hoping that neither Frank nor his dad might be there just yet. Having reached the door, I pushed at it but found it bolted from within, though almost at once there came the sound of footsteps from inside, followed by a low growl.

"I'm coming. You're early!"

I braced myself and stood there clutching my shawl about me, as the door was opened. My dad looked shocked to see me and took a few steps back. Then he sat down awkwardly on a stool and stared at the ground.

"What are you doing, here?" he murmured. "I'm 'shamed to face you, lass! Go away."

I stood there in the open doorway looking sadly at the mess of rough bedding on the floor. "But... but I'm still your daughter," I said at last.

"I don't deserve you," he whispered.

I stepped forward into the workshop then. "Well... you were very wrong to do what you did," I said, "but I was a fool to take notice of you. I make my own judgements now. Whatever anyone tells me to do… I decide."

He nodded slowly. "Yes," he said. "You are right, and I know what I have lost… the most precious thing I had… my family."

I sighed. "We are maybe not quite lost to you," I said.

He looked up then, as there came the sound of a door banging out in the yard, followed by the tramp of boots and voices. "I'm proud o' you, lass," he said and his mouth trembled as though he was in pain. "Proud of you, for despite the trouble I brought, here you are back in the yard, looking after the bairns and helping Kat."

"You're helping us too, with the money you bring," I acknowledged. "And maybe… in time…" I stopped, feeling that I couldn't promise more.

Frank and his father were arriving for work, but then they saw us there together and hovered awkwardly out in the yard.

"My family safe is all I want," Dad said.

"Aye."

I pushed quickly past Frank and his dad and went back to Kat's, where I found Bella and Joey eating porridge while Kat pulled the washtub out.

"Will you take them to Saltwick, again?" I asked, touching Bella's sleeve. "I know I ask a lot of you, but I need to try my hand at selling today. Frank has trusted me with this." I brought the box out of my pocket and set it on the table.

Bella lifted the lid and gasped, then touched the brooch lightly with her finger, looking wistful. "That's a really bonny brooch," she said. "And he's trusted you with it."

Doubt flooded my mind. "Will folk think I've stolen it… and slam doors in my face or set their dogs on me?"

Kat looked up at me and frowned.

Bella shrugged. "You go and try," she said. "You look fine in that gown and bonnet, Lina, I just wish it was me that could go out selling. You go and try your luck, and I'll take the others picking on the scaur."

I picked up the brooch that weighed so lightly in my hand. "Perhaps one day…" I said.

"Aye… perhaps one day," Bella said, with the faintest of smiles. "Maybe we'll go out selling jet together."

After they'd set out for the scaur, I began to wash and dress myself.

"Give me that old gown," Kat said. "And I'll see what I can do with it. I'll wash it while you're out and maybe I can patch it up a bit."

Having put on the black bombazine, I laced on the boots, tucked my straggly hair into the bonnet, picked up the brooch and set off.

I marched along Skinner Street and headed towards the Royal Crescent, where the big stone-built houses curve elegantly around to face the sea, trying to summon all the determination that I'd felt last night.

The promenade had recently been added to, with elegant newly laid-out gardens set high above the sea. Wealthy visitors strolled along to meet each other there while they breathed in the fresh sea air. The proportions of the houses were majestic, small palaces for the richest folk who wished to stay beside the sea.

CHAPTER TWENTY-NINE

On the West Cliff

My heart thundered and my stomach clenched as I marched up to the first house on the Royal Crescent. I knew that servants and trades people were supposed to go round to the back, but I wasn't dressed as a servant girl and needed to impress. I gathered my courage together and boldly approached the front door.

When I reached up and jangled the bell, the door opened almost immediately and a young maid looked out, surprised to find me there.

"Would your mistress like to buy a fine jet brooch?" I began.

"Traders round the back!" she said and shut the door on me.

I knew then that I had much to learn but turned away, refusing to be discouraged, and made my way round the side and through an archway that led to the back of the buildings. When I tried the first back door the same maid answered and this time she was ready with her speech.

"The mistress wants no jewellery," she said and shut the door again.

I went doggedly on to the back door of the next house and the next. Each time I received a similar reply, but I felt sure that the mistress of the house was never consulted or even knew that I was there. I spoke to kitchen maids, scullery maids, footmen and butlers, but the answers that I got were all the same. Working my way further along the row, I grew a little gloomier with each refusal. By then I knew that I'd been a fool to think it could be easy.

I recognised one of the maids, though at first she didn't know *me*. "Yes?" she said and bobbed a curtsey, but then she looked more closely. "I know you," she said. "Whatever are *you* doing here?"

"I'm selling jet," I said.

"Most likely stolen goods!" she cried, as she pointed an accusing finger at me. "It was jet that got you put in prison, I believe. Get away from here, before I call the constable!"

I turned and ran, back down the road in my dainty padded boots, sweating and breathless with fear. Glancing back again and again, I reached the corner, and only then did I dare to slow down to catch my breath. There were a few smartly dressed people walking in the gardens at the front of the crescent to take the air. At least there seemed to be nobody following me.

Utter misery welled up in me, and it was only pride that stopped me heading straight back to Turners Yard.

"Fine clothes fool nobody," I muttered, but just at that moment a well-dressed young man in a long coat, waistcoat, and cravat walked by and politely tipped his hat to me.

I stopped and hauled myself together. "That fellow tipped his hat to me," I whispered. "I'm a fool, I haven't even started yet!"

Ladies young and old were wandering through the gardens and along the promenade to take the air, some escorted by husbands and brothers, some followed by a maid; these were potential customers. I put a determined smile back on my face and approached the nearest old lady, who was walking slowly with a stick.

"Please, Ma'am," I bobbed a curtsey. "Would you like to buy a fine jet brooch, hand carved by a skilled local craftsman?"

She stopped and examined the brooch as I opened the box. "Let me see dear," she said. "Well now, that is beautiful. If I bought it from you, would you be able to give me a receipt for it?"

I shook my head, realising instantly that this was something that I should have thought about. "The carver would vouch for me," I said.

"Another day, perhaps," she said, smiling kindly. "I wouldn't like to buy without a receipt." And she walked on.

Remembering the young man who'd tipped his hat to me, I approached two more smartly dressed fellows out walking with a hunting dog.

"Buy a fine jet brooch for your sweetheart?" I asked.

They stopped and glanced at each other in an amused way.

"Well now, pretty miss," one said. "Let's see how it looks on you?"

"We can't buy without testing out the goods," the other said. "Pin it onto your neckline, so that we can see how well it looks."

I wasn't quite prepared for this, but I began to oblige, pinning it in place, just where the silk neckline scooped rather low. They glanced at each other grinning, and I saw that they simply made a goose of me. One got out a monocle and bent down to examine the brooch, pulling the edging of my dress out to glance further down at my breasts, while his companion burst with laughter.

I stepped away from them blushing furiously, feeling more of a fool than ever, and hurried on fast, realising that rich looking young men might not be the most suitable potential customers to approach.

I strode further up the promenade, feeling worn out and hungry as the sun moved towards the western horizon. It seemed I'd walked all day and achieved nothing. Fearful now that I must return empty handed to Turners Yard, I flopped down onto one of the wood and ironwork benches that had been set up along the walkway. Visitors would sit there to enjoy the views and I sat there too, feeling utterly miserable. Avoiding the thought of going home, I stared out to sea, where the warm colours of the sunset danced upon the rushing waves. I longed to be out there, where everything seemed to be fresh, golden and glistening.

I wasn't alone for long, for the sound of quick footsteps announced another presence and I glanced up to discover that a brisk and organised young woman had appeared at my side. She carried bags and books under her arms and looked not at me, but at the sea.

"Do you mind if I sit here with you for a while?" she said. "This is just the perfect spot, as I want to try to capture that sunset before it goes. Such glorious shades, such wonderful shapes."

"No, Miss," I said moving up a little. "Please do sit down."

I saw that the books she carried were the sort that artists use, with plain pages ready to be painted and drawn upon. Without further ado she sat down and un-stoppered a small flask of water, then opened a neat tin of colours. With a wide soft brush she spread water right across the thick paper and then, with a smaller brush, began to paint her colours into it.

Distracted from my troubles, I watched as the sunset in the distance, came to vivid life there on her page. I thought I knew who she must be, a woman still young, but old enough to be married, the daughter of the chief cashier at Green Gates Bank, who was also a respected artist. Her brother was a painter too, and the family were well known in Whitby Town.

"Miss Weatherill," I murmured. "You are Miss Mary Weatherill."

She glanced at me in a friendly way but never stopped her work. "And do I know you?" she said. "I feel as though I do. What is your name?"

"I'm Lina, Miss… Paulina, but I don't think you know me." I shook my head, fearful that she might recognise me for all the wrong reasons. "But everyone knows you. You and your famous father and your brother too, all artists, though I believe your father is in charge of Green Gates Bank."

She stopped her work and smiled, resting her brush on the small water pot for a moment. "My father longs to retire from the bank," she said. "He wants to devote himself wholeheartedly to his painting. And yes, I paint a little too."

I had never seen anything so magical as the way she'd brought that plain blank page to life, as I sat there and watched her work.

"Oh Miss," I said. "You do more than paint a little, I think."

"Well, thank you," she said. "And I can't help but notice that fine jet brooch you are wearing. That is carving of the highest standard, and with your colouring it suits you perfectly."

I reached up to touch the brooch, forgetting that I'd still got it pinned onto my dress. "Oh, it's not really mine, it's for sale," I added hurriedly. "I've been trying all day to sell it for the jet carver who shaped it, but I haven't managed it."

"Such a lovely thing?" she said.

I was so weary and despairing and she seemed so kind that somehow the truth slipped out. "I persuaded him to let me try to sell it," I confided, "but I've gone the wrong way about it. I see now that I need to give receipts and I hadn't thought of that. People are suspicious of me, offering just one piece, but… I needed to earn some money," I ended lamely.

She started painting again. "And how much did you want for the brooch?" she asked.

"We hoped for a sovereign," I said. "The carver thought it might sell for two sovereigns in a shop, though of course *he* wouldn't get that. I was trying to sell it straight to a customer for him, so he'd get a bit more, and perhaps I would get a bit too."

Mary Weatherill stopped, washed her brush and put it down, then laid her beautiful work out on the bench between us, leaving it open to allow the fresh paint to dry. She nodded thoughtfully as though she understood what I'd said and she sighed. "Yes, craftsmen rarely get paid what they should for all the skill and patience that goes into their work. Would you sell the brooch to me? I could give you twenty-five shillings for it. I cannot manage two sovereigns for, as you said, I'd be taking something of a risk, by buying without a receipt."

I stared at her for a moment and then hurriedly started to unfasten the brooch my fingers shaking. "Oh thank you, Miss, thank you," I said as I held it out to her.

CHAPTER THIRTY

The Sunset Lady

Mary Weatherill took the brooch from me and examined it closely.

"Intricate workmanship," she said. "Your man's a fine draughtsman. This is delicate, well-balanced, and worked with a light touch."

I was quietly pleased at the way she said "your man" and didn't contradict her. "His name's Frank Dunsley," I said.

"Ah, I think I know his father, a fisherman?"

"Yes, he *was*," I agreed. "But he's sold his boat and bought into the jet trade."

"It's sad to see the fishing going down," she said. "But with such a talented carver in the family, it was surely the wisest thing to do. Is your Frank the lad that suffered a fall a few years back?"

"Yes, he's the one."

"Well, he's done well," she said. "We lost a fisherman, but we gained a real craftsman." Then she felt around in her bag and brought out a purse and carefully counted twenty-five shillings out into my open palm.

"Thank you so much," I whispered, as my fingers closed around the coins.

She looked carefully at me again and I feared suspicion might have come to her, but what she said took me completely by surprise.

"I have another proposition to put to you," she said. "You say you need to earn money?"

"Yes, Miss, I do," I murmured faintly.

She closed her paintbox and gathered her brushes together as she spoke. "Well, I take a drawing and painting class for young ladies. They come for a few hours each week to the Bank House parlour, six or seven of them. Landscape is my best work, and I try to share what skills I've gained in that way, but these young ladies would also like to try their hand at drawing and painting portraits."

I stared, uncertain where this could be leading.

"You have a striking face, Lina, and unusual colouring," she said. "Would you come to model for us? And of course you would be paid for it."

My heart leapt at the thought of earning more money, but I felt unsure that I could do what might be required of me. "I don't know how to be an artist's model, Miss," I said.

She smiled and started to explain. "You would have to sit very still and do nothing at all, while the ladies draw or paint you."

"I think I could do that," I agreed.

"Well, keeping still can be more difficult than it sounds," she said. " It can really make your shoulders and neck ache."

"Oh, I wouldn't mind that," I assured her.

Then fear crept into my mind at the thought that her pupils' wealthy parents must surely object to their daughters painting a jailbird. As soon as they saw my shorn hair the game would be up, and I didn't suppose they'd want to paint me in a bonnet.

"I would like to, but..." I began.

She smiled thoughtfully at my hesitation. "I think I know what troubles you," she said. "As we've been sitting here talking, I've come to realise who you are. You're the girl who was sent to Northallerton."

I was touched by her kind way of putting it, but nodded and glanced shamefully down at the ground.

"I've also heard that it was not your fault," she said. "And this might be another way to help you to earn an honest living."

"But my hair…" I said, still deeply ashamed "It's shorn. It's what they do to you there, in Northallerton."

"May I see?" she asked.

I untied the strings of my bonnet and felt the sea-wind ruffle the loose clipped ends as I lifted it off. "I don't think your ladies would want to paint this," I said.

Mary smiled. "But your hair is a wonderful rich dark shade. Don't worry about it," she added thoughtfully. "I think I know just how to make it appear quite perfect. Here's my card, with the address of Bank House on it. Will you come?"

She handed me a small card that was covered in lettering. My reading was poor, but I knew well enough where Green Gates Bank was.

"Well, if you are sure," I agreed.

Mary Weatherill picked up her book and closed it carefully over the now dry painting. "Could you come tomorrow morning at ten o' clock?" she asked.

I nodded, my spirits lifting again.

And with that she turned and strode away, leaving me staring after her, an extraordinary young woman, skilled and clever, but oh so kind.

As I watched her go, I remembered how the constable's oldest daughter had told me on that terrible night, that life could be changed, and she'd been another Mary too. Suddenly my spirits seemed to leap with hope. Looking down at the coins in my hand, I counted them again.

My feet carried me fast along Skinner Street, down Flowergate, and back into Turner's Yard. I'd sold the brooch; not quite in the way I expected to, but nevertheless, I'd sold the brooch. The yard was hung with our washing, and Kat was busy gathering it in. I rushed straight past her and into the jet workshop to find Frank there with his dad. I counted the coins down onto the worktable.

"What's this?" Sam asked.

"I sold it," I said breathlessly. "I know you might think Frank shouldn't have trusted me, but he did and I sold it."

They both stared at the coins I laid out in front of them.

"How much is that?" Frank asked faintly.

"Twenty-five shillings," I said.

"Well done, lass," Sam said, sounding surprised. "That's more than we'd 'ave got for it in a shop. You can take three shillings back. That's yours by right, I'd say."

"Thank you," I said as I helped myself to the three shillings.

"Well, do you want to try again?" Frank asked.

"Yes," I said breathlessly, words tumbling out. "But I've learned a lot. We must provide them with receipts or nobody will want to buy, and I think we need a card with your name on it to show who the carver is. Customers need to know where the jet has come from, and I should have a few bits to sell, not just one brooch."

"Aye, but I fear I don't know how to write out cards," Frank said uncertainly. "You could take these three necklaces that you've finished along with you next time."

I thought too for a moment. "Our Bella can write," I said.

"Well, we seem to be in business then!" Frank said grinning at me.

"Aye, we're in business," I replied.

Back in Kat's home-place I hurriedly took off my dress and hung it up again. Kat watched me impatiently as I carefully removed the bonnet and shook out my raggedy locks, standing there in my shift.

"Well?" she asked. "Are you going to tell me?"

I nodded and held out my hand to show her the money.

She grinned hugely and put her knitting down. "I knew you could do it," she said. "That's a very good start."

"It was the artist lady, Mary Weatherill, who bought the brooch from me," I admitted. "And I don't know whether I can manage it so well again – there aren't many like her round here – but I've learnt so much. We need receipts to give in exchange and a decent way of displaying the jet."

I frowned then, my surging confidence ebbing a little.

"Do you mean the chief cashier's daughter?" Kat mused, impressed.

"Yes, and there's more, for she wants me to go to her father's house tomorrow at ten o'clock. I'm to model for her drawing class and I'll be paid for doing it. Look, I have the address on this card."

"Well, I never," Kat cried.

I looked around for my old gown and discovered that Kat had washed and patched it cleverly with scraps of old cotton, so that the stains didn't show anymore.

"Oh, thank you, thank you," I said, suddenly feeling worn and tired.

"Well, put it on," she said. "Let's see how that looks now."

"You've done wonders with it," I murmured. "I almost look respectable again in that."

"Go and meet those bairns and buy them a treat from Icy Tony. You all deserve it, when you've worked so hard."

"Aye, maybe I can do this," I said, forcing myself back to being hopeful again. I did as she said, hurrying across the bridge to meet them, and though they hadn't managed to find much jet that day, we sat together on the harbour side and ate ice-creams from the penny licks that Icy Tony provided. I slipped Sophia an extra sixpence when we set off home, just to keep old Grasper sweet.

Later that night I showed Bella the card that Mary Weatherill had given me. "Can you read it? I asked, uncertain again that it had really happened.

"The Bank House, Grape Lane," she said. "But why?"

"You know the lady artist, Mary Weatherill? She wants me to go to her house tomorrow, to be an artist's model and get paid for it."

There was silence for a moment.

"So, you're not coming down to the scaur again," she said sounding rather flat.

"No," I replied. "I can earn better money by threading beads and selling jet, and maybe modelling too."

"How much will you get for modelling?" she asked.

"I don't know yet," I had to admit.

"Will you take off all your clothes?" she asked.

"No," I said firmly.

She was quiet and thoughtful for a moment, and I wasn't sure whether she was angry or not.

"There's something that I need from you," I said at last. "People want receipts when I'm selling jet and maybe cards with information on them. Would you be able to write some cards for me?"

"I suppose I could write something," she said with a sigh. "I used to love to write at school, but I'd need pen and ink and some proper paper or card to do it now."

"I'll find you some," I said, satisfied that at least she seemed willing to help in that way.

CHAPTER THIRTY-ONE

Bank House

Late that night, when the others had all settled to sleep, I took a lantern and crept across the yard again. I pushed at the door, and it opened with a scrape to reveal my father rolled in a blanket on the floor and snoring softly. In sleep his face appeared younger, and I watched him for a moment, wondering once again how we'd got ourselves into this mess. I used to find him sleeping like that when he'd been out all night fishing, and I'd set a mug of ale at his bedside, all ready for him to drink when he woke up. After a moment or two he seemed to sense my presence, for he grew restless and then his eyelids fluttered open.

"Dad?" I called softly.

He stirred and I went inside and pulled up a stool to sit beside him.

"Lina, is it Lina?"

"Aye, it's me."

"Oh child…" he began. He pulled himself up into a sitting position and his face crumpled again.

"No," I said firmly. "I've not come to scold, it's something else, an idea that I can't get out of my mind. I've been thinking that you can maybe do better than this."

"I swear," he began. "Since Northallerton I've not touched a drop…"

"No," I said firmly and shook my head with conviction. "I'm not accusing you of drinking. Please listen and think a while on what I have to say. I remember well how neat and quick you used to be with your hands, when you mended nets and skeined those mussels and shelled flithers so fast. I used to watch you baiting lines with all those sharp hooks, and I swear that nobody could coil a baited line like you and set it on a skep."

He frowned and looked puzzled. "Are you saying I should go a flither-picking?" he asked.

I smiled. "No," I said, "though you'd maybe make a good 'un. No. I heard Frank and his dad say that they need a new bead-man to work with them. Why shouldn't that bead-man be you?"

He looked amazed. "Nay lass, they train up young lads these days for jet work, and they have to serve an apprenticeship. Five years I believe it takes to make a proper bead-man."

But I was ready for that. "Aye, but don't apprentices get ten shilling a week?" I said. "Are you getting that sweeping floors? Look at Sam Dunsley, he's not carving yet, but he's doing the other jobs and learning fast. And he's your age."

He shook his head. "Sam's put his own good money into the trade," he said. "That's different. What they need is a young lad, wi' a good strong body," he added.

I was ready for that too. "But you've seen Frank working at the wheel. His injury doesn't hinder him. That's one of the things that made me think of it. You don't need your legs to carve fine beads, just good strong hands and fast fingers, like you used for baiting lines."

He looked thoughtful at that and glanced down at his hands, flexing his fingers. I got up, feeling that I'd maybe said enough for the time being.

"Think on it, Dad!" I said and left.

The following morning was bright, and I rose early to make porridge for the others, for I'd struggled to sleep. As soon as Bella and Joey had gone off scavenging, I started to get myself washed and dressed in the bombazine. Kat patted a little lavender brew onto my neck and hands, and I set off in good time to find Bank House. It was a tall double-fronted building, set close to both the bridge and harbour on busy Grape Lane. One half of the building was the Bank, while the other half seemed to be a dwelling house, with an elegant front door, framed with a porch and patterned bricks and the words Bank House engraved into the glass. There was no way round to the back so, despite my fear of giving offence, I was forced to knock on the smart front door. I found myself greeted by a familiar looking maid, a girl I remembered from my short time at school.

"Eeh, I thought it were going to be you, Lina," she said, sounding quite friendly. "Come on in. I'm to show you straight up to Miss Weatherill's room and I'm to ask if you'd like a drink of coffee?"

"Oh no, no thank you," I said, too nervous to appreciate the kindness of the offer.

The staircase was wide and the bannister made of smooth polished wood. I couldn't help but stare about me at the elegant patterned wallpaper and the gold-framed pictures on the walls. The maid led me up two flights of stairs to find Mary Weatherill, who was waiting for us in her bedroom with a stool pulled up to a polished wood dressing table.

"Come and sit here," she said, smiling and patting the stool.

I did as she asked, feeling rather hot and overdressed in the bombazine, while the maid hovered curiously in the doorway.

"Thank you, Becca," she said. "Now let us see about this hair."

I gasped, for I saw then that laid across the dressing table was a thick black plait of hair, almost the same colour as my own.

"Is that real hair?" I asked, touching it carefully.

She smiled. "Real horse's hair," she said. "But look: the colour match is excellent, nobody will know the difference. I once dressed as an Egyptian princess to go to a fancy-dress party and used this hairpiece. Take off your bonnet and let me see what I can do with it. Trust me, I'm good at these things."

And I did completely trust her. She parted my hair neatly at the front and combed it flat, fixing it down at the sides with pins, then brushed the rest back smoothly to form a little tuft that she managed to gather up with thick black cotton thread. The short tufty tail stuck out at the back of my head.

"Now then," she said. "This is the best bit."

She loosened the plait and combed it through carefully, then plaited it again and fixed it firmly into place, so that it completely covered my awkward tuft. Mary picked up a hand mirror and moved it around the back of my head so that I could see the effect.

"How's that?"

I gasped with pleasure to see myself suddenly transformed. I looked something like the many fashionable ladies who copied the styles that Princess Alexandra wore.

"Oh… thank you, Miss," I whispered. "That's made me feel decent again."

"The colour's perfect, as I thought it would be. Now, time to go down into the main parlour, where I hold my drawing classes."

I followed Mary nervously down through the huge house, stepping on soft woollen carpets with my too big boots and into a wide parlour, to find a room like no other I'd ever seen. The wide space was filled with little polished tables and stools and comfortable chairs upholstered in deep rich-coloured brocades. Heavy drapes hung at the windows, printed with a pattern of leaves and small creatures, all coloured in deep shades of green and blue. Peacock feathers stood in a vase, and shells, rocks, and fossils were displayed on the windowsills and even on the splendid gold-painted mantelpiece. I stared entranced at a round grey stone that had been cut open to reveal a waterfall of glittering silver and purple gems.

"Is that amethyst?" I asked, for I thought I'd seen something like it in one of the most expensive shops that sold jet, though never a lump as large as that.

"Yes, amethyst," Mary said.

I caught my breath, knowing that it must have cost a great deal, though many of the other things on display could easily be found on our own scaur –ammonites both large and small, differently shaped shells, and some lumps of sea-washed jet. It was a room filled with warmth and plenty, and I tried not to stare too rudely at it all.

"Now, when the young ladies arrive, I will ask you to find something to look at," Mary said. "And I'll want you to sit very still for a while. There will be two short poses first, and then I'll ask you to hold a longer pose. Can you do it, do you think?"

"You ask me to sit still and do nothing and be paid for it?" I said, smiling.

"It will be harder than you think," she warned.

When the young ladies started to arrive, I went very quiet and felt shy as I saw them glance inquiringly in my direction. Their voices sounded soft and refined, and I felt rough in comparison. I didn't dare to speak, but Mary introduced me kindly as her friend and quickly got them settled down in the seats, ready to draw me. I perched on a stool in the middle of the room and looked at the splendid mantelpiece, holding my position for just a few minutes while they whispered to each other and made quick sketches.

"That was excellent," Mary said. "Now a second pose."

She asked me to stand and look out of the window so that the light fell on one side of my face, while they drew again rapidly. That time they fell silent and I could only hear the slide of their pencils against the paper and the milkman crying his wares outside.

"Now take a short break, Paulina," Mary told me. "Move a little, before we settle for the longer pose."

I wriggled my shoulders and gazed out onto Grape Lane where I watched the milk cart moving into the distance and the chimney sweep pulling his little trolley along. The ladies chatted politely behind, while dogs ran up and down the street outside and a familiar gang of fisherwomen passed carrying their buckets, with baskets on their heads. Maids came out into the street to beat carpets, and the everyday life of Whitby continued out there, while inside the Weatherill's parlour my life seemed to be changing fast.

"Are you ready, Paulina?" Mary asked at last.

"Oh yes, Miss," I assured her.

CHAPTER THIRTY-TWO

The Artist's Model

Polite murmurs rose around us as Mary Weatherill settled me in the most comfortable chair, placing cushions behind me; I felt like a queen, with all the young ladies watching me so intently.

"Now you must turn your head in whichever direction feels easiest for you, so long as you think you can stay like that for quite a while."

I turned my gaze towards the curtains, feeling certain that I could stare at those astonishing intricate patterns forever.

"Yes, that is perfect, a gentle, pensive expression," Mary said. "And the light from the window falls onto your face in an interesting way. Now can you stay like that until I ask you to move again?"

"Yes, Miss," I whispered.

"Then let us begin!"

There came the rustling sounds of papers, followed by a few sighs and then quietness, other than distant street cries and the faint soft scrape of pencils. Mary had been right of course; it was harder than I expected it to be, for very soon I began to want to scratch my nose. I dared not do it, though I wriggled it a bit and that seemed to help. After that my shoulders began to ache, though why they should do so when they weren't doing anything at all, I couldn't understand. I tried to listen again to the soft scuffing sounds the pencils made, and eventually, almost magically I seemed to drift into a bit of a dream that took me into the enchanted forest depicted in the curtain patterns, where strange beasts peeped from luxuriant plants and gorgeously feathered birds flitted from tree to tree. I was happy in that wonderful place, but then was sadly compelled to leave it, as my neck began to feel as though it had turned to stone. I dreaded being forced to complain but then discovered that with a few tiny movements the sensation eased a little, and I became aware of Mary's soft comments to her pupils.

"That's it Selina, you need to round the shoulders a little here and there."

"Well shaped hands, Frances. I like that look."

"Lighter around the cheek, perhaps…"

"Margaret, I should save those heavy dark lines for the brow."

"Oh yes, Phyllis, excellent hair, such a contrast. Our model is striking to look at, don't you think?"

Those words made me drift again into a pleasant dreamland where I was considered beautiful and maybe even respectable, until I began to sense a restless gathering together in the room and realised that Mary was speaking to me. "That's it! Thank you Paulina. You may stand up now and move around. That's enough for today. Everyone has worked so hard."

I rose warily to my feet and rolled my shoulders back and forth. They ached a little, but it was nothing compared to the pain of the treadmill.

"May we have our model again next week, Miss Weatherill?" a voice piped up, and I glanced gratefully at the young woman who'd suggested such a thing.

Mary looked around to gather assent. There were more nods and smiles and at last she turned to me.

"Yes, Sylvia, if our model is willing?"

"Oh yes, Miss," I agreed. "I'd be glad to do it again."

The young ladies nodded politely to me as they left the parlour. I made a quick bob to each of them, fearful to speak in case I said the wrong thing.

"Not easy is it?" Mary said, as the last one left. "I sometimes sit for my father and brother, so I know how hard it is. You will earn your money doing this."

"It's made my shoulders twinge a bit," I admitted, "but I'd be glad to do it."

She took out her purse and counted two shillings into my hand. "I hope that will be satisfactory," she said.

"Oh yes, Miss," I said. "Thank you very much, but…" and I hesitated, afraid that what I wanted to ask might seem too rude. "But I wondered, Miss… if I might ask a bit o' help of you?"

She nodded and waited patiently. I swallowed hard and hoped that what I'd say would make sense. "You see, Miss… I've learned that I must give receipts, if I'm to sell jet, but I'm not sure what a receipt ought to say. I couldn't write it for myself, though my sister Bella is clever that way and she says she can make the letters for me."

Mary looked thoughtful for a moment and then nodded. "Follow me," she said.

We went back up two flights of stairs and into a tiny square room at the very top of the house. Pictures of all sizes were stacked under the eaves, filling every nook and cranny. There was just enough floor space left for a small table that was strewn with brushes, pencils, paintboxes, tubes, tins, and bottles. The whole made me think of Frank's workshop rather than a lady's room. The wide roof window flooded the place with light, and I wrinkled my nose at the strong smell of oil and turpentine.

"My studio," Miss Weatherill said. She laughed at the surprise on my face. "Yes, it's time I cleaned a bit and tidied it up," she said.

"Oh, I never meant…" I started.

"No offence taken," she assured me firmly. "One day I'll sort it out, but not today! Now then, receipts; I have just what you need, somewhere here."

She pulled open a drawer in the table and lifted out a quill pen, a small grey clay bottle and a handful of neatly cut squares of paper. She put these things down on the corner of the table, pulled up a stool, and sat down.

"Now then, Dunsley's is the name, is that right?"

"Yes, Dunsley's Jet Ornament Manufacturer's."

"I'll write what I put on my receipts when a customer buys a painting from me, but instead of my name, I'll put Dunsley's Jet Ornament Manufacturer's at the top."

"Oh, thank you," I said. "May I take it with me? Then Bella will be able to copy it."

"Yes, that's the idea. I'll write the first one as a receipt for the brooch I bought from you, then your sister will know what to put, I think."

She dipped the pen into the ink and her writing came out looking beautiful, with regular loops and curls.

DUNSLEY'S JET ORNAMENTS

Turners Yard – Whitby

Received in exchange for one hand-carved jet brooch in the form of a rose

The sum of Twenty-five Shillings

Signed………..

"And you must sign your name there," she said, blowing on the paper to dry the ink.

I was glad she didn't ask me to do that there and then, for I'd have struggled to get it right, but I knew that with a bit of practice I could manage it.

"Now then," she asked, "have you pen and ink at home?"

"No, Miss," I said, shaking my head.

"Well, you'll need a slate and piece of chalk for practicing, but your young man in the jetworks should have such a thing, and I'll give you these cards all cut to size."

When we went back down the stairs, I had a good stack of paper squares, a quill pen and a small bottle of blue/black ink, all stashed in a little basket that Mary had given me. An older man stood in the hall at the bottom of the staircase, wearing a neat suit and waistcoat. He watched us as we ascended, looking amused, and I felt overwhelmed as I realised that it must be Mary's famous father.

"Oh, Sir," I said, hurriedly curtseying when I reached the bottom step.

"Oh, Miss," he said, making a gentlemanly bow.

"This is Paulina, she's been modelling for my ladies," Mary said.

"Yes," he murmured, thoughtfully. "Yes, yes, I quite see why, jet and ivory; you have a striking complexion, my dear."

Mary opened the front door for me, and as I stepped outside I remembered the hairpiece, still pinned to the back of my head, and my hand flew up to touch it.

"No, no," Mary said smiling. "It's only horse-hair. You keep it. It looks perfect on you and you can use it when you come to model for us again."

I didn't argue for I wanted it so much. "Oh thank you, Miss, thank you, so much," I murmured. "But I should pay you for these cards and inks."

"It can come out of your next lot of wages," she said cheerfully as she closed the door on me.

CHAPTER THIRTY-THREE

Quite the Opposite

I strode home fast, to find Kat waiting and anxious to know how I'd got on.

"Well?" she asked. Then she blinked, uncertain that she saw me right. "Your hair!"

My bonnet swung in my hand and I grinned and turned around slowly to show her the hairpiece. "It's made o' horsehair," I said. "And Miss Weatherill told me to keep it. I don't think any o' the young ladies guessed that it were not my own."

"Oh, that *was* kind of her," Kat said. "I've seen those hairpieces for sale and they cost quite a lot. Some o' them are made of real hair, and to have to sell your hair…"

Her voice faded and she saw from my face that her words had sent me straight back in my thoughts to the day I'd been shorn.

I looked at her sharply. "Do you think they sell the prisoners' hair?" I asked. "I'd think mine would have been worth a shilling or two. Maybe I could have sold my hair for Mam's medicine, rather than go out stealing jet. Why didn't I think o' that!"

Kat put up her hand to halt my thoughts. "Stop!" she said firmly. "Don't think that way. You're back with us now and doing well; it was respectable modelling, wasn't it? Not shameful to be sitting for the artists?"

I smiled at that concern. "They offered me a cup of coffee, though I refused it," I said. "Sitting still like that made my shoulders ache, but it doesn't trouble me. I'm to do the same again next week. And look," I said holding out my hand, "two shilling for a morning's sitting, along with paper, ink and a pen for the jet receipts."

"That's grand," she said, but then she frowned.

"What is it?" I asked, sensing there was something else troubling her.

"Sit down a moment. There's more to say," she said.

I sat down and my stomach tightened. "What's fretting you?" I asked, troubled by her serious look.

"While you were at Bank House, I went to see Maria," she admitted.

"What… you walked up to the ropery?"

"I managed it," she said. "And I'm glad I did. She's feeling stronger, much better now, and the workhouse doctor has been round to examine her. He's said that she's to leave at the end of the month, or she must go into the main block to be put to work and they'll send the bairn to the baby farm."

My stomach gave a sharp twist. "So, the time has come," I said.

"If need be, we will somehow cram them both in here with us," Kat said.

But I looked around at the tiny space we'd got and couldn't see how we'd manage. "I should use Frank's money now," I said. "I could put down a deposit for our old place next door, and then with what we're earning, we might just manage to cover the rent."

"Aye," Kat said, with a sigh. "Well we've three weeks to get it sorted."

"I'll get going now," I said.

Feeling that there wasn't a moment to waste, I hurried out of my good clothes and over the yard to the workshop. "Have you a slate and a piece of chalk?" I asked breathlessly as soon as I arrived.

Frank pointed to a shelf above the workbench but said nothing.

"I need to learn to sign my name on a receipt," I said by way of explanation.

"Aye, as you wish," he said.

I dashed back across the yard with my chalk and slate, not wanting to disturb him and his father further while they were working together, then sat all afternoon, trying to write my name. I wrote and wiped, wrote and wiped, and at last threw down the chalk, exhausted.

"Some folk just make their mark, they make a cross," Kat said.

"I'm not making a mark," I said. "I'm going to do it right."

"Then ask for help," she said and she nodded meaningfully towards the doorway, as we heard the shrill sound of voices in the yard.

Bella arrived back with Joey, cheerful that they'd got a good haul of small jet pieces to give to Frank.

"Look 'ee," Joey cried and held out both grubby hands to show us.

"No thanks to Sophia," Bella said resentfully. "She wouldn't come today, just poked her head out o' their battered door and said she wasn't coming."

I sighed at that, but I was more concerned with what I was trying to do and couldn't spare the time to go rushing round to New Way Ghaut to discover why Sophia was being awkward.

Bella looked over my shoulder to see what I was doing. "What's this?" she asked.

I sighed heavily again. "I'm trying to write my name and I need you to write out some receipts for me. Miss Weatherill has done one for us to copy from."

Bella silently took the pen from my hand, lent over the table and began to copy the careful wording. The result was almost as beautiful as the artist's own hand.

Kat gave me a gentle nudge. "See what I mean?"

"Aye… you'd best sit here," I said.

I got up, so that she could sit in my place and then stood and watched while she wrote out more cards. A sudden catch rose in my throat. "I didn't know… I didn't know you could write like that, Bella," I said softly.

She paused briefly. "Miss Ruswarp taught me how," she said wistfully. "I can write you all the receipts you're going to need, and I can write your name out too, so you can copy it. Here's the sign for pounds, this for shillings, and this for pence. All you need to do is write the numbers down and sign it."

She picked up another square of card and began again.

"Ah Bella," I murmured. "You really *ought* to be in school. You're a clever one you are, like the constable's daughter, Mary Linskill. You could maybe get to be a teacher or a governess to wealthy folks' bairns."

Bella shrugged and paused again. "But I wouldn't want to go away from here and leave you all," she said sadly.

I tried to put my arms around her then. "Bella… I'm so sorry," I whispered. "If it weren't for me and what I did, you'd still be in school."

She put down the pen, got up and hugged me properly.

"It weren't just what *you* did," she said and we rocked together, smiling and wet-eyed. "It was Dad as well… and you did it for Mam."

When we pulled away, we saw that Kat and Joey were both smiling to see us being proper friends again.

"Good lasses," Kat said quietly.

We smiled, sniffed a bit and dabbed our eyes.

Bella sat down, took up the pen and began to write again. "I heard that Mary Linskill had a story published in a magazine," she said brightly. "They paid her for it too."

"Aye well," Kat said. "Maybe one day…"

But before any of us could say more, there came a knock at the door. Joey ran to open it and I heard Frank's voice. "I've got more beads," he said, sounding rather sharp. "More beads to thread if your Lina is willing. That's if she's got time to spare, from these other things."

I went to him at once. "'Course I will." I said. "But I thought I'd done 'em all."

"I found more," he said. "Enough to make another set, so if…" and his voice drifted away as he shifted his weight from foot to foot, looking slightly uncomfortable.

"I'll come straight over," I told him.

"Aye, if you can."

I picked up my shawl then, ready to follow him out.

"'Careful now, lass," Kat murmured as I passed her.

I followed Frank across the yard and into the dusty workshop that flickered with candlelight as darkness gathered inside. When I sat down as usual in front of the beading board, I saw that the beads he'd found were dusty and looked as though they'd spent ages lying in dark corners or on the floor.

"These'll have to be cleaned first," I told him. "I'll need a damp cloth."

He scrabbled about beneath his workbench and clumsily threw a grubby damp cloth at me. I stood up then, hands on hips, sensing that something seemed very wrong. "What's troubling you?" I asked. "Do you want me to finish this necklace or not?"

His glance seemed resentful when he looked at me and he shrugged. "Never mind those beads," he said. "Who is this artist you've been modelling for?"

My stomach immediately tightened with anger that he should think it any of his business, but then I glimpsed the impression that he might have received. My mouth twitched a little, for suddenly I wanted to smile and a feeling of warmth spread through me.

"Why should it bother you?" I asked softly.

"It don't bother me," he said and went to sit at the wheel.

CHAPTER THIRTY-FOUR

Dusty Beads

I waited quietly for a moment or two, wondering if that was all that Frank was going to say, but he soon turned round again and spoke softly. "It does bother me," he admitted.

"Why?" I repeated.

"I didn't go all the way to Northallerton, for you to do that."

"For me to do what?"

He tried again. "I didn't follow you to Grasper's filthy den and haul you out o' there for nowt," he admitted. "I saved that money, so you wouldn't be having to do things like taking off your clothes for men."

My stomach leapt and twisted, but the feeling was not wholly unpleasant. I went swiftly to his side and put my hand on his arm.

"You're jealous," I said.

He turned away, as though he couldn't bear to look at me.

"Well… are you?" I demanded.

"Yes," he growled out the word, through gritted teeth. "Yes… It was all I thought about," he admitted in a husky voice. "*You* were all I thought about, all the time you were away, ever since that moment when I grabbed at you in the dark and I'd have given anything not to have…"

"It was not your fault," I said and pressed his arm. "I know it was not your fault." I waited for him to turn around, my heart beating fast, and at last he did.

"You were so… so warm and soft and scared," he said. "And I was too late… too late to stop it all from happening. When I saw you in that courtroom, I wanted to grab tight hold of you and run away, for the two of us to go… anywhere!"

I couldn't speak, just shook my head.

"What a fool you must think me," he said.

"No…" I grabbed at his shoulders and suddenly we were hugging each other tightly.

"Eey… now then," he whispered in my ear and then softly he kissed my cheek.

"I thought of that moment too," I whispered. "When I was locked up in Northallerton Jail, I thought of your hands on me and sometimes couldn't sleep for thinking of it. Such a fool I was, to do what I did."

He gave a small sigh and hugged me tighter still.

I pulled back then. "There were moments when I hated you," I admitted. "But mostly, I was angry with myself and then, when you gave me that money, and you made me come back to the yard… You befriended me when I needed it most."

"I hoped that in time you'd forgive me," he said, and the husky tone crept back into his voice. "And maybe come to like me… a bit!"

"I have forgiven you," I said. "And I *do* like you… that's what I'm telling you. I like you very much!"

"But…" he protested, and his voice grew resentful. "But now you have this artist that you're modelling for, and I can't bear the thought of it!"

I laughed softly then. "The artist I'm modelling for is Miss Mary Weatherill," I said quickly. "I think you know of her, and the job is a most respectable one. I'm sitting fully dressed for the young ladies in her drawing and painting class. Miss Weatherill pointed out to them the folds of the material in my dress and how she liked the way they draped and fell."

"Oh," he said, covering his eyes with his hand. "Now, I'm the fool."

I reached out for him again and somehow found myself sitting on his knee. I pressed my cheek against his cheek and felt the pleasant scratchiness where his stubble rubbed against my skin. A sense of contentment washed over me, warmer and more real than any of those disturbing dreams I'd had. I turned my face towards him and we kissed each other properly. The sensation was sweeter than anything I'd felt before.

"I was jealous," he whispered. "And I'm ashamed o' it."

We kissed again and then Kat's whispered warning came back to me – "be careful, lass". Old Kat knew about such things. I wanted to stay there on his knee all night, but it wouldn't do.

"There's beads to be sorted and sewn," I whispered.

He stared at me and smiled. "You're a crafty woman," he said.

I nodded slowly. "Like my gran… I mean to be," I said. "And when…"

But before I'd finished my words, we both turned sharply at the sound of footsteps in the yard. I leapt to my feet at the scraping sound of the workshop door opening. My dad was standing there, his cap in his hand.

We all three stood in silence for a moment, and I wondered what he'd heard, but Dad simply nodded at us.

"I've had a good think," he said. "'Bout what you was saying to me, lass."

He came further in, and I backed away and went to sit on my stool by the bead-board and waited.

Dad turned to Frank. "I've been talking to Sam," he said. "He'd be agreeable for me to try working as your apprentice bead-man, if you were willing too. I could still manage to do your cleaning in the evenings – but you are the gaffer here."

Frank looked faintly puzzled, but I could see that he was relieved that my father didn't seem to have noticed the sudden warmth that had been there between us.

"I'll get off now and do my sweeping," Dad said. "'Give you time to think it through and," he turned to me then, "'I just wanted to let you know, honey, that I gave a bit o' thought to what you said."

"I'm right glad of that," I said quietly.

After he'd gone, we seemed to turn suddenly shy again.

"I'd best get on wi' these beads," I said.

"Aye," Frank agreed. He sat down at his wheel and set to work on another facetted brooch.

"But I need a clean cloth and a bit of water," I said. "These beads are filthy."

Frank looked at me and laughed. "I scraped them together from every dust-filled corner, just to have an excuse to get you over here," he admitted. "I went crawling beneath all the work benches to find them."

I shook my head and chuckled. "Then I'm not the only crafty one," I said. "But I'll sort and thread them, for I need every penny I can earn. Mam must leave the infirmary ward in the ropery in three weeks' time, and if we cannot find living space for her here, our new bairn might get farmed out.

He frowned at that and looked concerned. "I owe you for three strings o' beads and that will be the fourth," he said. "I can help out wi' this."

"You've done enough already," I said.

"But I want to do more."

"Thank you," I said. "But Dad and I… we are the ones that must put things right."

He picked up the cloth he'd thrown, dipped it in a jug of water and squeezed it out thoroughly, then began cleaning the beads for me. "We'll work on it together," he insisted.

I set to work when he went back to his wheel, feeling happier than at any time since that terrible night. Sometimes I glanced at him and found him watching me, but we worked steadily until it was dark and I heard Kat calling my name in the yard. I got up hurriedly and went to the door.

"Just finishing off!" I called back to her.

Frank stopped the leading wheel and began to pack up.

"That's one string o' beads finished and another half done," I said.

"And here's a facetted brooch for you to sell," he said. "But this old wheel is likely to break at any time. Maybe we need to look for a better place with a workshop too, in a tenement so there'd space for us all to live together."

"That'd be grand," I said with a sigh, for it was a lovely thought. "I'll be back in the morning, as early as I can."

When I moved to the door, he snatched my hand and pulled me back, so I kissed him goodnight. When I got back Kat was worriedly waiting up for me.

"It's alright," I said. "We've been working hard… well, most o' the time."

"Most of the time?" she asked with a lifted eyebrow.

"You were right," I confessed, for I couldn't keep the contented smile from my face. "He was a little jealous and he's sweet on me, but it's nowt that you need fear. He wants to help us find a place and the money for it too, so that maybe we could all live and work together."

"Aye," Kat said. "And would you want that too?"

"I would," I said.

"He's a good 'un then. I've always thought that. Now get to bed, hon. You need your sleep."

CHAPTER THIRTY-FIVE

An advantageous offer

The next days passed in a frantic blur. I rose early every morning and went straight over to the workshop to spend an hour or two sorting and threading beads. The scraps of jet that Joey and Bella scavenged from the beach were ideal for bead-making, and Frank began to show my dad how to turn and cut the pieces. It got very hot and crowded in the ramshackle work-shed, and the fishy stink of glue and dust that hovered in the air gave us all bad coughs. Dad's hands were soon covered in sores and cuts, but he bandaged them up and carried on, his fingers flying fast as I knew they could. Each night he swept the whole place clean. It was strange to see Frank and my dad hobbling about the workshop together, each steadying a treadle with the foot that suited him best.

At eleven o'clock each morning Kat would call me and I'd wash myself and dress in my excellent bombazine. With my hairpiece fixed in place I'd walk out onto the West Cliff, carrying a tray that Frank had made for me suspended from a ribbon round my neck. The best sellers were the small facetted brooches and strings of beads, for we didn't try to charge too much for them and could turn them out at a faster rate. I strode up and down the promenade so regularly that people began to expect me to be there. Some people greeted me like a friend, while others grumbled that it wasn't right to have a jailbird there, but I kept my hurt feelings hidden and smiled and nodded and handed out receipts; a model of respectful courtesy.

212

One morning as I walked down Skinner Street, past the funeral directors that we called the Coffin Shop, a lad came running out and grabbed my arm.

"Hey, there!" he called. "Is it Lina?"

I shook him away, annoyed. "Paulina," I corrected him. "Leave me be, Lanky Jack, running out and grabbing folk like that!"

"No, stop," he said. "My mester wants a word wi' thee."

"I've done nothing wrong," I protested.

"He says to step inside a moment," he hurried on breathlessly. "I'm to say that it would be to your advantage."

I looked up at the neat sign above the doorway, puzzled as to what they could want with me. It said "Garbutt and Sons, Funeral Directors". Mr Garbutt was the most respected funeral director in Whitby Town, despite the blunt name we'd given his establishment. I looked properly then at Lanky Jack and saw that he now had on a neat black suit, unlike the rough cord trousers and fisherman's gansey that I used to see him wearing. His hair was combed back from his face and tied at the back of his head with a thin black velvet ribbon.

I reached out to touch his jacket. "Is that bombazine?" I asked.

"Aye," he agreed, surprised that I should recognise the material. "A bit hot and itchy though. Will you come and speak to Mester Garbutt?" he asked more politely.

"I can't stay long," I warned, "for I've beads to sell."

He stepped back and allowed me to go into the Coffin Shop ahead of him.

Mrs Garbutt appeared through some draped dark velvet curtains. "Glad you caught her," she said. "Take that tray off, lass!"

"Oh, no. I must keep it with me," I insisted.

She shrugged and turned to knock on a door at the back of the shop, then opened it. "She's here!" she announced.

More mystified than ever I followed her inside. Mr Garbutt got up from behind his desk. "Ah, yes," he said, and he seemed to be looking me up and down. "Just right," he murmured. "She looks just right. Put your tray down girl."

I clutched it even tighter then, baffled as to why they seemed to want to take my jet wares away from me.

Mrs Garbutt touched my arm. "It's alright, Lina," she said. "We only want you to put it down for a moment, so we can see how you look without it. We need a new female mute, and we've seen you walking past our shop and thought you'd maybe be right for the job."

"You're offering me a job?" I asked.

"It wouldn't be full time," Mrs Garbutt went on. "You'd have to come to us with just a few days notice, but we'd pay you by the hour. It isn't a job that many like, but..."

"I'll take it," I said.

I set my tray of goods down carefully then on the desk and stood up as straight and as tall as I could, my hands by my side.

"The gown she's wearing would do well," Mr Garbutt said, "but we'd need to provide a veil and measure her for a white dress too."

I glanced at his wife uncertainly. "Yes," she said hurriedly. "And we need to work fast, for there will be a young girl's funeral next Wednesday and they want an angel mute. Could you do it?"

"Yes," I said. "But would I have to pay for the white dress?"

I thought I saw Mrs Garbutt's mouth twitch a little then and realised that I must sound very grasping, though I had my reasons.

"No," she said firmly. "The white dress will be our property, kept here to be laundered and starched each time. If we're agreed now, you must come with me to be measured, for there's no time to lose."

I picked up my tray and followed her deeper into the building, down a corridor and into a small room strewn with materials, mainly dark. There were silks and satins in black and purple and just one roll of fine white cotton.

"Take off your bombazine," she ordered.

I hurried to obey, but felt a little shamed to be standing in my shabby shift. She made me turn this way and that and at last seemed satisfied with her measurements, but when she reached out and touched my hairpiece

I froze. "My hair…" I began, fearing that it might lose me this unexpected opportunity to earn more.

"No problem," she said, holding up her hand to stop me. "I know what they do at Northallerton, honey, but for a young girl's funeral the hair must be loose. Take the hairpiece off and let me see."

I hated doing it but removed the hairpiece and released my poor hacked locks. Mrs Garbutt stared for a moment, then picked up a comb and a pair of scissors, from the table. I flinched away from her.

"Do you want this work?" she asked, looking resolute.

"Aye," I said.

"Trust me then, hon," she said quietly.

And for some strange reason I did trust her and stood like a lamb, clutching my precious hairpiece in my hands.

She snipped away, combed and snipped. I shut my eyes. She snipped some more and then stopped to push my hair into the shape she wanted. I gritted my teeth and opened my eyes, as I felt her positioning something light onto the top of my head.

"Now, then," she said at last. "Look here!"

I opened my eyes and gasped, for she held up a mirror for me to look into and I saw a soft dark halo of hair, cut into a wide fluffy shape, like one of the angels that I'd seen in a famous painting. My springy curls were now topped with a white velvet band that held a silver star in place, above my brow.

"That will do well for Wednesday," she said. "But now I'll help you smooth it back for the hairpiece."

"Thank you," I murmured.

"The funeral procession begins at twelve o'clock," she went on, very business-like. "Come here at ten and I'll dress you and take you round to the house."

"What should I do at the house?" I asked.

"Well," she said hesitantly. "Usually they want the mute to stand outside the front door for the hour before the funeral procession begins, but for this little lass, they want you to stand by her coffin. Can you do it?"

"Aye," I said quietly. "I saw the little 'uns Mam lost in their tiny coffins."

"I expect you did," she said. "And I'll be there to tell you what to do."

"Yes," I said. "I'll do it."

"Well, tha'd best be away for now then."

She removed the star-band and combed my hair back in place, then helped me with the hairpiece. Picking up my tray again, I set off to try to sell my wares, my thoughts in more of a jumble than ever.

"Mind, Lina," Mrs Garbutt said quietly, as I stepped down from their front step. "If anything goes missing from our shop, you know who'll be the first to be suspected?"

"Aye… I know," and I hurried on my way.

CHAPTER THIRTY-SIX

For the Right Person

Kat looked a little uncertain when I told her about the new job I'd been offered.

"Can you manage it, lass?" she asked. "It's true, we need the payment it will bring, but it's not a pleasant way to earn money."

"No," I said. "But I'm stronger now, and Mrs Garbutt was not unkind."

"No, she wouldn't be."

I frowned at the strange tone of her reply. "Why do you say that?" I asked curiously.

"You mustn't speak of this to anyone," she said, pointing a gnarled finger in my face. "But Nelly Garbutt once saw the inside of Northallerton Jail. A small theft of food, when she were nowt but a child."

"Nobody shall hear of it from me," I said, though I was truly surprised. "She looks as though she's thriving now and most respectable."

"You'd do well to take note o' that," Kat said.

I sat up late beside our hearth that night, threading beads after Frank had packed in his work. Bella sat up with me, scratching away with her pen, carefully writing out receipts for us.

"Did Sophia go with you today?" I asked.

"No," Bella said. "She still refuses to come with us, and I can't make her. Maybe she don't want to come wi' us because you're not there. She says old Grasper's ill and that she must stay to look after her, but..."

I frowned. "But where's she getting money from then?" I murmured.

Bella shrugged. "Maybe thieving again."

"She'll end up back in Northallerton Jail," I said regretfully.

"Aye, she probably will!" Bella agreed.

I resolved to try to find the time to go over to New Way Ghaut and see Sophia for myself, but what with jet-selling, bead-threading, modelling for the artists, and now working as a funeral mute, I couldn't see when it could be done.

We fell into bed exhausted, no time even left for sweet thoughts of the few stolen kisses I'd managed with Frank.

When Tuesday came, I almost forgot to sit for Miss Weatherill's art group. I arrived in a hurry feeling dishevelled, having already done two hours at the beading board. Miss Weatherill welcomed me kindly as ever. I sat for a few brief sketches and then settled down for a longer pose. The young ladies placed themselves around me, and I perched on a stool with my face towards the stunning mantelpiece. The mirror was magnificent and reflected much of the room, surrounded by a frame carved into the shape of fruits and flowers. When they started to draw I kept very still and examined with interest the exotic ornaments on the mantelpiece. My shoulders began to ache, but I remembered to let them droop back and drifted into a dream again. I took little notice of the gentle chatter that surrounded me, until suddenly my ears picked up on something that jolted me wide awake.

"So, if anyone knows a trustworthy jet worker who needs a place to rent, my aunt says to let her know," a soft voice said. "My aunt would make the rent very reasonable, if she could find the right person. She needs somebody she could trust to look after the place and act responsibly, for it's got a fully equipped workshop, situated directly below the house."

"Which terrace, did you say?" Miss Weatherill asked.

"It's the end house on the fine new row they've built above Elbow Yard. They call it Aelfleda Terrace. Such a strange name, I don't know why they've called it that."

My mouth dropped open a little, and I couldn't help but move my head in order to see reflected in the mirror which lady it was that had spoken.

A soft laugh followed. "Our model seems a little distracted today," Mary commented.

"Oh, sorry, Miss," I murmured, hardly daring to move my lips.

"I'm only teasing," she said. "You're doing well, Paulina." A quiet pause followed, but then Mary spoke again. "Aelfleda should not be a strange name to us, for Aelfleda was the second Abbess of Whitby and a king's daughter too. She lived in Saxon times, and our famous Abbess Hild was her foster mother."

"Well, Miss, I never knew that," came an awed reply.

After that I was impatient for the drawing session to be over. It was Sylvia who'd spoken of the house to rent, and I wanted to leap from my stool and demand to hear more. Since I'd walked up to the ropery that day, those new houses on Aelfleda Terrace had been my dream, but far beyond our reach. But "somebody trustworthy" the lady had said. My spirits flagged for nobody could consider either me or my father trustworthy, but then... maybe Frank and his father? I should be unselfish and think of them.

When the drawing class drew to a close and I was free to move again, I took a deep breath and approached the young woman called Sylvia.

"Please, Miss," I asked with a respectful bob. "Are you the lady that spoke of Aelfleda Terrace?"

"Yes," she said. She glanced up at me with interest as she packed her papers and brushes away into her bag. "Do you know somebody suitable?"

"I do," I said. "Frank Dunsley is a most respectable young man and his father Sam Dunsley owns a jet ornament manufactory, but they are in need of new premises."

"Well, Anne Trowsdale is my aunt," she said. "And a widow woman now. Aunt Anne has bought one of the houses on the new terrace as an investment for her future. The workshops there are wonderfully well set up, with new wheels and lathes and all that's needed for the work."

"Why don't you give Paulina your aunt's address, Sylvia?" Mary Weatherill intervened.

The girl rummaged in her bag and brought out a black-edged card that she handed to me, the kind that widow ladies use when they go visiting.

"Oh, thank you, Miss," I said, and bobbed dutifully again.

I raced back to Turner's Yard, clutching the card, with two more shillings in my pocket. Frank stopped the wheel, when I appeared in the workshop babbling excitedly about new houses and a seemingly rich widow. My father too looked up from the chopping out table.

"Do you mean those new houses, up above Elbow Yard?" Frank asked.

I nodded eagerly.

"But we could never afford owt like that!" he said.

"No, but the lady said it could be let quite cheaply, to someone she could really trust."

"I doubt that would be us," said Frank.

"Aye, lass," Dad said with a sigh. "Surely, not for us."

Their glum words floored me and my spirits plunged, for they had brought me swiftly down to earth and I could see that our uncertain reputation would be bound to surface.

I sighed. "Maybe you are right, Frank. Not for me… or Dad, but I was given this card by the niece of the lady who owns the place." The card slipped through my fingers and floated down to settle in the dust at my feet. "Mrs Trowsdale wants a tenant that she can trust, and they say that for such a worker the rent would be good… so, perhaps it could be you?"

Frank got up and took hold of my hands. "Don't fret," he said kindly. "It was a lovely thought, but if we find a place, we'll go together."

I went back to Kat, feeling foolish to have hoped even briefly for something so impossible. I took of my dress, hung it up carefully, and started to thread beads again.

CHAPTER THIRTY-SEVEN

The Funeral Mute

On the morning of the funeral I scrubbed myself clean and set off in good time to the Coffin Shop. The white dress was ready and waiting there for me, draped over a velvet-backed chair. It fitted perfectly and made me feel fresh and decent. There were soft white slippers for my feet, and Mrs Garbutt combed and fluffed up my hair, patting it into place with a handful of jellylike liquid. I watched her with renewed interest, knowing what Kat had told me. She was brisk, practical and efficient, and I didn't mind at all that she ordered me about.

"I can smell fish," I said.

"That's fish gum to hold your hair in place. You'll have to wash it when you get back home, but this'll smell better for now," she said and picked up a glass bottle to spray me with a violet-scented cologne.

I smiled and breathed in the sweetness of the smell. Having fitted the star onto my brow, Nelly Garbutt stood back and nodded. "You'll do," she said. "But wipe that smile from your face and remember: say nothing, not a word. You're mute."

I nodded vigorously and made as solemn a face as I could.

"Come now!"

She took me by the arm and we marched along Skinner Street and up the smaller back road, where carriage houses stood behind the elegant new mansions. We arrived at the kitchen door of one of the houses Kat sometimes visited.

A familiar-looking maid opened to Mrs Garbutt's knock, giving me a second, disapproving glance that told me I was recognised.

"Well, she *does* look the part," the girl admitted. "I'll say that for 'er."

"Take us to the parlour," Nelly Garbutt said, ignoring the remark.

The maid in the grand house hurried ahead of us and let us into a huge front room furnished with black velvet drapes; even the tables and chairs had dark brocades thrown over them. Everything was elegant and expensive, though I thought it dull compared to the Weatherill's rooms in Bank House.

"Come," Mrs Garbutt said, and she guided me to where the poor child's body had been laid to rest in a coffin. She was dressed in white silk, a posy of white lilies in her hands and a wreath of smaller white flowers on her head.

I'd braced myself to feel nothing at the sight of an open coffin but found it harder than I'd expected, for she must have been about the same age as our Joey. I remembered too that I'd seen her walking in the West Cliff gardens with her nursemaid when I'd been out selling jet, and recalled that she'd sometimes given me a small wave.

Mrs Garbutt arranged stools and chairs around the coffin, with practicality, while I hovered there uncertainly.

"Right. I'll set you up now," she said at last, "'then bring the family in. You must stand here and hold your hands so."

She stood at the head of the coffin and clasped her hands against her chest. I took her place and tried to copy the stance. "Is this right?" I asked.

"Yes, but you must look up at the ceiling, as though you are looking up to heaven where the little one has gone."

"Am I supposed to be an angel, then?" I asked.

I saw her mouth twitch in slight amusement. "Aye, just for today," she said. "Now you *must* keep still. No words, no smile. I'll fetch the family in."

I thought that after sitting for the drawing class, it would be easy to keep still and look up at an ornate ceiling, but it wasn't. My eyes explored every plaster garland and bowl of fruit so cleverly carved into shape, but my shoulders and neck began to ache as usual, and I felt a desperate need to shuffle my feet. I could hear soft whispers all around me but dared not look, though I was aware that the grieving mother had come to sit beside the coffin. The father stood on the other side. There came faint sounds of movement, the rustling of silks and quiet condolences, as mourners came and went from the room. Mrs Garbutt had said it would be for an hour, but it seemed longer and just when I thought that I must move, the sound of soft sobbing arose beside me. Those sounds touched me deeply. I forgot the aches and pains that came with keeping still, and a tear crept down my cheek unbidden, then another. I did not dare to move, but a huge and overwhelming wave of sadness seemed to wash over me, so that I sorrowed for the poor little girl whose life had been cut short, but sorrowed too for my family, my mam in her lonely workhouse bed, the tiny weak child beside her, my sister who should be in school, and even for my dad in his rough blanket on the workshop floor. I wept in silence and tears ran down my cheeks, which I could not wipe.

"It's time to go now, Sir," I heard Mr Garbutt say quietly to the father.

There came a sense of change and purposeful movement around me, though I still feared to take my eyes from the ceiling. A hand grasped my arm, which seemed at last to give permission for me to move my head, and I found myself face to face with the grieving mother.

"I thank you for your tears," she said softly, then turned to follow her husband out of the room. The coffin had already gone.

"Come," Mrs Garbutt said. "Time to go. The funeral procession is forming up outside and you must walk at the front of it. Here carry these flowers and walk behind the carriage, slowly mind."

"I'm sorry…" I began. "I couldn't seem to stop myself from crying."

"Don't be sorry for tears," she said. "You must never be sorry for tears."

The rest of my work as a funeral mute passed quickly. It was a relief to be out in the open air and moving at the head of the procession, even though the pace was slow. Once the mourners had vanished inside the church, Mrs Garbutt hurried me back to the funeral parlour, where I changed into my shabby clothes, still feeling a little shaken by the unexpected emotion that had overwhelmed me.

I arrived back at Kat's with red eyes, a basket of bread rolls, a pot of meat paste, and two more shillings in my money pouch.

"What was it like?" Kat asked.

I shook my head. "It made me ache," I said. "And it made me sad."

"Aye, it would," she agreed. "That lad has been looking in here for you."

"Who, Frank?" I asked.

"Of course, him," she said, with a small knowing smile.

I wrapped my apron around me and went straight over to the workshop. Frank's dad was there, as well as my dad – and they seemed to be waiting for me.

CHAPTER THIRTY-EIGHT

Anne Trowsdale

"Well," I asked. "Have you got more beads for me to sort and thread?"

"No," said Frank.

I saw then that he'd picked up the visiting card that I'd dropped on the floor, and though it was now rather dusty he waved it at me and pointed to his dad.

"Is this the same Annie Trowsdale whose husband used to own three fishing boats?" Sam Dunsley asked.

I looked at him, surprised. "'Not sure," I said. "I know only that she's a widow lady and has bought the new house as an investment."

"Dad thinks he knows her," Frank said, and there was a touch of excitement in his voice.

"Now then," Sam started, and cleared his throat. "I heard that John Trowsdale had collapsed and died a few months back. I heard too that his boats had been sold on. If this is his wife – and I think it must be – I worked on their boats as a lad and lodged in their attic."

I looked from one to another, unsure what this might mean.

"We're thinking that maybe Sam should apply to rent the house," Dad said. "I've told them, don't fret about us, we'll find summat in time."

"Aye, of course," I agreed, unsure whether to be pleased or not.

"But it sounds as though there might be room on that terrace for us all," Frank said. "If the lady could just be persuaded to take us on. Dad and I have our cottage and workshop to sell, so we could put down a deposit for the rent."

"Yes, you must do it," I said. "The young lady said to write a letter to Mrs Trowsdale."

Sam took the card but shook his head sadly. "I could no more write a letter than read one," he said.

"Our Bella can do it though," I assured him.

Sam looked up and smiled. "Bless 'er," he said.

That night Dad, Bella, and I went over the yard to the Dunsley's cottage carrying ink, paper, and pen. After much thought and discussion, Bella produced a carefully worded, neatly written letter.

To Mrs Anne Trowsdale,
Widow of the Ship Owner Mr John Trowsdale

Dear Mrs Trowsdale,

Mr Samuel Dunsley, once a Whitby fisherman, now the proprietor of a small jetworks off Flowergate, would like to inform you of his interest as a possible tenant of Number 7 Aelfleda Terrace. He wishes to thank you greatly for your many kindnesses in the past and also for the many benefits bestowed upon him by your revered husband, now departed.

Yours sincerely,

Your obedient servant,

Samuel Dunsley

We watched as Bella shaped each letter with care.

"This lass should be in school," Sam said. "I'd think they'd be wanting to make her a pupil teacher before too long."

Bella gave him a shy smile but then looked disconcerted. "We need an envelope to make it proper," she said.

We sat there looking uncertain for a moment, until Frank picked up the spare sheet of paper that we'd brought with us and folded it carefully into the shape of an envelope. "Just a dab of fish glue will fix it," he said. "I've plenty here."

Bella folded the written sheet and slipped it into the homemade envelope, then copied the address from the visiting card.

"I'll take it to her straight away," I said, impatient to see it done. "It's one of the houses at the end of New Buildings, and the sooner the better I'd think."

Frank snatched up his jacket. "I'll come with you," he said.

We walked up Flowergate arm in arm and on to where the grand new houses began. "You're a sharp one, you are," Frank said, grinning at me all the time.

"But we haven't managed to persuade the lady yet," I warned.

"No," he agreed. "But something good suddenly seems possible, now."

We found the house at the far end of the road, a little more modest than the biggest ones at the bottom of the hill, but still like mansions to us. We hesitated at the front gate, wondering if we should go round to the back, but then the front door opened and a maid in a neat black dress came out leading a little dog. Yet again it was a girl I knew. She stopped when she saw us, surprised to find us standing there.

"Yes?" she said.

"We've come to deliver a letter to Mrs Trowsdale," Frank said.

"She's very busy," came the reply.

Frank took the letter from me and handed it to her. "Please would you give her this letter?" he asked politely.

"Have you written it?" she asked.

I wanted to tell her sharply that it was no business of hers, but instead I smiled politely. "My sister has written it," I said.

"She writes well," the girl admitted grudgingly.

"Will you see that Mrs Trowsdale gets it?" Frank asked.

"Yes," she said.

We turned and wandered back down the road. "Do you think she'll give it to her?" I asked.

"We'll have to wait and see," he said.

Once again as I marched past the Coffin Shop, Lanky Jack ran out to call me in.

"Do you want me as a mute?" I asked, as Nelly Garbutt bustled out of her sowing room.

"Aye," she said. "It's a poor lady died in childbirth this time, and the bairn too. We'll need you to come in your bombazine, and I thought I'd let you know, they were asking me about buying some jet. I said I'd send you round to them."

"Oh thank you," I said breathlessly. "I'll go at once."

I hurried straight round to the house and sold half my stock in one go, providing facetted brooches for the aunts to wear and three necklaces of threaded beads for the surviving daughters. It seemed that Kat was right: death provided good business for some of us.

We waited with agitation to get a reply from Mrs Trowsdale, and we'd almost given up hope when, a week later, the maid we'd given the letter to appeared in our yard along with the dog and a written reply for us. We had to wait until Bella had returned from the beach to be sure that we'd understood what it said.

To Mr Sam Dunsley,

Thank you for your application, wishing to be considered as a possible tenant for Number 7 Aelfleda Terrace. Mrs Anne Trowsdale invites Mr Sam Dunsley and his son to meet her at the house in question on Thursday 24th at 11 o'clock. The lady has pleasant memories of a hard-working and polite young man.

Yours sincerely,

Annie Trowsdale

"Don't get your hopes up, honey," Dad warned. "For though the lady might offer the house and workshop to the Dunsleys, it's unlikely that she'll want us there too."

I braced myself to be pleased for Frank, but Sam intervened. "No. We need you with us," he said. "I've no wish to start looking for new workers when we've got a long way training up both you and your dad. It's a case of we all go, or none of us go. I want this lass to dress up smart as I know she can, and come along with us to meet Annie Trowsdale."

"Are you sure?" I asked.

"I'm sure," he said.

CHAPTER THIRTY-NINE

Sophia

When Thursday morning came, Bella and Joey set off as usual to hunt for jet. Frank and his father brought their only good suits to Kat, who cleaned them free of stains and brushed them thoroughly. She applied lavender water to the cloth so that they would smell fresh, while I combed and clipped Frank's hair. Then I dressed as usual in my black bombazine, with my hairpiece fixed in place.

When eleven o' clock approached, we set off to walk down Flowergate. A few familiar faces turned sharply as we passed, surprised to see Frank and his dad in suits when it wasn't Sunday. We had to hurry to get across the bridge, just in time before it closed to allow a tall-masted schooner to pass into the Upper Harbour. My stomach churned as we set off up Grape Lane, towards the long flight of steps that would lead up to Aelfleda Terrace.

When we reached the far end of the lane, there came the sound of running feet behind us and a familiar voice shouting out. "Stop. Lina, stop!"

I turned around, astonished to find Bella racing after me, her hair flying wildly and her face all pink.

"What is it?"

"Stop!" she gasped.

Our Joey followed behind her, his little face quite pale and anxious looking.

"I saw you turn the corner," Bella panted. "You must come with us. Now!"

"But we're on our way to see Mrs Trowsdale," I reminded her, annoyed that she didn't seem to understand the importance of what we were doing. I exchanged a sorry glance with Frank and his father, for they too were upset by this interruption of our business.

Bella grabbed my arm and continued to pull at me, gasping breathlessly.

"What is it?" I repeated.

"It's Sophia," she managed to say at last. "I told you she wouldn't come with us, not for ages, and now we know why. Her grandmother is dead and they've carried her body away on a cart. Sophia's been turned out of her home and she's gone, vanished, I don't know where!"

"Oh no!" I said, trying to stay calm and understand what this must mean. "I'll come and look for her later, but not now!"

"I'm sorry to hear of this trouble," Sam Dunsley intervened. "But we mustn't be late to see Mrs Trowsdale."

"You don't understand," Bella howled. "Her grandmother has been dead for days and Sophia's been hiding inside the place with her. It was the smell that fetched the landlord there, and then bailiffs came to break down the door. We saw it all and it was terrible... terrible!"

Joey clapped his hands to his nose. "The stink so bad," he cried.

"Sophia ran out between the men's legs... she ran like a rat,' Bella cried. "And the bailiffs shouted after her – 'get to the workhouse brat!'"

My heart broke for Sophia when I heard that, knowing her fear of the place. I could see what must have happened – old Grasper gone, she'd stayed there in that hovel, terrified that she'd be sent to the workhouse when she was discovered.

"Why didn't she come to me?" I murmured, but I knew the answer to that: I'd been too busy trying to see the family right – and see myself right too.

I turned to Frank and his father. "I must go," I said.

"Yes," Frank agreed. "Go find the lass and bring her to Turners Yard. We'll find a place for her there, somehow. You cannot leave her out on the streets, so fright'ed and alone."

Sam nodded. "You go, lass. We'll speak to Mrs Trowsdalc and do the best we can. I hope you find the child."

They turned and crossed the road, marching purposefully off towards the yards and steps. Joey took my hand and we hurried back along Grape Lane, up Sandgate, and then across the marketplace to New Way Ghaut.

"Which way did she go?" I asked. "When you saw her last, where was she heading?"

"To the sea, to the sea!" Joey cried.

"That's why I feared so much…" Bella began.

"No," I cried. "Not that … she wouldn't do that … surely not."

We had to slow up a little when we got to New Way Ghaut, for I saw the door to Grasper's den lay smashed upon the cobbles. The bailiffs were still there, arguing over the old woman's rocking chair. The stench of death was everywhere. We slipped past them and rushed down towards Tate Hill Sands, where all three of us ran out onto the beach calling out Sophia's name, while the scavengers stared. A few asked what the matter was and there were shrugs and frowns, though a few of them joined our search.

I looked everywhere.

"Sophia," I cried. "Sophia, come to me! Come to Lina! I'll not let them take you, hon!"

I scanned the incoming tide but could see no sign of a dark head bobbing amongst the waves.

"She wouldn't do that, surely," I whispered out loud.

At last we went back towards New Way Ghaut, striding boldly through the yards, still shouting out her name.

"She's not in here wi' us, honey!" came the reply.

"Old Grasper is dead and her girl is lost," I bellowed, for like her or not, I knew they wouldn't want to see her drowned.

A small crowd gathered around us all calling out her name, and Fishtail Lizzie came marching up the steps from the sands with a bucket of bait in one hand and a coiled long line in a skep on her head.

"What's up?" she asked.

"Old Grasper is dead and her girl run away," I said. "We need to find her fast, for she's mad with grief and I fear she might do anything."

"Eeh dear, old Grasper dead! I can't believe it. She's looked half dead for years, but she still went on. O' course the little lass will be in our coal-hole. That's where she goes."

And as she spoke I remembered from long ago the gloating face I'd seen in Blackburn's Yard, on the day I came back from the Court House. The small, dark space where coal was kept, set between two of the cottage walls, crammed into Blackburns Yard.

I turned and ran back up through the marketplace and into the narrow alleyway. The coalhole was dark and half full of coal. I peered into it but could see nothing there; then as my eyes got used to the darkness, I began to make out a small dark shape huddled in the far corner. I sighed with relief. Sofia was curled up tight, her face turned to the wall, looking more like a dirty bundle of rags than a child.

"Sophia," I called softly. "Don't be afraid. It's me, Lina. I've come to find you and take you back to Turners Yard wi' me. Nobody's going to send you to that workhouse, I promise you. We won't let them do that. You're coming home with me."

Nothing moved and for a moment I feared I'd come too late, but then a small wavering cry came from the darkness, more like the mewling of a kitten than a human sound. I reached inside the coalhole to touch her curled back, and my heart filled with pity as I felt the knobbly bones and remembered how it had been when she came into my cell in Northallerton Jail.

"I'm still here, hon, and won't ever leave you now."

At last she turned and reached out to me with another faint cry. I pulled her into my arms and sat myself down on the piled-up coal, just as Bella and Joey appeared in Blackburns Yard. Fishtail Lizzie followed behind them.

"Y' see, I knew she'd be 'ere," Lizzie said. "S'truth, look at the state of 'er."

Joey and Bella stared too, for despite the coal dust that covered her, we could see she'd become pitifully thin.

"You stayed with granny?" I asked quietly.

"Mmm," came the same weak kitten-like cry.

"How long?" I asked.

"Don't know," she whispered.

"What did you eat?"

She simply shook her head.

I glanced at Lizzie and she immediately set aside her bucket and basket. "Come wi' me, you two," she told Joey and Bella. "Bread and milk is what she needs!"

Bella and Joey followed Lizzie into her cottage and returned quickly with a bowl of milk with small bits of torn up bread soaked in it.

Lizzie came out again looking concerned and handed me a spoon. "Go steady wi' this," she warned. "You don't want to choke her."

"Just a bit now," I warned as I lifted a spoonful of milk-softened bread to Sophia's lips. "There will be plenty more to come, whenever you want it."

She opened her mouth and took a little, regarding me warily as she chewed and swallowed. Her eyes glinted like light blue glass in the coal-blackened face.

"Now a little more," I said and fed her again.

Bella dashed a tear away and Joey put out a hand to stroke Sophia's grizzled hair. "You can come and live wi' us," he said.

She looked up at me, doubtfully.

"Yes," I said firmly. "Wherever we go, you will come with us."

"They s… said go to the ro… ropery," she gulped. "And they've taken Granny away fro' me."

Lizzie put her hands on her hips and shook her head. "No ropery for you, my lass. If you get weary o' this lot, you can come and live wi' me instead."

Bella and Joey smiled at her words, while I fed Sophia a few more sops. Suddenly the door of Constable Linskill's house flew open and the constable and his wife came out, aware that something was happening in the yard.

"What's this?" he asked.

Sophia jumped in my arms and grabbed at me, terrified. I held her tight, fearful that she'd run again. Lizzie folded her arms across her chest. "This poor lass's gran has died and they've taken her to the mortuary and turned the young 'un out o' her home."

"But I will take her home with me," I told him hurriedly.

"Yes, she's coming back wi' us," Bella said determinedly.

The constable and his wife exchanged a glance and nodded.

"If she's found wandering, you know what we must do," the constable warned. "We don't want vagrancy."

"Yes," I assured him. "We are taking her now."

I stood up and set Sophia on her feet, where she swayed a little. I took one of her arms and Bella took the other, and we walked her out of Blackburns Yard between us and headed for the bridge.

CHAPTER FORTY

The Meeting House

Kat made no comment when we appeared in Turners Yard half carrying Sophia between us. She simply looked the child over and began ladling warm beef broth into a mug.

"Sit her down here," she said.

Sophia sat at our table, watching anxiously as the mug was placed in front of her. Her hands shook wildly as she lifted it, but she supped eagerly.

"Is she going to be alright?" Bella asked.

"Aye, I think she'll do," Kat said.

Neither Frank nor his father had come back from their meeting at Aelfleda Terrace, so I explained to Kat what had happened.

We sat together then, waiting anxiously for their return, and when there came a knock at the door we all jumped up. It was my dad, aware that I'd arrived back in the yard without Frank or his father, and he too was wondering what might be happening.

We related it to him, all speaking at once.

"So Lina couldn't go to see the lady," Bella said firmly.

"She can come an' live wi' us," Joey finished, and he put his hand on Sophia's shoulder, giving her a gentle pat.

Kat and dad exchanged a glance.

"Aye, o' course she can," Dad said. "But I'd best go back to work again, as it seems we've more mouths to feed."

Sophia emptied the mug of broth and gave us all a wavering smile.

"You're welcome," Kat told her firmly. "But if you're going to be staying here wi' us, you must be clean. There's an old shift of Bella's in the box that'd fit you, but you must be washed."

Sophia looked rebellious for a moment but then nodded, and Bella went straight away to rummage amongst our old clothes, while I struggled out of my bombazine.

"We won't wash her at the pump," I insisted.

"No, indeed," Kat agreed. "She can get washed in the basin, and we'll make the water nice and warm."

We set our biggest basin on the floor and filled it with cold water from the pump, while Kat set a kettle to boil.

"Lina, do it," Sophia begged. So I helped her to take off her filthy smock, and when I peeled away the flea-ridden rags, we were shocked to see how thin she'd become. She stepped into the basin and submitted patiently to my scrubbing, though I tried to be as gentle as I could.

I scrubbed her knotted hair with Kat's green soap and rinsed it thoroughly. "Fetch me the flannel towel and those things of yours," I called to Bella.

I combed Sophia's hair, talking gently all the time and when she was dried and dressed again she looked a great deal better, but suddenly tears started to pour down her cheeks.

"What is it?" Bella cried.

"Is it your granny?" I asked.

"Yeh! They took Granny away," she sobbed, "and said she must be thrown into a pit of lime."

Kat looked distressed. "A pauper's burial," she murmured.

We tried to comfort Sophia, but we knew that what she said would most likely be the truth and none of us could spare the money to pay for a decent burial space. I had the money

239

in my bag, but we needed that desperately to help us find somewhere for Mam to come home to. I thought resentfully of the elaborate funeral of the little girl for which I'd acted as mute, but business is business, and despite Nelly's small kindnesses, the Garbutts had their living to earn.

Kat sat quietly looking thoughtful.

"There's just one possibility," she said. "And I don't want to build your hopes up honey, but sometimes the Quaker Friends have helped people with funeral costs. Someone would have to go round to the Meeting House to speak to them and as they've taken old granny away, I daresay there's no time to lose."

I got up at once. "I'll go and ask," I told Sophia.

I didn't much relish going begging to the Quakers again, but needs must.

"Best put the bombazine on again," Kat suggested. "And straighten your hair."

I dressed myself again and hurried back down Flowergate, catching a glimpse of my reflection in the polished glass windows of a shop. My hair was a little wild, but my hands and fingernails were clean from scrubbing Sophia and the dark bombazine didn't show the coal dust stains that I knew must be there. I raced across the bridge and was relieved to find the door that led into the Friends Meeting House still open.

As I went in, I was reminded of that humiliating day when I'd first gone there to beg to be given soup. Just as then, two ladies looked up from the table where they were sitting, so clean and neat in their plain grey gowns and starched white cuffs and collars. A younger girl moved behind them, less severely dressed: she seemed to be stacking cups and plates away in a cupboard.

"I haven't come for soup," I said.

They stared at me, puzzled. "No," one of them said. "There is no soup today. What have you come for then?"

I patted my hair, trying to make myself look a little neater, like them, and took a deep breath. "I've come to ask help of a different kind," I said. "I think you will know of the beggar girl, Sophia Goodchild, who lived with her granny in New Way Ghaut?"

They glanced at each other and nodded. "Only too well," one agreed.

"I've come to speak on the girl's behalf."

"You'd best sit down," one of them said.

They indicated a plain wooden bench and I sat down gratefully and began to try to explain what had happened that morning. They listened quietly and exchanged a few uncertain glances as my story of poverty and hardship came to its dreadful end. They both sat in silence for a moment.

"A very sad story indeed," one of them acknowledged at last. "I think we'd best consult with Annie…"

The younger woman who'd been clearing plates away came forward then, and it was clear that she'd been listening to what I'd said.

"Do you remember me?" she asked. "You were our model that day. I am Sylvia."

I felt foolish that I hadn't recognise her at once; the young woman from Miss Weatherill's painting class, who'd spoken of the house for rent and given me Mrs Trowsdale's visiting card. I felt more aware than ever of my rather dishevelled state.

"Oh, Miss," I whispered. "I am so sorry… and you were so kind to me. I was going to visit Mrs Trowsdale this afternoon, but on my way I heard about Sophia and had to go to find her and see her safe."

"I think you were quite right to do that," Sylvia said kindly.

"Did Annie say…?" one of the women began.

"Why yes," the girl replied. "My aunt told me to wait for her here. She said that she'd come to the Meeting House after she'd conducted her business up at the terrace. I'll go and look for her now." And Sylvia hurried out onto the street.

I sat there frowning, uncertain what to do. One of the Quaker ladies got up and went to pour something into a mug.

"Here take a sip or two of water," she said. "For I think you've had a hard day too, as well as the poor beggar child."

I took the mug and sipped the cool, clean water, but found that my hands had begun to shake and would not stop. Then something of a commotion arose outside the Meeting House and an older lady whom I distantly recognised appeared, followed by Frank and his dad.

I stared at all three in astonishment, feeling dazed.

"This is Mrs Anne Trowsdale," Sam Dunsley said.

I put down the water, struggled to my feet and tried to make a respectful curtsey.

The lady smiled and nodded; like the others she wore a plain Quaker gown.

Frank watched me for a moment with concern, but then came to me and insisted on taking my hand. "All's well," he said quietly. "We have the house. And your family can come to live with us there, too."

I looked from him to his father, unable to believe what I heard.

"It's right," Sam Dunsley said. "It's agreed. We'll take the tenancy of Number 7 Aelfleda Terrace and the use of the workshop down below. Your family may join us there, for we've a deal of work to do."

"Oh, lady…" I gulped. "It… it is so very kind of you."

Anne Trowsdale shrugged. "Well, my husband's left me comfortable," she said. "Not wealthy, but comfortable and my own needs are small. I have no children, sadly, and I wish to share what I can. Now then, Paulina – have I got the name right?"

"Yes, Ma'am," I said, nodding my head vigorously.

"Well," she said. "I understand why you didn't come to inspect the house today. My niece has told me about the beggar girl and I think I can help with that too, for it's part of my belief that everyone should have a decent burial. Please tell the child that I'll pay for a modest burial plot, up at the cemetery. My niece will go to the Garbutt's and speak to them, so they can take charge of the poor woman's body."

I stared at her unbelieving for a moment. "Oh thank you, Mistress," I managed to say shakily.

"All I want, is that you look after my house, for me," Anne Trowsdale said.

Sam Dunsley nodded and smiled. "Now then, lass," he said. "Let's go to find your dad and give him the good news."

CHAPTER FORTY-ONE

Aelfleda Terrace

Mrs Trowsdale was as good as her word and Sophia's grandmother was given a modest, but decent burial. Most of the occupants of Turners Yard turned up, soberly dressed and Sophia, brushed, washed and wearing an old gown of Bella's, watched it all with quiet satisfaction.

During the third week in September we moved into Number 7 Aelfleda Terrace. It was a huge palaver carrying our belongings over the bridge and up the steep flight of steps that led to the new terrace. We hired a cart for the work tools that were needed for the jet workshop, but to save money we carried as much as we possibly could. Kat stayed in Turner's Yard all day, packing and sorting things, while Bella and I went back and forth with loaded baskets and bags. We put knapsacks on both Joey and Sophia, and they trotted along beside us, uncomplaining for we were all so excited that at last we were to get a proper home again.

It had been agreed that Kat would take the smaller of the two rooms on the first floor and that I would share the front room next to it with Bella, Joey, and Sophia. We were delighted as it meant that we'd have the most wonderful aspect overlooking the Upper Harbour.

Frank and his dad would take the larger front attic – though of course they'd spend their days in the workshop with the new grindstones, polishing boards, breeching-straps, and stoves. My dad would sleep in the smaller back attic, hoping that Mam might soon be able to join him there with our new babe. The scullery and the parlour would be common to us all, though Kat would be in charge and she'd do her best to provide us workers with breakfasts and an evening meal.

It was an exhausting day, and Kat joined us on the last journey over the bridge and up the steps. I thought she looked a little wistful as she locked the door on her now empty home-place, ready to hand the key back to the landlord.

"Are you sad to leave?" I asked. "You've lived in this place so long."

"Nay, lass," she told me firmly. "Always look forward, never back!"

So we crossed the bridge and struggled up the steep flight of steps, ready to start our new life.

Kat had planned it well; we had bowls of soup for our evening meal that she'd prepared that morning and carried over the bridge in her largest jug. There was fresh bread too, and we all sat together round the long trestle table set up in the parlour. We talked and laughed as we ate, delighted that we were all there at last in our spotless new home.

We cleared the table and washed the dishes. Kat left us to it and went to sit in her rocking chair, where a small fire crackled in the clean new grate beside her.

"You'll be tired, old lass," Sam Dunsley said.

"Aye, tired," she agreed with a sigh. "But happy to be here."

I looked up a moment later and saw that she was sleeping, a gentle smile there on her face. She was sleeping still, when we eventually got up to go to bed.

"Bedtime, Kat," I said and went to take hold of her hand and pull her to her feet, but she didn't move – couldn't move – her hand was cold.

"Oh Kat," I cried. "Not now… now that we are all here at last and safe again."

Everyone gathered round us, and Joey and Bella burst into tears while Sophia looked terrified.

"Shall I fetch a doctor?" Frank offered.

Dad took Kat's hand and gently stroked her cheek. "Nay, lad," he said. "Too late for that I'm afraid; there's nowt that a doctor can do for her now. Look at her peaceful face; she's gone from us."

"No… no," Bella cried. "How will we manage without her?"

I grabbed hold of her and Joey and we clung together, for I too couldn't see how we'd manage. Sophia watched us, white-faced and silent.

"Let's sit down for a moment and have a think," Sam said.

We sat down quietly then, glancing all the time at Kat, shocked and devastated by what had happened.

"Gran's smiling," Joey said at last.

"Yes, she looks contented," I had to agree.

"What should we do?" Bella asked again.

None of us knew how to answer her, but then Dad spoke gently. "Let's carry her up to her room, so that at least she can spend this night in her new home-place. Tomorrow will be soon enough to do what must be done."

"Yes," I whispered. "Let her be in her new room tonight."

Frank put his arm about me, and we all stood up. Sam Dunsley and my dad carefully carried Kat up the stairs and laid her on the bed. We followed them and stood around the bed for a while. I saw that Sophia hovered in the doorway, so I reached out to take her hand and pull her forward.

"Don't be scared," I said. "Whatever happens now, you'll still be safe with us."

"Aye," Bella added as she linked her arm through the crook of Sophia's elbow.

"Cover Gran up and keep her warm," Joey insisted, his face still wet with tears.

So we searched amongst the unpacked baggage until we found Kat's old patchwork quilt, and once we'd covered her with it she looked as though she was sleeping comfortably there in her new home. We lit a candle and left it burning by her bed and then, reluctantly, went downstairs again. We lit more candles and sat around the table talking quietly, for none of us could face going to bed. At last Joey fell asleep on my lap.

"You know what Kat would say," Sam said. "She'd tell us to get to our beds, for there'll be much to do in the morning."

We got up quietly, knowing that he was right.

I woke early the next morning, feeling more distressed than ever as the hugeness of our loss sank in. I got up and washed and dressed myself, for I couldn't rest, and told Bella that I was going to see Nelly Garbutt. I walked over the bridge, so many pictures of Kat flying through my mind. When I got to the Funeral Parlour, Nelly listened to me patiently as I told her what had happened.

"Your Kat shall have the funeral she deserves," she said. "Don't fret about it; leave it to me. I'll send the men over to Aelfleda Terrace and we'll arrange it all for you. The charge will be modest, special rates for those we employ."

"Will Mr Garbutt agree to that?" I asked.

"He will!" she said sternly. "Go back now. They'll be needing you there."

I hurried back to Aelfleda Terrace, overwhelmed with the responsibility of it all, for Nelly was right: Kat's death must leave the little ones more dependent than ever on me. I should find a way to tell my mother too, for Kat was her mam and she had a right to know that she'd died.

When I got back, we didn't have long to wait before the men arrived with the funeral cart. After they'd carried away their precious load, I thought that I'd set about getting the house straight. Frank, Sam, and Dad went down to the workshop, for we knew that we needed to get the jetworks up and running. I couldn't think how I'd feed them all that night, fearing porridge might have to suffice.

I'd set Bella to scrub the table and Sophia and Joey to wash the bowls we'd used that morning, when there came a knock on the door. I sighed, for I knew that none of the men would knock and we really didn't want visitors, however sympathetic they might be, so I opened the door reluctantly and stood there shocked. There on the step stood my mam, with little Robbie in her arms and a small sack dumped at her side.

"Mam!" I whispered and burst into tears.

"Mam... Mam!" Bella and Joey both left their work and rushed to fling themselves at her.

"Oh Mam," I whispered, my voice gone all hoarse. "What are you doing here? It isn't the end of the month just yet!"

"Here take the babe," she said and thrust little Robbie towards me. I took him, relieved to feel the weight of him in my arms, while my mother hugged Bella and Joey.

"But Mam... do you know?" I tried to find the words.

She looked up at me and nodded sadly. "Aye, I know about Kat; the matron told me," she said. "I got straight out of bed there and then and told her, I'm going... my family need me."

I saw that she was trembling, but there was steely determination in her voice and in her eyes.

"Oh Mam," I agreed. "We *do* need you! We do!"

I went to her then and we all hugged again together, so that Mam almost toppled off the step and the baby gave out a strong wail.

"Careful!" I warned. "The bairn."

Then suddenly we were all laughing, though our cheeks were wet with tears.

The noise we made brought the men out of the workshop, and they stared up at us from the terrace down below. Dad hovered uncertainly behind the others when he saw our mam.

"Dad," I called to him. "Come up here!"

Mam turned around and saw him hesitating there. Frank and his dad went straight back inside the workshop, kindly giving us a private moment. I stood by the doorstep with the baby in my arms, as Mam walked towards the top of the workshop steps. Joey made a move to follow her, but I hauled him back.

"No… you stay here, wi' me," I said.

Dad came up to meet her but wavered again as he reached the top. "I'm sorry," he said. "I'm so very sorry. I can never…"

Mam opened her arms to him. "My mother is gone," she said. "I need *you* now… I need all of you."

They held each other tightly for a moment, cheek to cheek, while we stood quietly and watched. At last Mam pulled back a little and linked her arm through Dad's in the old way, as they turned towards us.

"Well now, I have to say that you've found us a grand place to live," she said. "I never dreamt of such a place."

"That's our lass… done that," Dad acknowledged.

"How did you know where we were?" I asked.

Mam smiled. "Half the town knows where you are. I asked those I met ,and they directed me here."

She stopped again, seeming to glance past us and into the house. We turned to find Sophia peeping nervously round the open door.

"I know *you*," Mam said, pointing at her. "Kat told me about you!"

Sophia looked frightened and vanished inside.

"No… come back here!" Mam ordered. "*You* must come and give me a hug now, like the others have, for you're to be part of my family too."

Sophia appeared again still looking nervous, but she moved obediently down the steps and received a hug.

"Come inside!" Joey cried impatiently. He took Mam's hand and pulled her in through our front door.

I went to Dad and put baby Robbie into his arms.

"Thank you, lass," he said, and he dropped a soft kiss on the baby's head.

EPILOGUE

Kat's funeral was long remembered in Whitby Town, not for its lavishness but for the surprising number of mourners who turned out for it.

We trusted the Garbutts to make the arrangements and we needed their help, for there was so much to be done to get the house and the workshop up and running. We were terrified too that if we didn't look after Mam, she might fall sick again.

The day before the funeral, Bella and I worked hard, baking funeral cakes and getting all our clothes pressed and looking fresh. Mam handed out advice, but we made her sit most of the time, allowing her only to nurse little Robbie and see to him.

Nelly Garbutt produced neat black hired gowns for Mam, Bella, and Sophia to wear and a smart black suit for Dad. Frank and Sam already had their best suits. I wore my bombazine of course, and I fought back tears as I dressed myself, remembering the care that Kat had taken to make it fit me.

The morning of the funeral we gathered together on the front of the terrace, and I sensed a bit of tension amongst us, which was not surprising in the circumstances.

I was a little startled when Frank came to stand in front of me, bowing formally. He looked smart in his suit and held something hidden in his hands. He opened up his palms to reveal a beautiful rose-carved jet brooch, very much like the one I'd sold to Mary Weatherill.

"For you," he said.

"Aye… just… for today," I agreed, feeling pleased that he'd thought of that.

"No," he whispered. "This is for you to keep. Rich ladies are given a ring when they promise to marry a lad. I have no ring to give, only this brooch… if you will accept it… and me as well?"

I struggled to speak, for I was surprised and overwhelmed, but he looked so lovely and kind and handsome in his suit, that I flung my arms about his neck. "Of course I'll have *you* as well," I managed to say.

There came a quiet ripple of approval from the others, as he fastened the brooch onto my gown and kissed my cheek.

"Time to go," Dad said, and he held out his arm to Mam.

I insisted on carrying Robbie carefully down the steps, and we walked along to the bridge where we'd arranged to wait for the funeral procession. We'd made sure that we'd be there in good time and all was quiet at first, but then at last we saw a horse-drawn hearse coming towards us, with Mr Garbutt walking slowly in front of it. Another carriage followed behind, driven by Lanky Jack and Nelly Garbutt walking beside it.

We stared, for following behind the carriage came a great multitude of people. Many that I couldn't recognise at first, for they were all so smartly dressed. Fishtail Lizzie strode across the bridge towards us, her hair plaited neatly and no apron on that day. There followed a gang of flitherpickers, all turned out in their best gowns and shawls. There were fishermen, old mates of Dad's, all walking slowly and respectfully in their dark suits and caps. Mary Weatherill was there, with Sylvia and her aunt – our landlady now. Other young ladies from the drawing class followed behind, all beautifully dressed but looking very sad for us. There were Quaker wives and kitchen maids, and I was quite shaken and startled to see that Constable Linskill was there with his wife and Anne, and he kindly lifted his hat to us.

The carriage driven by Lanky Jack stopped right beside us.

"For Mr and Mrs Raw," he announced formally.

I glanced gratefully at Nelly Garbutt.

"You get into the carriage," I told my mam, relieved that she wouldn't have to walk too far. "And you, Dad," I said, "take Robbie with you."

Mam stared at me, looking tearful and amazed. "However are we going to feed this lot?" she asked.

"Don't you fret, Maria," Nelly said. "It's all in hand."

Still looking stunned, they climbed into the carriage, and I passed the baby up to them; Bella and Joey squeezed in too.

"There's room for you," I offered Sophia, but she shook her head.

"Are you walking?" she asked.

"Yes," I said.

"I walk with you," she said and grabbed my arm.

As the carriage moved off, Frank took my other arm. "Come," he whispered. "You must lead the way. Let us be glad that Kat is going in such style."

I lifted my chin and walked at the front of the procession with him.

"Yes," I said. "Always look forward, never back... Kat would be proud I think."

ACKNOWLEDGEMENTS

The author would like to thank the following people for their help and advice with this project:

My thanks to Mike and Tricia Shaw for help and advice with the photographs, which are not intended to depict the fictional characters in the story, but to give an atmosphere and impression of the place and the time.

Photographs by Frank Meadow Sutcliffe
© The Sutcliffe Gallery
www.sutcliffe-gallery.co.uk

Sarah Caldwell Steele, of The Ebor Jetworks Whitby, Consultant Gemmologist at Whitby Museum, for advice on the history of jet – www.eborjetworks.co.uk

Pete Thompson, former lifeboat coxswain and curator of Whitby Lifeboat Museum, for information and advice on the Whitby Lifeboat disaster.

Dave Wharton for advice on Victorian Whitby.

Christine Pybus, artist and art historian, for advice and information on Mary Weatherill.

Chris Dowson for lending me her precious copy of THE ROWING LIFEBOATS OF WHITBY, by Arthur F Humble.

Wendy Havelock for advice on Whitby jet.

Anthea Dove for her unfailing support with editorial advice and encouragement.

To Caroline Domingo for her careful reading and copy editing of the text.

The following books have provided a great deal of useful information:

HOUSE OF CARE – A History of Northallerton Prison, by Stephen Wade, ISBN 1-905373-20-1

WHITBY JET, by Helen and Katy Muller, published by Shire Publications ISBN 978-0-7478-0731-5

WHITBY JET THROUGH THE AGES, by Mabel McMillan, published by the author, 1992, ISBN -13: 978-0951875902

THE ROWING LIFEBOATS OF WHITBY, by Arthur F Humble, published by Horne and Son, 1974, ISBN – 10: 0900476087

AUTHOR'S NOTE

Paulina's family and most of the main characters in the story are fictional, though Mabel Macmillan recorded in her book, WHITBY JET THROUGH THE AGES, the case of a father and daughter who were apprehended for working together to steal jet from a local workshop.

However, Mary Linskill, the writer, her father, a Whitby constable, and her family are loosely based on real people who lived in Whitby during the 1860s.

The character of Mary Weatherill is based on the artist, who lived in Whitby but also travelled widely. She was the daughter of George Weatherill, well known for his watercolour landscapes and Whitby studies.

The character of Sophia is loosely based on a set of records held by North Yorkshire County Records Office. This interesting information has been used for study in a project for young offenders.

The records state that 11-year-old Sophie Constable and 20-year-old Fanny Goodchild stood accused of obtaining by false pretences a threepenny loaf of bread from a shop in Church Street, Whitby, in October 1872. Both girls were apprehended and pleaded guilty to the offence, stating that it was only through hunger that they had resorted to theft. Sophie received three weeks in prison followed by four years in reformatory school. Fanny Goodchild received one month in prison with hard labour.

www.theresatomlinson.com

ALSO BY THE SAME AUTHOR

Life is hard for all the close-knit fishing families on the north-east coast. Here in one volume are two of Theresa Tomlinson's gripping novels about the fisher folk of Sandwick Bay, in which the sea and the pull of the tide ultimately shape all their destinies.

Of THE FLITHER PICKERS

"A gritty, touching novel of the North Yorkshire coast"
the Guardian

"A most distinguished novel which is also a convincing piece of historical reconstruction"
Marcus Crouch – Junior Bookshelf

Of THE HERRING GIRLS

"Utterly absorbing"
Michael Morpurgo

"A good, honest, unadorned voice reminiscent of Laura Ingalls Wilder"
George Hunt – Books for Keeps